"A top-notch new series that deftly demonstrates Ashley's mastery of historical mysteries by delivering an impeccably researched setting, a fascinating protagonist with an intriguing past, and lively writing seasoned with just the right measure of dry wit." —*Booklist*

"An exceptional series launch. . . . Readers will look forward to this fascinating lead's future endeavors." —*Publishers Weekly* (starred review)

"A smart and suspenseful read, *Death Below Stairs* is a fun series launch that will leave you wanting more." —Bustle

"This mood piece by Ashley is not just a simple murder mystery. There is a sinister plot against the crown, and the race is on to save the queen. The characters are a lively, diverse group, which bodes well for future Below Stairs Mysteries, and the thoroughly entertaining cast will keep readers interested until the next escapade. The first installment is a well-crafted Victorian adventure." —RT Book Reviews

"A fun, intriguing mystery with twists and turns makes for a promising new series." —Red Carpet Crash

"What a likeable couple our sleuths Kat Holloway and Daniel McAdam make—after you've enjoyed *Death Below Stairs*, make room on your reading calendar for *Scandal Above Stairs*." —Criminal Element

Titles by Jennifer Ashley

Below Stairs Mysteries

A SOUPÇON OF POISON
(an ebook)

DEATH BELOW STAIRS

SCANDAL ABOVE STAIRS

DEATH IN KEW GARDENS

MURDER IN THE EAST END

DEATH AT THE CRYSTAL PALACE

THE SECRET OF BOW LANE

SPECULATIONS IN SIN

A SILENCE IN BELGRAVE SQUARE

The Mackenzies Series

THE MADNESS OF LORD IAN MACKENZIE

LADY ISABELLA'S SCANDALOUS MARRIAGE

THE MANY SINS OF LORD CAMERON

THE DUKE'S PERFECT WIFE

A MACKENZIE FAMILY CHRISTMAS

THE SEDUCTION OF ELLIOT MCBRIDE

THE UNTAMED MACKENZIE
(an ebook)

THE WICKED DEEDS OF DANIEL MACKENZIE

SCANDAL AND THE DUCHESS
(an ebook)

RULES FOR A PROPER GOVERNESS

THE SCANDALOUS MACKENZIES
(anthology)

THE STOLEN MACKENZIE BRIDE

A MACKENZIE CLAN GATHERING
(an ebook)

ALEC MACKENZIE'S ART OF SEDUCTION

THE DEVILISH LORD WILL

A ROGUE MEETS A SCANDALOUS LADY

A MACKENZIE CLAN CHRISTMAS

A MACKENZIE YULETIDE
(an ebook)

THE SINFUL WAYS OF JAMIE MACKENZIE

A
SILENCE
IN
BELGRAVE
SQUARE

❖—·—❖

Jennifer Ashley

Berkley Prime Crime
New York

BERKLEY PRIME CRIME
Published by Berkley
An imprint of Penguin Random House LLC
1745 Broadway, New York, NY 10019
penguinrandomhouse.com

Book design by Laura K. Corless

Library of Congress Cataloging-in-Publication Data

Names: Ashley, Jennifer, author.
Title: A silence in Belgrave Square / Jennifer Ashley.
Description: First edition. | New York: Berkley Prime Crime, 2025. |
Series: Below stairs mysteries
Identifiers: LCCN 2025009532 (print) | LCCN 2025009533 (ebook) |
ISBN 9780593549933 (trade paperback) | ISBN 9780593549940 (ebook)
Subjects: LCGFT: Detective and mystery fiction. | Novels.
Classification: LCC PS3601.S547 S55 2025 (print) | LCC PS3601.S547
(ebook) | DDC 813/.6—dc23/eng/20250325
LC record available at https://lccn.loc.gov/2025009532
LC ebook record available at https://lccn.loc.gov/2025009533

First Edition: August 2025

Printed in the United States of America
1st Printing

The authorized representative in the EU for product safety and compliance is
Penguin Random House Ireland, Morrison Chambers, 32 Nassau Street,
Dublin D02 YH68, Ireland, https://eu-contact.penguin.ie.

A
SILENCE
IN
BELGRAVE
SQUARE

1

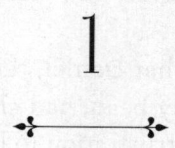

Late on a rainy night in May 1884, Daniel McAdam paid me a visit.

The kitchen was dark and thankfully quiet, the only sound the quiet pattering of light rain on the high window and a sputtering of candle wax. I'd turned out all the gas sconces, as the mistress of the house was inclined to be fussy about the expense, and had lit a single candle. Under this warm glow, I sharpened my knives and made my notes on the meals of the day.

Mrs. Bywater, the aforementioned mistress, had been rather tiresome about a fish dish she'd claimed tasted off, though the family and guests had eagerly downed it. I'd used fresh coriander leaves, which apparently some people believe have the taste of soap. Mrs. Bywater appeared to be one.

She'd lectured me for some time about ingredients and had insisted I take her over the larder and show her how I stored my herbs and vegetables.

I'd been weary after this session and grateful for my assistant, Tess, who carried on with the work while Mrs. Bywater distracted me. I liked to keep to an exact routine in order to finish all our tasks on time, and Mrs. Bywater's interference put me behind.

I was also grateful that Daniel, the ostensible man of all work and, I suppose, my beau, had chosen tonight to visit. I hoped I could vent my frustration to him, but one look at his face when he sat down in the circle of my candlelight stilled my words of vexation.

"What is it?" I asked.

Daniel tried to beam his disarming smile. He'd pulled off his cap when he'd stepped inside, revealing tousled dark hair in need of a trim. His blue eyes warmed me even through my sudden concern.

"Are my thoughts so plain?" Daniel made the question sound like a jest.

"Only when you are truly worried about something. Tell me what it is at once."

I thunked a plate in front of him of leftover stew filled with chunks of beef and roasted vegetables, with a soft bun for sopping up the juices. The fish dish was entirely gone, in spite of Mrs. Bywater's objections to the taste, as the others in the household had made short work of it. That was fine, because Daniel preferred fish when it was covered with batter and wrapped in newspaper, served alongside a load of crispy chips.

Daniel, being Daniel, did not answer me until he'd taken a mouthful of the savory stew, followed by a bite of bread.

"Oh, Kat." He heaved a long sigh. "That is heaven."

"Never mind the flattery." I poured tea for both of us, adding sugar and a bit of cream to the cups. "What has upset you?"

Instead of explaining, the wretched man gazed around the kitchen, taking in the dresser with its crockery and the large black stove crouching like a beast against the wall. I'd grown fond of that stove, though it was temperamental and needed coaxing some days. Copper pots hung above it, gleaming in the faint light. Behind me stood another dresser filled with various cooking implements, including empty produce crates I'd have the strong footmen tote back to the merchants I'd obtain orders from.

My scrubbed but scarred kitchen table, where Tess and I chopped vegetables, kneaded bread, and rolled out pastry dough, had become another friend, a place to relax and enjoy a meal in the evening. Every night I reposed here to contemplate the day gone by and plan for the one to come.

Tomorrow was Thursday, my favorite day of the week. I had the entire day out, from morning until evening, to enjoy with my beloved daughter, Grace. I'd hoped to enjoy it with Daniel as well.

He shattered that hope by stating, "I will miss this."

My heart sank. "Do not say you are being sent to the ends of the earth again to do things for your unreasonably demanding boss. Where is it this time? Scotland? Ireland? Somewhere on the Continent where people are rising against their rulers instead of staying home and minding their own business?"

"Some rulers are fairly terrible people and should be risen against," Daniel said in a reasonable tone. "You'd be the first to lead the charge, I think, striding out with your rolling pin aloft."

I was not in the mood for his humor. "Do not be ridiculous, and tell me where you are going."

"Belgrave Square."

I stared at him. I'd expected him to name a far-flung out-post of the empire, not a nearby district of London.

"This is not such a great distance." I made myself lift my teacup without it trembling. "From Mount Street it is perhaps a quarter of an hour walk, if you do not stop to chat with friends or look into shop windows in Piccadilly."

"It is not distance that will take me away, but time." Daniel laid down his spoon. "I will be moving in to the home of one Viscount Peyton, who leases a house on the south side of the square. I am to be his secretary—a dull-witted but efficient young man trying to earn my living."

"While you discover what he is up to?" Daniel was often sent to nose around in other people's affairs.

"Which might be nothing at all. Viscount Peyton spends his days in a wheeled chair, attended by a young man who is strong enough to carry him about when necessary. His previous secretary has vanished, and I am to replace him."

"Vanished." My heart thumped, and I set down my teacup with a decided click. "So Mr. Monaghan will send you in to see if you vanish as well?"

Daniel had the audacity to grin. "He might not have been done away with and buried in the cellar, like in a tale in a sensational magazine. He might simply have become impatient with the post and departed. The previous secretary was the son of an aristocrat and possibly didn't enjoy being ordered about like a footman."

"Whereas *you* take orders without qualm?"

"I do when there might be something dangerous in play." Daniel resumed his meal. "I don't know how long it will take before Monaghan is satisfied that nothing is amiss in the household of Viscount Peyton. I could be there some time."

"Daniel." I placed my hands onto the table and regarded him sternly.

"Mm?" Daniel glanced up, his jaw working as he enjoyed the stew. "This is truly wonderful, Kat."

"You never reveal this many details when you inform me you are off on a mission. You usually tell me you are departing for a few weeks, then return and explain you were in Dublin or Glasgow or some remote farm in Northumbria. You remain vague about the assignment, and I do not tax you for more information, knowing you are unable to provide it. Why are you now telling me exactly where you will be and with whom?"

Daniel made a small gesture with his spoon. "To alleviate your worries. Also to prevent you from trying to find me or calling out to me if you happen to see me peering into shop windows in Piccadilly."

"You are prevaricating," I said. "Mr. Davis's dictionary says that means being maddeningly imprecise while pretending to be straightforward." I leaned to him, the table's edge pressing into my abdomen. "This is the last assignment, isn't it? The one you will do to fulfill your commitment to Monaghan and make him release you from his power. Am I correct?"

From Daniel's silence as he drew his spoon through the stew, I knew I was.

My heart constricted. Mr. Monaghan was a coldly cruel man, who blamed Daniel for the death of a colleague—wrongly blamed him, that is. In retaliation, Monaghan sent Daniel on dangerous assignments for the police, to ferret out people who made bombs and planned assassinations and other perilous missions. Often Daniel went alone to spy on these people, with no guarantee of help if he was caught.

Monaghan had promised that one day, Daniel would work

off his guilt and be free of his obligation. We both knew that the last commission would be the most dangerous of all.

"There is much more to this than you watching an elderly gentleman in a wheeled chair, isn't there?"

"Yes." The fact that Daniel didn't evade the question made me still more worried. "Someone in that household, or connected to that household, is supporting a project that might damage not only the queen's person but the cabinet, members of Parliament, and anyone else who gets in their way, including innocents on the streets. Monaghan has wind of such an undertaking being planned, and all threads in the web lead back to Peyton's home in Belgrave Square."

I knew Monaghan and his colleagues were not ones who jumped at shadows. They had rounded up very dangerous criminals in the past, usually using Daniel to do much of the hazardous work. They would not suspect Lord Peyton or someone who worked for him without careful scrutiny first.

"Suppose it was the secretary?" I suggested. "Who is now conveniently gone? He might have realized Monaghan had caught on to his evil deeds and fled to a far corner of the earth."

Daniel shrugged. "In that case, I will do tedious work as a legitimate secretary until Monaghan pulls me out again in disappointment."

I sipped tea, trying to calm myself. I did not like the idea of Daniel walking into a lion's den. Unlike his biblical namesake, I couldn't be certain the Lord would make the beasts inside tame for him.

"I do not suppose Viscount Peyton's household needs a cook," I said in a casual tone.

Daniel clattered the spoon into his nearly empty bowl. "No, Kat. The cook has been with Peyton for years, and he trusts her with his digestion. You are going nowhere near that house. These sorts of people kill to protect their secrets, and they would not hesitate to murder you. They are ruthless."

"Which means they'd not hesitate to murder *you*," I pointed out.

"I do not have a choice. This is the work I do to keep Monaghan from trumping up charges against me and putting me in prison, or worse. Please, do not try to stop this."

"How could *I* stop it?" I pressed one hand to my chest. "I am a cook below stairs, not the head of the Home Office."

"Oh, there are many things you could do if you put your mind to it," Daniel said darkly. "Please do not discuss this with anyone at Scotland Yard, not Inspector McGregor, not Constable Greene when he visits Tess. Not Tess either."

Daniel's eyes held a steeliness I'd never seen in them, a grim determination that had no softness, even for me.

"I am only expressing concern for your well-being," I said, somewhat stiffly. "I know there is damn-all you can do about undertaking this task."

Daniel let out breath, trying to relax, but he couldn't quite. "I only ask that you do not try to interfere. I would like to focus my entire attention on the case at hand without having to fear for your safety at every moment. I gave you as many details as I did so you would not rush to Inspector McGregor to try to find me when I didn't come around as often."

Now he was making me cross, though I admitted that if he'd simply disappeared, I would likely have expressed my concern to those I could approach at Scotland Yard. I did realize that if Inspector McGregor, who intensely disliked Monaghan, raised a commotion about what had happened to Daniel, things might not go well for Daniel.

"Interfere," I repeated. "Is that what you suppose I have

been doing all this time? I'm very sorry if my interference has helped you in various cases, or saved my friends from the gallows or from being murdered themselves."

Daniel's shoulders sagged. "Kat . . . Damnation, I knew I should not have come here. I only wanted to see you before I had to keep from you for who knows how many weeks. Or months."

My anger fell away with a crash. I rose from my chair and moved to kneel by his.

"My poor Daniel." I slid my arms around his waist and rested my head on his lap. I'd never taken such a daring pose with him before, and I was momentarily distracted by the strength of his legs beneath me. "You are so very worried about this mission, and all I've done is twit you about it. I am thinking only of myself and the hole in my life if I lost you."

Daniel laid a gentle hand on my hair. "And I, the emptiness if I lost *you*. I never should have lingered the day I first delivered goods to your kitchen. I should have returned to business and forgotten all about you. I knew I'd regret coming to know the pretty cook with the warm eyes, but somehow, I couldn't help myself."

He'd melt me with all his flattery. Daniel had a way with him, I'd always said.

I raised my head to see all hardness in his expression gone. His eyes held a bleak light, and behind it, fear.

"I will stay out of your way," I assured him. "Think of me here, baking all sorts of treats for your return."

The humor returned to Daniel's voice. "The cakes and things might grow moldy before I can eat them."

"That is not what I meant, and you know it, silly man. I will try various recipes and choose one for us to celebrate with when you are finished."

I started to rise. Daniel caught me, pulling me down to his lap. I hoped the rest of the staff truly were in their beds and not ready to pop in and catch me in so compromising a position.

I forgot all about them in the next moment when Daniel kissed me more fervently than he had in many a day. I clung to him without shame and kissed him back, fearing in my heart that I was seeing him for the last time.

When Daniel departed the house a quarter of an hour later, I was dangerously close to tears. I bravely held them in, smiling my good-bye to him and wishing him well.

Thursday morning dawned, but instead of waking with my usual joyous anticipation, I opened my eyes to a feeling of dread. For a moment, I couldn't remember why, and then the details of Daniel's nocturnal visit came flooding back to me.

"No good borrowing trouble," I told myself as I rinsed and dried my face at the washbasin and reached for my hairbrush. "Daniel knows exactly what he is about. Today, I shall visit Grace and be happy."

Daniel had been accompanying me on my visits most Thursdays, joining Grace and me for walks, treats at our favorite tea shops, or lively conversations in Joanna's sitting room. I felt his absence as I made my lone way across London toward Cheapside.

On the other hand, Grace was the most important person in my world, and when I embraced her, my courage returned.

"Is Uncle Daniel coming with us today?" Grace asked me as we ventured into the soft May sunshine, the rain of the previous night having abated.

I did not want to fob off my daughter with light falsehoods. Keeping in mind Daniel's warning about secrecy, I waited until we were walking, hand in hand, in a quiet area behind St. Paul's before I spoke.

"He is investigating something for his inspector. We might not see him for some weeks."

Grace wrinkled her nose. "For that awful man who followed us to the tea shop that day?"

"Indeed, Mr. Monaghan." Who had accosted me one afternoon I was with Grace and tried to pry answers out of me about my relations with Daniel, as if it were any of his business.

"I don't like him," Grace declared. "Or the sound of this new task. Uncle Daniel should chuck it."

"I do not like it either, and young ladies should not use such slang."

Grace put on her stubborn expression. "There are too many things young ladies should not do. So many that I do not want to become one."

I could not argue with her. Ladies had few choices in this world, though happily they had more now than when I'd been young. Grace would very soon be old enough that I would have to decide which direction her life would take. Not something I wanted to think about at the moment, on top of my worry for Daniel.

"Will you be helping Uncle Daniel?" Grace went on as I pondered. "I think he'll need you, Mum."

"I'm afraid I'll not be able to visit Daniel in the house where he'll be staying, nor can he come and go as he pleases. Also, you must not discuss this with anyone, not even Joanna."

"I never do." Grace swung my hand. "I know Uncle Daniel does dangerous work for the police, and that it is safer for him if I don't mention it. As long as you tell me all about it when it's over."

Her request was so like what I often said to Daniel that I laughed, feeling better.

"You ought to become cook in the house, wherever it is," Grace suggested as we emerged into Ludgate Hill.

"I thought of that, but no. The cook has apparently been in place for a long time and not likely to leave. Besides, it would be impractical. I'd have to give up my post in Mount Street without knowing if I could have it back when I was finished. And of course, Daniel has already warned me off such a course."

I must have looked downcast because Grace patted my arm. "You will think of something, Mum."

Her confidence heartened me. By the time we reached Lincoln's Inn Fields and Sir John Soane's interesting museum, I'd formed an idea. It was audacious, and Daniel would not thank me when he learned of it, but if I was successful, I'd have eyes and ears in that house. Whenever Daniel was in danger, I'd be able to act.

After we'd looked over Sir John Soane's collection of scale models of ancient buildings, Grace and I had a longer walk and a lovely tea out before I returned her home.

I was always heavyhearted when I said good-bye to Grace on Thursday evenings, but today I walked to busy Cheapside with renewed purpose. Eventually I found an empty hansom and stepped aboard.

"Where to, missus?" the cabbie called to me as I closed the door and settled the lap robe.

"Portobello Road," I told him. "Hurry, before the market shuts for the night."

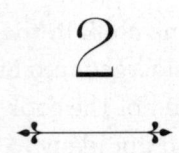

2

Portobello Road lay in Kensington, north of the palace there, and led up a hill that ultimately ended in a burial ground and the prison of Wormwood Scrubs. A market for fruits and vegetables and other goods often set up in Portobello Road, including a few stalls for trinkets and sundries—nothing valuable but nice to have.

It was one of these bric-a-brac stalls that I made for as the afternoon merged into a long, late-spring twilight. I walked slowly along the road, pausing often, as though I browsed for curios. I did spy a lovely comb and brush set on one table that I contemplated purchasing for Grace, if I decided it was worth the thruppence asked for it.

But I was not here to buy things. I halted for a time in front of the stall I'd sought, without letting on why I was there. The stall's table was strewn with bits and bobs of all sorts—thin chains with lockets, colorful little boxes, finger rings, pen and ink trays with inkpots missing their lids, mirrors and brushes, empty perfume bottles, and cracked and faded cups celebrating Queen Victoria's coronation more than forty years ago.

Lounging in a chair behind the pile of trinkets was a lady with a black jacket buttoned to her chin, her long legs stretched out under a bright blue skirt. She had very dark hair, its color due more to artifice than nature, and a pair of lively blue eyes under a worn feathered hat five years out of fashion.

Those eyes focused on me, at first shrewdly—a seller deciding how to entice a customer—then with a jolt of recognition. She sprang to her feet with a swing of skirts and gaped at me over the table.

"Well, if it ain't Katie bloomin' 'Olloway, come to slum in the Portobello Road," she screeched to all and sundry.

"Kat," I corrected her, though she knew exactly what my name was. "How are you, Hannah?"

"Keeping. I'm keeping." Hannah Dunnett grinned at me, showing clean but crooked teeth. "Nothing on this table's nicked, if that's what you've come up this 'ill to twit me about. Leastways, not by me. I pick things up here and there, so who knows? How about you, me dear old darling? Widowed now, ain't ya, poor thing, with a little girl to bring up on your own."

"I am doing well, thank you for asking." I hadn't spoken to Hannah in years, but her infectious friendliness made me wonder why I'd waited so long. When one struggled, I supposed, one felt that one had to do it alone. "My daughter is growing tall and so beautiful."

For a moment, I forgot everything difficult in my life. Grace had told me today she did not want to be a young lady, but she already was one. She was almost as tall as I was, with her brown hair sleek and curling, her face holding the adult beauty she would soon achieve.

"Aw," Hannah said as she studied my expression. "I'm glad for ya. I'd love to see her."

"An excellent idea. I'll bring her along one day."

"No, ya won't." Hannah bellowed a laugh. "You've forgotten all about your friends, haven't ya? Dragging yourself from hoity-toity Mayfair, where you're queen of cooks. I've heard all about you, Katie H., in your bloomin' mansion."

"Cease with your bloomin' this and bloomin' that," I admonished her. "You sound ridiculous."

"That's the way us Cockneys are supposed to talk. Innit?" Hannah laughed again, her warmth of character I remembered so well filling the space.

"You can sound like anyone you wish," I told her. "I've heard you do it."

"That's true. I can talk like a toff if I want." Hannah drew herself up and took on the stuffy tones of a lady of breeding. "How do you do, madam? May I tempt you with a fine piece of jewelry for your charming daughter?"

"I have few coins to spare." I turned over one of the little boxes, which held a painting of a girl with golden curls on it. The girl reminded me of Grace when she was younger, though her hair was a different shade. The box was the least worn of those on the table, and the tiny hinges and catch still worked. "But I might have this."

"A penny for it." Hannah relaxed into her own voice, which hailed from the same part of London as mine. "I know that's dear for such a trinket, but I have it on authority it used to belong to a duchess."

"It never did, and you know it." I reached into my coin purse and extracted a copper penny. "These are turned out in a factory somewhere in the north. But it's pretty enough."

Hannah chortled as she snatched up the coin and tucked it

into her pocket. "You were always sharp, weren't ya? Now, I know you didn't make your way to me 'umble little stall to pass the time of day and buy a present for your girl. What'cha want, Katie?"

"Do you do domestic work any longer?" I asked, as though idly curious. "Or are you a merchant only now?"

"Ah, me." Hannah collapsed into her chair and heaved her cracked leather boots onto an upturned crate. "I never took to life in service. I only got myself into that house as upstairs maid so I could pinch things, and you know it."

Hannah had been working in a large house where I'd been hired as a kitchen assistant before my marriage. Her name had not been Hannah at the time—she'd given our mistress a false one. I'd never suspected her as anything other than a prim and rather disdainful upstairs maid in her starched cap and pinafore, until the night I'd walked into the second-floor sitting room and found her calmly robbing the mistress's desk.

Both of us were meant to be in bed, but I'd been worrying about my ill mum and wandering the silent house to calm my nerves. I'd heard a noise in the sitting room and had peeped inside.

My initial thought had been worry that the faultless Hannah would see *me* in this upstairs room where I had no business being. Then I'd noticed Hannah pocketing several valuable trinkets before she turned around and spied me.

She'd tried to call my bluff, asking haughtily what I thought I was doing above stairs, but I called hers. We'd had a whispered argument about who was more in the wrong, until I threatened to call the butler—a petty and cruel man—to make her turn out her pockets.

Hannah then broke down with a sobbing story of having to

steal to feed her old dad and seven brothers and sisters, which was as much a fabrication as her references to obtain this post in the Montagu Square mansion.

Once we'd come to an agreement that we wouldn't peach on each other—as long as Hannah put back what she'd taken—we went down to the kitchen and had a cup of tea and a long natter.

After that, we became fast friends. That is, until she'd vanished one morning, along with some of the best silver spoons. The master had summoned the police, but as Hannah had told no one but me her real name and had forged all her letters of reference, they searched for her in vain.

I'd caught up with her a few years after my husband's death, when I'd ducked out of the rain into a pub in Maiden Lane. Hannah had been a barmaid there, and we'd had another intense chat. She was one of the few who knew of my ignominious sort-of marriage and the existence of my daughter.

Hannah had been gone when I'd returned to the pub a few months later, and the landlord told me she was bunking in with a man who had a stall on the Portobello Road. I'd lost track of her after that.

I saw no sign of the man today, but the stall was here and so was Hannah.

"Are you still in the business?" I asked her. The confidence game business, I meant, and she knew it. "Or are you walking the straight and narrow?"

Hannah lifted her chin. "I'm an honest trader now, love. Was going about with the man who ran this stall, but *I* run it now. I bought him out." She laced her fingers behind her head and regarded me beatifically.

"I see." I touched a pocket watch that was finely made but I could tell was not expensive. Something else churned out in factories by the dozen. "I was hoping you hadn't forgotten all your old tricks."

"Oh, yes? Well, if you came here to ask me to rob the house you cook in, no thank you. I'm out of *that* business. I never stole those spoons, by the way. It must have been old Lady Mortimer, who was staying in the house at the time. She was constantly sliding little trinkets into her pockets, which her lady's maid would quietly return. Lady Mortimer was right off her nut, though I heard she's gone now, poor soul. Blaming me for them spoons was to save her from humiliation."

I believed her. At the time, I'd reasoned Hannah would never do anything so obvious. However, no one had been interested in the opinion of an under-cook, and they'd ignored me when I'd spoken up for her.

"No robberies necessary," I said. "But I would like it if you could become a maid again, a proper one, in a house in Belgrave Square."

"You are intriguing me now." Hannah swung her legs down and surged to her feet, snatching up a cloth to drape over her wares. "Come around behind here, Katie, me friend. I'll fetch us a pint from across the road and you can tell me all about it."

I refused the pint, as I did not really like ale, but I accepted a cup of tea from another vendor. The tea was weak, the leaves reused too often, but I did not complain.

We sat together behind Hannah's table, me on a rickety folding chair. Hannah sipped her dark ale, her feet up once more, as I told her what I wished her to do.

I was as cryptic as I could be, keeping in mind the danger to Daniel and the secrecy of his mission. Though I trusted Hannah more than almost anyone else I knew, I told her only that my friend Daniel had gone to work in this house and might be in peril from its inhabitants.

Hannah realized I was leaving much out, but she listened patiently, nodding as I explained.

"Be a new adventure for me," she said when I finished. "Not used to being a spy."

"It's much the same as being a confidence trickster," I told her. "Learning things, watching, and noting, while pretending to be someone you are not."

Her laughter rang out. "I always liked you, Katie, even when you bristle when I say your name wrong. You're easy to tease, love." Her eyes sparkled. "You have my interest. I'll do it."

"Please be careful," I admonished. "As I say, it could be quite dangerous, for both of you."

"Me first husband was more a danger to me than any toff in a big house ever could be, even if they are villains." Hannah winked at me. "They'll never know I'm anything but a prim and proper maid with her nose in the air. How d'ya want me to report to you?"

"You'll have a day out, like any other maid. Mine is Monday afternoon and all of Thursday, but if they do not let you match that, have no fear. We can meet at a market or chance upon each other in a tea shop. Two domestics having a chat. Nothing wrong in that."

"Someone might try to follow me," Hannah pointed out. "To make sure I'm what I say I am."

I'd thought of that. "Hopefully they will not believe they need to. But if so, I am confident you can give them the slip. Or perhaps you can let them watch you do whatever a maid would do on her day out. Peek in at a music hall, go to chapel."

"Chapel." Hannah's smile flashed. "Well, I suppose they'd

think me blameless if I sat in a pew for evening prayer." She patted my knee. "Don't you worry none. I'll get to you, with no one the wiser."

"Thank you." I set aside my half-drunk tea. "You have relieved my mind already."

"Anything for an old mate. You kept yourself from me for too long, you know. I'll pretend it don't hurt me feelings."

"You are difficult to keep track of." I rose and straightened my skirts. "And I have been very busy. Meals to cook, a daughter to raise."

"Life rolls around all of us." Hannah jumped to her feet and caught me in an embrace, her arms strong around me. "You keep yourself well, Mrs.—are you going by Bristow now?"

"Holloway," I said, my voice going tight. "Mrs. Holloway."

Hannah released me, her approval beaming forth. "You've kicked his dust from your boots, have you? Good for you, duck. I know he was a hard one."

"He was." I'd never been able to keep the truth from her.

"Good riddance to 'im. Now, don't puff up and tell me I'm a bad'un because I'm happy he's shuffled off his mortal coil. The world's better without some people in it." Hannah squeezed my shoulders. "I'll get into that house, Kat, me darling. Don't you worry."

I thanked her profusely, then we said our good-byes. I left her stall and walked back down Portobello Road, the little box wrapped in a handkerchief in my pocket.

As I searched for a hansom, I wondered if I'd been wise to recruit her. But I could think of no other way of inserting eyes into the Belgrave Square house with none, including Daniel, suspecting.

As I climbed into the hansom and instructed the cabbie to take me to Mount Street, I reflected that I trusted a known thief and confidence trickster more than I did the police inspector who'd knowingly sent Daniel headlong into danger.

The only trouble with my plan to put Hannah in the Belgrave Square house was that I'd have to wait and stew until she could come to me. Until then, I could have no idea what was happening only streets away from me.

As I carried on with supper for the family when I returned Thursday night and preparations for the next day's breakfast, I tried not to picture Daniel being taken into an attic room or a deep cellar to have his throat cut for being a police informer.

These visions troubled my sleep, and I was testy the next morning. When Lady Cynthia strode into the busy kitchen, I continued slicing vegetables, not in the mood to exchange pleasantries.

Cynthia wore a frock today, a subdued one of slim lines that she'd taken to in the past year or so. At any other time I'd tell her she looked fetching, but I was too distracted by my own troubles. So distracted that I almost missed the deep lines of worry etched on her face.

I ceased chopping the slim spring carrots I'd add to a roast for dinner. Tess had stepped into the scullery, her voice and Elsie's risen in friendly chatter, leaving Cynthia and me relatively alone.

"Is something amiss?" I asked her in concern.

"I'm not certain." Cynthia scraped a wooden chair from the work table and sat down, propping her elbows too near a smear of butter. "It is Auntie, you see. She's in a state."

"Oh?" An upset Mrs. Bywater could take her unhappiness out on the staff, noting the minutest speck of dust left on a mantelpiece, a tiny smudge on a polished floor. Or she might march downstairs to demand I prepare a ridiculous meal of overly complicated dishes to dazzle whomever she worried about impressing.

"It is a letter she received," Cynthia said. "She did not tell me of it, but I happened to catch her reading it. She became as pale as the paper in her hand. When I asked if it was bad news, she nearly flew at me and commanded me out of the room with much waving of her arms. I almost thought she'd strike me. I retreated as bade, but when she was at the theater last night, I stole into her sitting room and had a peek."

Cynthia's expression changed from triumph at her own cleverness to worry for one of her family. "It was an awful letter, Mrs. H. Accused Auntie of all sorts, including being unfaithful to Uncle—which is mad. Auntie has no use for men at all, except for Uncle, upon whom she dotes. But the language they used was horrible."

I listened, both disquieted and puzzled. "Your aunt and I have had our differences, but she is the most upright woman I have ever met. What on earth could this poisoned pen say that was true? Also, why wouldn't Mrs. Bywater dismiss such a thing as nonsense?"

"Judge for yourself. Auntie is out again today, so I fetched the letter and brought it with me." Cynthia slipped a stained envelope from her pocket and held it across the table to me. "Go on, Mrs. H. Read that."

3

While I hesitated at reading another's correspondence, especially that of the mistress of the house, my curiosity got the better of me. I reached for the missive.

Instead of ripping out the letter and reading it immediately, I carefully studied the envelope, as I'd learned from long association with Daniel. It told me nothing, except that the paper was cheap, such as could be obtained at any stationers in the Strand. That and the fingers of whoever had carried it had been dirty, though no fingerprints could be seen, only smudges.

The envelope bore a penny stamp, which meant it had come by post like any ordinary letter. The stamp had a cancellation mark on it, so no one could use it again, and the back of the envelope had been marked with the date it went through a post office—two days ago. The direction on the front said *The Lady of the Household,* with the address of 43 Mount Street.

While Cynthia watched me impatiently, I withdrew the letter and unfolded it.

What I read made me flinch. The letter writer accused Mrs. Bywater of many and varied reprehensible things, using quite foul language, as Cynthia had indicated. It was a repellent, abusive missive that would sicken even the hardiest soul.

"I understand your aunt's reaction," I said. "But also, I do not. If she has done none of these things—which I am certain she hasn't—why would she not simply thrust it indignantly on the fire?"

"Read to the end," Cynthia urged.

I had ceased perusing at the bottom of the first page, my senses already offended. I flipped the paper over and read the writing that filled the top half of it.

The writer demanded that Mrs. Bywater leave him or her a sum of money—one hundred guineas, to be precise—at a location to be disclosed in the next letter.

"Drat," I said.

"My words were more unfortunate," Cynthia said. "What an awful thing to send to poor Auntie. Not to mention trying to pry money from her. Strange they'd believe she'd pay up. Everyone knows how parsimonious Auntie is."

I folded the paper to shut out the awful sentences. "I exclaimed because I am unhappy they did not tell us where to leave the money in *this* letter. If they had, we could lie in wait for whoever it is to collect the funds and then fetch a convenient policeman."

"They have thought of that." Cynthia quoted from the letter: *"Tell anyone, and your sins will be exposed to the world."*

"Your aunt hasn't told anyone, I am guessing. Who would?

If you can find the next letter when it comes, perhaps it will lead us to this horrid person."

"I will watch out for it," Cynthia promised. "And lie in wait for this person, as you say. Whoever they are, they will be sorry they upset Auntie in any way."

I agreed with her. Cynthia began to reach for the letter, but I opened it again and made myself read the lines once more.

Cynthia wrinkled her nose. "You can't mean to go over it again. I am made of stern stuff, but it nauseated me."

"This letter writer is amazingly specific at some points, did you notice? They are not spewing general abuse." I picked out a few phrases. *"I saw you and your foul lover at the lake in Holland Park . . . I witnessed what you did under your secret tree on Hampstead Heath . . ."* I regarded Cynthia over the paper. "I very much doubt your aunt conducted trysts in either of these places. She scarcely likes to get her feet wet."

"That is true," Cynthia agreed.

I folded the pages and slipped them into the envelope. "Why does this writer believe Mrs. Bywater will pay to keep quiet about things she never did?"

Cynthia shrugged. "To prevent them spreading lies? Auntie's friends are prudish in the extreme. If any believed she'd conducted these sorts of affairs, even in the distant past, they'd shun her."

"Or laugh," I said. "At the absurdity that anyone could think so. It is ludicrous." I studied the envelope again. "The address says *The Lady of the Household.* As we know your aunt has done none of the things she is accused of, the logical conclusion is that the letter writer did not mean it to go to Mrs. Bywater."

Cynthia looked puzzled, then her eyes widened. "Good Lord—you don't suppose they are talking about *me*? I've never had trysts of any kind, not on Hampstead Heath or in Holland Park or in any other green refuge London has to offer. More's the pity. How awful they'd think so."

"No," I said gently. "Not you. The previous lady of the house, before your aunt came to look after you."

Cynthia drew a sharp breath, then her chest ceased moving at all. "The mean, foul, nasty *bitch*."

Her voice was tight but loud enough that Elsie and Tess glanced in from the scullery, startled.

"Say nothing to your aunt," I instructed Cynthia, motioning Elsie and Tess to go back to what they were doing. "You keep a lookout for the second letter, and we'll have him. Or her. But please keep this between us for now. If you must rant, do so to me, or perhaps Mr. Thanos, who is discreet, but no one else. It is important."

Cynthia continued to splutter in outrage, but I held her with a stern gaze, and finally, she nodded. Her rage was high, but she was wise enough to grasp that if she went on a rampage, she'd frighten away the culprit, and we might never catch them.

She jammed the letter into her pocket. "I don't like that Auntie has to continue believing this is about *her*."

"Perhaps she doesn't." I wanted to pat Cynthia's shoulder or some such and comfort her, but I could not do so to the daughter of the house in the middle of the kitchen. "She must realize it has nothing to do with her. Perhaps she is so upset because she knows who they *do* mean."

"Oh." Cynthia stilled again. "She might. Auntie is oblivious much of the time, but she is no fool. But hang about, Mrs. H. Why send a letter trying to extort money from my poor sister, when she has been gone from us for three years?"

"That might be the most intriguing question of all." I

grasped my knife, preparing to continue chopping. "Put the letter back, say nothing, and watch for the next one. We'll have this person." My knife came down and severed the leafy head of an unfortunate carrot.

"Right you are. Thank you, Mrs. H. I'll keep you informed." Cynthia saluted me and dashed from the kitchen, nearly running down Mr. Davis on her way.

Mr. Davis stepped aside in deference, then scowled at Cynthia's back once she'd passed him. He was quite fond of Cynthia but sometimes disapproved of her impetuous ways.

"She'll come to grief running about like that," Mr. Davis said to me. "I agree with the mistress that she should take a husband, but only if she finds a gent who likes her temperament."

"That would be best." I continued to slice carrots with vigor. "None who will try to break her spirit. Or I shall break *him.*"

Mr. Davis unbent enough to shoot me a wry smile. "I too, Mrs. Holloway."

He turned from the kitchen and disappeared back down the hall to his demesne of the butler's pantry.

I puzzled over the letter and its purpose as I continued preparing the midday meal.

The *Lady of the Household* meant Cynthia's younger sister, Lady Rankin—Lady Emily Shires, that was. She'd been married to Lord Rankin, who held the lease on this house. Lord Rankin, a lofty baron, was not the best of men, but he'd truly grieved when Emily had died.

Lady Emily had been the one to originally hire me on as cook, with dire consequences, I am afraid. Though I suppose the events would have played out whether I'd come here to work or not.

I made myself cease chopping the carrots before they were too minuscule for use and move on to the next task.

"Everything all right, Mrs. H.?" Tess asked me. When she'd finished her conversation with Elsie, she'd begun mixing flour and yeast for a special bread I intended for tonight's sweet. At the moment I couldn't remember for the life of me what else went into it.

"I cannot tell you. I'm sorry, Tess." I scraped the carrot bits from my chopping board into a bowl. "It's nothing to do with me, and private."

"Did someone send Lady Cynthia a nasty letter?" Tess added the warm water I'd left out and a bit of finely pounded sugar to the dough and began working it into a clump with a wooden spoon. "I saw you passing one back and forth."

Tess was quick, her guess almost exact. "I do not wish to speak of it without Cynthia's permission."

I stared into the bowl as I stated this, wondering what I'd intended with all these carrots. I was most distracted today.

"If they're fussing at her for wearing trousers, I'll have at 'em." Tess pounded the dough with her spoon. "Why shouldn't a lady wear what she likes? They're more practical sometimes, trousers. Ain't they? I knew a lass who lived on a farm, and she was always in breeches to do her work with the animals."

"It was not about Cynthia and men's attire. I really can say no more than that."

Tess continued to beat the dough with vigor. "That's all right. I'm dead curious, but I don't want to upset her ladyship. She's been good to me. If she needs any help though, you look to me. Caleb as well."

It was kind of her to offer, even if it was partly from inquis-itiveness. "Please do not mention this to Constable Greene," I said quickly. "At least, not yet."

"You know me." Tess cheerfully made a sign of locking her lips, smudging the upper one with flour. "I'll say nothing till you give me the word."

"Thank you, Tess." I calmed enough to at last recall what I intended for the bread. "Work that butter I melted and one egg into the dough, then turn it out and knead it—gently—and we'll put it aside. When it's risen, I'll show you how to make it into a star shape, which we'll fill with sugar and cinnamon."

"Mmm." Tess poured in the butter, then cracked an egg into a small bowl before stirring it into the dough. She'd learned not to crack an egg directly into a batter, in case the egg was bad or it sent bits of shell cascading into the other ingredients.

Tess turned a well-mixed ball onto the floured table and began to work it. "Please say we can have some of this."

"I will make any leftover dough into small portions for us." I continued to hold the bowl of carrots, still unable to remem-ber the next step with them.

"Weren't you going to rub them carrot bits with spices?" Tess asked me. "And put them in with the roast?"

"Yes, of course." I bustled to the stove, where the meat was waiting to go into the oven to sear slowly all afternoon. "You have a good memory for the recipes now."

Tess beamed. Whether she believed I'd been testing her or knew I had truly forgotten what I was about, I couldn't say. She was kind enough not to tell me.

I saw no more of Cynthia that day. Mrs. Bywater, who made it a habit to come downstairs to ask me about menus, my expenditure, and what quantities I was buying of the comestibles, did not appear either.

I wondered if Mrs. Bywater's distress over the letter was because it could shame Lady Emily posthumously, and by extension Cynthia, and even Mrs. Bywater herself. Mrs. Bywater had never approved of either Emily or Cynthia—the entire Shires family, actually—though she was pleased her husband's sister had married an earl and his niece had married a baron. However, Mrs. Bywater had never been happy with her in-laws' characters.

She already was having difficulty enough interesting young men in marrying Cynthia. A blackmailer threatening to expose Cynthia's sister's indiscretions could ruin Cynthia's chances entirely.

By the standards of the upper classes, Cynthia was already on the shelf, unmarried at nearly thirty-three. *She* was not bothered by this state of affairs, but Mrs. Bywater found it embarrassing and disgraceful. Was this what had Mrs. Bywater so unhappy about the letter's threats?

I confessed I was a bit surprised that Emily, Lady Rankin, had found the energy to conduct liaisons outdoors at Hampstead Heath and Holland Park. She'd been a frail thing, barely able to lift her hand to eat her meals. This was the image she'd cultivated, at least. I knew Lady Rankin had been more robust by the actions she'd taken, but even so, antics with a man in various parks seemed out of character.

I wondered very much who that man was.

These thoughts stayed with me as Tess and I assembled meals for the remainder of the day. Underlying my musings was profound worry for Daniel beginning what I called His Last Ordeal, and pondering whether Hannah would successfully find employment in the house and then how she would report to me.

I roused myself from fretting to teach Tess how to shape the cinnamon bread. After the dough rose, I showed her how to divide it into quarters and then roll each of those quarters into a perfect circle. Much flour cascaded over our aprons, hands, and faces, and onto the floor before Tess accomplished it.

I'd mixed some cinnamon, cardamom, and a bit of brown sugar with melted butter in a bowl. We painted this over each circle before stacking the next one on top of it. The final circle was left bare.

"Now for the prettiness," I said.

With the dull side of a knife, I carefully marked the stack of circles into sixteen equal wedges, then sliced these all the way through, making certain the wedges remained joined in the center.

"We take two pieces." I gently picked them up in my fingers and bade Tess take two on the opposite site. "And twist them away from each other a couple of times. Now we seal the ends together."

Tess copied my movements, awkwardly at first, then she caught on how to manipulate the pieces of dough. Between us we quickly twisted and sealed the pieces all the way around.

We had to let the bread rest and rise again while we finished the clear soup and side dishes of vegetables for the evening meal.

"A dusting of finishing sugar on the top, and then the bread goes into the oven," I said once the dough was puffy enough. I carried it there myself, on a paper-lined tray. If Tess dropped it, there would go an entire afternoon's work.

Tess was smiling when I turned from sliding the bread safely into the oven. "Can we do more like that?"

"Let us see how this one turns out first." I hadn't mentioned that I'd never attempted such a pastry as this before. "Now for our portion."

We'd had to cut away some of the dough to make the circles exact. These bits I rolled out again, brushed with the butter and spices, and then curved into pinwheels. I let these rise while we took out the roast—the carrots had caramelized nicely and would lend a mellow flavor to the meat.

Once we sent up the meal on the dumbwaiter to the dining room, I removed the star-shaped bread from the oven, sent it up on its own, and popped our portion into the oven to bake.

Not long later, Tess and I sat down to our meal of leftover salt pork from the day's lunch, boiled potatoes, and our cinnamon bread.

"None better." Tess closed her eyes as she chewed the pinwheel, a drop of butter trickling down her chin.

"Just a simple bit of dough," I said with pretend modesty. "Nothing a high-placed chef would applaud."

In spite of my words, I was quite pleased with how the bread had turned out—a perfect star shape streaked with cinnamon. I longed to show it to Daniel and share some with him. I swallowed on heartache.

"More fool your stuck-up chef." Tess stuffed a large portion of roll into her mouth, her cheeks puffing out as she chewed.

I drew a breath to warn her against gluttony but closed it again as Lady Cynthia, clad in a man's frock coat and trousers, skimmed into the kitchen. Cynthia hesitated and glanced at Tess, the only one in the kitchen with me, clearly impatient to tell me something.

I set aside my fork and rose. "Will you excuse us, Tess? Shall we go to the housekeeper's parlor, Lady Cynthia?"

Cynthia shook her head and continued her charge to the table. "Don't disturb your supper, Mrs. H. I don't mind if Tess knows. Judith received one of those horrid letters as well. She told me so this afternoon. Same envelope, same writing, same foul accusations. What do you make of that?"

4

As I regarded Cynthia, and Tess gaped at her, I was gripped by dire foreboding. "A strange occurrence indeed," I managed to say.

Cynthia dragged out a chair and plopped breathlessly into it. "A damned strange one, I'd say."

Miss Judith Townsend was a young lady from a very wealthy family, an artist, and she lived without chaperonage with her friend Lady Roberta in a large town house in Upper Brook Street. I could well imagine a threatening letter coming to her because of her scandalous lifestyle, but one hard on the heels of what Mrs. Bywater had received could hardly be a coincidence.

"Did Miss Townsend show the letter to you?" I asked, resuming my seat. My supper tried to entice me, but I was no longer hungry.

"She did. I confided in Judith about the letter Auntie received. She expressed surprise, then rummaged in her desk and produced her own letter, which she said had come yesterday. She'd had a laugh over it with Bobby and then forgot about it."

"Did the letter demand money for silence?"

"Indeed it did." Cynthia balled her fists on the table. "Judith let me read it. The writer went on for some time about her misdeeds—as Judith lives unconventionally, they had much fodder. Told her she had to give them a thousand guineas, in a location to be disclosed. If not, they'd expose her and shame her family."

"A thousand guineas?" Tess repeated in shock. "The cheek."

"I agree, Tess." I set one of the sweet rolls on a clean plate and pushed it toward Cynthia. "Eat this and calm yourself. I assume Miss Townsend has no intention of paying it."

"None whatsoever. Judith said that she didn't put it on the fire right away, because she enjoyed herself reading the more salacious bits out to Bobby." Cynthia snatched up the roll and stuffed it into her mouth as inelegantly as Tess had. Her face changed as she chewed. "I say, Mrs. H. This is scrumptious."

"Ain't it though?" Tess rhapsodized. "The one that went up to table was twisted into a star shape."

"I'm sorry I didn't see it—I dined with Judith and Bobby. But this is fine." Cynthia made short work of the rest of her roll. "Judith is intrigued now that I told her Auntie had one of these letters. She instructed me to rush home and consult you about it."

I pushed away my plate and turned to my sweet with more composure than my companions. "Would Miss Townsend let me have a look at the letter?" I asked.

Cynthia nodded. "I'm certain she would. Do you have an idea, Mrs. H.?"

"None at all," I answered truthfully. "But it is very odd. Neither Mrs. Bywater nor Miss Townsend have received the second letter telling them where to leave the cash?"

"Not yet, apparently. I wonder if the writer was happy to vent their spleen with the first letter, and have left off. Perhaps they've convinced themselves they've rattled the receiver and have decided it's not worth the bother of the second."

"Possibly," I said with doubt. "A letter spewing invective and making vague threats is upsetting, but a specific request to leave a certain sum of money in a certain place becomes a criminal offense. In that case, one stands trial for blackmail. Perhaps the writer is reluctant to cross that line."

"Judith would be happy for you to look into it," Cynthia said. "She'd have handed the letter to me to bring home to you, but she wants to see you in person instead. As her guest for tea, whenever you are able."

"That is very kind." I was flattered, but Cynthia and her friends did not always understand that a body had to work for a living. "Please warn her that I will not be able to take leave until Monday."

"Never worry. I'll fix it with Auntie, and you can pop to see her tomorrow."

"Tomorrow is Saturday," I said with patience. "Tess's day out. I will not be able to leave the kitchen."

Tess looked stricken. "I can stay if ye like, Mrs. H. Wasn't going to do much—"

"No," I said firmly. "One thing you must learn as a domestic, Tess, is that you guard your days out fiercely. Once you give one up, the household will believe it not important to you and expect you to work without ceasing. You visit your brother on your days out, do you not?"

Tess nodded, flushing. Her brother was slow and needed looking after. He lived with a trusted friend, but Tess took him some of what we baked and little gifts, and I imagined he treasured her visits. She also used the time to stroll about London with her beau, Constable Greene, who also had Saturdays free.

"Miss Townsend will have to wait, I am afraid," I told Cynthia. "If she is too impatient to give me until Monday, I could possibly take tea Sunday afternoon, after the midday dinner, of course. Mr. Bywater will not give up his Sunday roast with all the trimmings so his cook can pay calls."

"Calm your pride, Mrs. H." Cynthia finished up the roll and licked her fingers. "Judith is not completely oblivious—she does have staff of her own, and understands. You bake up another of these delicious breads and take it to her on Monday afternoon. She'll be more than pleased with that."

Monday afternoons I spent with Grace, but if I could slip away a bit early, I could carve out a half hour to take Miss Townsend the bread and read her letter.

"That can be arranged," I said. "Please tell her to expect me early Monday afternoon for tea."

"Done." Cynthia beamed. "Any more of this bread about, Mrs. H.? I could dine on it."

Tess leapt to her feet at my nod and brought the rest of the rolls to the table. She and Cynthia, with my permission, gobbled them up, while I sat back and contemplated. Things were becoming intriguing indeed.

One reason I'd decided to become interested in the problem of the letters—though I would have, in any case—was to ease my mind from constant worry about Daniel.

Not knowing whether he was well or in danger or simply working through tedium kept me ill at ease. I snapped more than I should have and glowered at Tess when she came home later than usual on Saturday. She explained that she and Caleb had been visiting with her brother, and her brother hadn't wanted her to leave.

I had compassion for her and her brother both, but I am afraid I testily told her she should have sent word. I apologized later, relieving her of duties after supper, but Tess was put out with me, and I could not blame her. I also could not explain to her the reasons for my grumpiness.

Sunday morning, a grubby boy knocked on the back door with a soiled piece of paper, demanding a penny to give it to the cook.

I heard Elsie arguing with him, declaring a penny was too dear a price. I jerked my hand from the dough I'd been shaping into bread and hurried into the scullery.

"Here's a ha'penny." I thrust a floury coin at him and snatched the paper from his hand. The lad scowled at me but decided to cut his losses and charged back upstairs.

Elsie shook her head and returned to her sink. "Cheeky beggar. Not bad news, I hope?" she added as she caught a glimpse of my face as I read the paper.

"No," I said breathlessly. "It is good."

I thrust the scrap into my pocket and returned to the kitchen, leaving Elsie baffled.

The note had been written in carefully printed letters, consisting of three simple words: *I am here.*

Early on Monday afternoon, as soon as I dared, I donned my best frock and tucked the little box I'd purchased from Hannah for Grace into my pocket. Downstairs, I took up my basket with a warm star-shaped bread wrapped in a towel, and walked from Mount Street to Park Street and turned from there into Upper Brook Street.

The May weather had become fine, with the sun shining hard and a few puffy clouds drifting overhead. Because of the warmth, fewer fireplaces burned, which meant less smoke in the hazy air.

Mrs. Bywater would soon begin her yearly debate about whether to remain in the hot and smelly city for the summer or retreat to the cooler countryside. On the one hand, she lived in London fairly cheaply, as Lord Rankin did not charge the Bywaters rent to live in his house.

The air in Somerset was much more salubrious than London's, but the Bywaters' house there was sparsely staffed. If Mrs. Bywater took any maids or footmen from this house to Somerset with her, she'd have to pay them, as their terms with the agency were for Lord Rankin's London house only.

She'd once tried to chivy us all to the country with her, with no promise of pay at all, but Mr. Davis had put his foot down about that. Also, the Bywaters' country-house servants might have severely objected to us descending on them, though Mrs. Bywater had not considered that.

Servants were at the mercy of their masters, it was true, but only to a point. If we decided we were being unfairly treated, we could be plenty obstinate. Mrs. Bywater had backed down from Mr. Davis's objections—he supported by Mrs. Redfern and me. Now whenever Mrs. Bywater took servants to Somerset with her, it was only one or two, and those were paid extra wages.

Thinking of Mrs. Bywater returned me to speculations on the letter she'd received, and I sped my steps to Miss Townsend's tall house in the middle of Upper Brook Street.

The elderly butler, Hubbard, whose stiff manner hid a soft heart, opened the front door and ushered me into an elegant hall. Whenever I'd attempted to visit Miss Townsend through the below-stairs kitchen door, she'd overruled me and insisted on me entering through the front, claiming I was arriving as a guest. I found this odd and uncomfortable, but Hubbard welcomed me as courteously as if I'd stepped down from a lord's carriage.

I handed Hubbard the basket. "That's for Miss Townsend's tea. There's extra pieces for the rest of the household."

Hubbard gave me a cool bow of thanks, though I swore I detected a gleam of anticipation in his eyes. Basket on his arm, he stepped across the hall to a speaking tube that hung within an elaborately carved frame. He lifted the mouthpiece, blew into it, and spoke.

"Mrs. Holloway has arrived, madam."

I heard a muffled voice from the other end of the tube before Hubbard hung up the receiver.

"You are to proceed to the studio, Mrs. Holloway. Lady Cynthia is already there."

"Thank you, Hubbard."

I turned to the stairs and steeled myself to march up them to the top floor. I should be used to such exertion, as my bedchamber was in the attic of a house as large, but I puffed as I stepped off the final landing.

Miss Townsend had converted her attic rooms into one large studio, with skylights to illuminate it. I'd once wondered idly where her servants slept, and Cynthia had told me they each had a comfortable room on the house's third floor.

While I was happy with my own place, I sometimes wished Miss Townsend's cook wasn't so devoted to her. I'd relish working in a house where I had a real bedroom with a window. It was small wonder that Miss Townsend's staff all adored her.

When I entered the studio, Miss Townsend, a slim lady with very dark hair and brown eyes, sat before a canvas as tall as she was, her brush poised as she contemplated where to put her next stroke. The canvas was at such an angle that I could not see the entire composition, but I spied colorful draperies and a very naked young woman in the middle of them.

I did not recognize the model in the picture, but she was no doubt one of Miss Townsend's and Lady Cynthia's rather scandalous friends.

"She's here, Judes," Cynthia announced from the depths of a sofa where she lounged. She wore her man's suit this afternoon and was buried in an issue of a racing newspaper.

Miss Townsend swung around on her stool and bathed me in a warm smile. "Welcome, Mrs. Holloway. Please, sit. I have instructed Hubbard to send up a scrumptious tea."

"I cannot stay long." I took the indicated chair, which was soft. It felt good on my legs after the walk, but I perched on its edge, unwilling to become too comfortable. I wanted to leave as soon as I was able.

"We know." Miss Townsend rose and went to a small chest-on-stand and opened a drawer, her every move elegant. "Here's the letter. Have a look and see what you make of it."

She handed me an envelope similar to the one Mrs. Bywater had received. As I studied it, the door banged open, and another young woman in a frock coat and trousers strode inside.

This was Lady Roberta Perry, Bobby to her friends. She'd shorn her brown hair close and had her suits tailor made. With her soft abdomen and square face, a person who didn't know her wouldn't guess she was female.

"Ah, the poisoned-pen letter is already out." Bobby nodded a greeting to me, then moved to the sofa. "Budge up, Cyn."

Cynthia obligingly swung her legs down to make room for Bobby to sit next to her. Both watched me intently, as did Miss Townsend, as I finished with the envelope—of the same cheap stationery as had enclosed Mrs. Bywater's letter—and slid out the paper inside.

I grimaced as I went over the lines, which said very nasty things about the good-hearted Miss Townsend. The letter ended with the demand for cash, the details to be given in the next letter.

"This is awful," I said as I folded the paper. "I am so sorry you had to read this, Miss Townsend. It's foul."

"My skin is rather thick," Miss Townsend said easily. She resumed her stool, crossing her legs and clasping paint-stained fingers around one knee. "I've endured similar abuse since I was very young and decided to be an eccentric. Admittedly not so much packed into one short letter in one go."

I was no stranger to slurs myself. Those in the working classes are perceived to be dull-witted and poorly skilled, and to have no understanding of finer feelings. We are never clever, only crafty. Women, in particular, are expected to be willing to put aside virtue if a man of a higher class demands it, and then are punished for it.

I'd learned how to defend myself, but what had been hurled at Miss Townsend was worse than anything I'd heard directed toward myself. This was even more repugnant than the letter meant for Lady Rankin that Mrs. Bywater had received.

"They had no excuse for writing it," I stated. "I hope we find the person so I can express my displeasure."

Bobby barked a laugh. "I'd love to see that."

"Two more of my friends have had similar letters," Miss Townsend said. "Not quite as bad as mine, but venomous enough. Viola laughed it off." She indicated the canvas, from which I understood that the lady depicted was the said Viola. "But Delia was very upset. I am quite annoyed on their behalf." Her serenity slipped for a brief moment, giving me a glimpse of the steely, determined woman beneath it.

"Funny thing," Bobby said from where she'd slumped into the sofa. "*I* haven't had a single note. I prance about town in these rags and openly live with Judes, and yet, this poisoned pen hasn't bothered to mention me. I'm not even in *that* letter." She waved at the one I held. "I might grow offended, if they're not careful."

I set the paper and envelope on the table beside me, no longer wishing to touch them. I was happy I was wearing gloves, though now I wanted to clean them.

"That is quite interesting, actually," I told Bobby. "While I would not wish such a thing on anyone, please let me know the instant you receive a letter, your ladyship, if you do."

"Right you are," Bobby said cheerfully. "Cyn hasn't gotten one either."

Cynthia scowled. "No, they chose to castigate my sister."

"No directions about where to leave the money?" I asked Miss Townsend.

"Not as yet," Miss Townsend replied. "Neither Viola nor Delia have received such instructions either." She sent me a humorless smile. "The letter writer is wise to be careful. I could have a number of policemen watching over the spot where we deposit the cash, ready to snatch them when they come to collect."

"I do wonder if they will take precautions against this," I mused. "They might send a go-between, but the go-between could be followed, of course. Perhaps this difficulty is why no one has received specific instructions about the money."

"Well, if they only meant to upset me, they missed their

mark." Miss Townsend gave me a decided nod. "Though they struck gold with poor Delia. She's shut herself up in the house and will not emerge, no matter how I try to persuade her to shrug it off."

I was not familiar with Delia or Viola, and Cynthia, realizing this, filled in the details. "Delia is married to the Marquise of Hayfield, a stiff-necked, punctilious human being. When I had my debut, he actually made overtures in my direction, but my father didn't like him, thank the Lord. Delia mostly ignores him, but if he read a letter like this about her, he'd believe every word and lock her in the cellar."

"Which is why he will never hear of it," Miss Townsend said firmly. "Viola's husband pays no attention to her and already believes the worst of her, so she's not bothered."

"Viola's chap, George Donnington, is a friend of my brother's." Bobby rolled her eyes. "Second son of a duke—his father is even a cabinet minister. Quite the catch."

"Hm." I longed for my notebook to record this information, but I would have to wait until later. "Lady Cynthia, I wonder if we could have Mr. Thanos look at the letter and envelope. He might be able to tell us something about the paper, ink, handwriting—those sorts of things."

Mr. Thanos was a genius in so many areas that I could only believe he'd lend insight into this problem as well.

Cynthia pursed her lips. "I'm not certain we should show these awful things to Thanos. He becomes very upset when someone is disparaging to ladies, bless him."

"We could show him only a part of the paper," I suggested. "A torn-off bit with more innocuous words. The envelope, certainly."

"What could Thanos hope to tell us?" Bobby asked in curiosity. "He's not a stationer."

"I do not know, in truth," I admitted. "But I would like his opinion."

The opinion I truly wanted was Daniel's, but he was out of my reach at the moment. Blast Monaghan. The safety of the realm was important, of course, but so was Daniel's safety.

"Thanos has amazing knowledge," Cynthia said. "We'll tear up Judith's letter and take it to him."

"Thank you," I said. "And please, Miss Townsend, if you receive further instructions about delivering the payment, send word to me or to Cynthia."

I rose, ready to depart, but at that moment, Hubbard arrived. He rolled in a cart loaded with a teapot and cups plus my star bread, laid out on a plate and cushioned by a checkered cloth.

Bobby leapt to her feet, rubbing her hands. "You can't leave now, Mrs. H. The repast has just arrived, thanks to you. It looks magnificent."

"It tastes even better than it looks," Cynthia avowed. "But Mrs. Holloway needs to race away."

"Yes, indeed." Miss Townsend, the exemplary hostess, left her stool and came to me. "You were kind to give us these few moments of your time, Mrs. Holloway. I will do as you instruct. We will find this letter-writing fellow and rout him."

"Or her," Cynthia put in.

"Or her," Miss Townsend said. She held out her hand, and I clasped it politely. "Thank you very much for coming, Mrs. Holloway. And for bringing us your lovely bread. We will enjoy consuming it."

I hoped they didn't intend to stand about and admire it—enriched bread spoiled quickly—but I only squeezed Miss Townsend's hand in return and gave her and the others my farewells.

I forbade Miss Townsend accompanying me downstairs, assuring her I knew the way. The three ladies were ready to forget about nasty letters and tear into the sweet treat, and so they should. Little was more important than enjoying good food with treasured friends.

Hubbard ushered me out of the studio, but he remained to serve the tea while I trudged down the many flights of stairs. A footman awaited me on the ground floor, guiding me out the front door.

Outside, I breathed a sigh of satisfaction. I had the rest of the day free, and I would spend it with Grace. I'd give her the little gift I'd bought her, and we'd talk and laugh and be a family.

I made my way east, skirting Grosvenor Square and up North Audley Street to Oxford Street. Crowds and vehicles surged around me as I walked along that busy thoroughfare packed with shops, houses, servants, and masters.

Despite the throng, I became aware, as I passed New Bond Street, that someone followed me. They were clever and furtive, but not enough to deceive me.

I ducked into the nearest lane, pressed my back against the brick wall there, and waited.

5

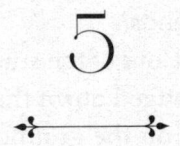

The fellow after me was sharp. He slowed outside the passage I'd slipped into and peered around its corner, perhaps making certain he was not walking into an ambush.

I left the shadows and stepped into his path.

"It's rare that I catch you out," I told the towering youth. "Why are you following me, James? Couldn't you simply walk with me?"

James McAdam, Daniel's son, grinned down at me. He was several inches taller than Daniel now, his voice deep, his handsome face guaranteeing many ladies would break their hearts over him. At nineteen, he was fully a man now, and who knew how long it would be before he announced he'd marry a lady he'd charmed?

"Sorry, Mrs. H." James leaned his lanky frame against the wall where I'd hidden. "Dad's asked me to look after you while he's away. I've taken over much of his delivery route for him, so I have to watch you when I can."

"Oh, did he just?" I asked in indignation, but I could not be surprised. Daniel was as concerned about me as I was about him, though I considered his danger to be far greater than mine. "I have been looking after myself for many years, thank you."

James flushed but was not defeated. "It's all my life's worth to tell him I won't do it. Besides, I want to make certain you're well too."

It was kind of him, and I climbed down from my pridefulness. "You are good to me, James, but you can call on me in the usual way, you know."

"True, but when you wander through the metropolis on your own, who knows how many cutpurses and ruffians might mean you harm? I already warned one pickpocket away."

My face heated in some embarrassment. I was usually keen-eyed, but I'd been distracted by worry for Daniel and these odd letters, plus eager to get on to see Grace, and hadn't noticed.

"I am grateful," I said with sincerity. "I am hardly wandering about the metropolis, though perhaps not paying as much attention as I ought. It is Monday, so you know I am walking with purpose to Cheapside."

"I'll go with you then, all right?"

I clasped James's offered arm, which I noted had changed from a bony boy's to a man's solid limb in the few years I'd known him. He made me feel quite aged.

"I do welcome your company, James," I told him. "And not only to keep the ruffians away."

"Always my pleasure, Mrs. H." He meant it, the good lad.

We returned to Oxford Street and strolled companionably toward Holborn. People pressed around us, everyone hurrying to be someplace different.

"Do you hear anything from your father?" I asked as we went.

James bent to catch my words, then shook his head. "Not since he started his mission. He had a chat with me before he went and told me he'd be having one with you too. Said I wasn't to come nigh, that it would be too dangerous for me, and for him," he finished in frustration.

"He told me the same." I debated whether to confess to James about Hannah, but though I trusted him, I decided I could help Hannah best by keeping my knowledge of her secret, at least for now. "I do not like it, I am not ashamed to say," I continued. "Daniel closeted with someone who might be the devil himself, and he uncertain which person is the fiend."

"That's not to say I haven't gone." James flashed me a defiant look. "No one notices me when I don't want them to." His grin returned. "Except you."

"Because I'm wise to your ways." I tightened my hold on his arm. "What have you found out?"

James glanced cautiously around us. While I doubted the harried wives and housekeepers, grooms and valets, who rushed about on their own business, planned to overthrow the queen and her cabinet, one never knew with spies. Many at Scotland Yard were aware that Daniel and I had a close friendship, and some villains must have that information as well. Likewise, most of London knew James was Daniel's son.

We'd reached High Holborn, and I tugged James to the side of the road. "Let us find a hansom, and you can regale me as we ride."

James agreed. I prepared to make for the nearest hansom stand, but James stepped into the street and let out a shrill whistle. The blast cut through the din of traffic, making people stop and turn. Some scowled at him, but others smiled at the handsome James, who waved at the nearest cabbie. He was so like his father that tears briefly stung my eyes.

A hansom with a black-coated, high-stepping horse made its way to us. Daniel often used a cabbie called Lewis to help him move about town—and had told him to transport me several times—but this driver was not he. Still, he recognized James.

"How are you, lad?" the man called from his perch behind the seats. "Where to?"

"Cheapside," James said. "I'll signal ye where to stop."

"Right you are."

Before I could offer the fare, James tossed a coin to the cabbie, then assisted me into the hansom as though I were a highborn lady and he my footman.

"It is really not necessary for you to pay," I said as we settled in and the cab jolted forward. "I have enough to take us to Clover Lane."

"Dad would skin me if I fobbed a fare from you, Mrs. H." James settled the cab's lap robe over my skirt. "This way is better. I get to keep my hide."

"You know your father would never hurt you," I admonished. "Not even in anger."

I'd realized this soon after I'd met James and seen him and Daniel together. Daniel not only would never harm James, but he'd never harm me. He was vastly different from my not-husband, Joe Bristow, in so many ways.

"Tell me everything," I commanded James as the cab bounced onto the Holborn Viaduct and descended toward Newgate. "Leave nothing out."

"There's not much to tell, unfortunately." James removed his cap and rumpled his hair, which was dark red. Daniel's was deep brown, so James's mother's must have been flaming red.

"The house is plenty luxurious, as you'd expect, but not many come and go. I thought I'd try making deliveries there, but there's only one van stops by every third day, with two men. One drives the horses, and the other unloads the goods and takes them down to the kitchen. He don't stay more than enough time to set down the boxes and sacks, and up he comes again, and they're off. No one but they are allowed down. That's what the scullery maid said when I tried to offer my services to fetch whatever the kitchen needed."

Instead of admonishing him to leave well enough alone, I went through other possible ways of getting him into the house. "Perhaps these deliverymen could employ you," I suggested. "What is the name of their company?"

I pulled out my notebook, the lovely one Joanna had given me last Christmas, extracted the stub of a pencil, and prepared to write.

"Mercer and Son," James said, and I scribbled it down. "But I've already tried. They only deliver to dukes and the like. Even the royal kitchens sometimes. Weren't looking for casual labor, they said."

"Put on airs, did they?" I'd met such merchants, who held themselves in high regard because they did business with the aristocracy. No one who didn't have a listing in *Debrett's* could so much as speak to them.

"They did. Sent me off with a flea in my ear. Other than them, a kitchen maid goes in and out to shop for whatever can't be delivered, or to nab something the cook wants at the last minute."

"As you do for me sometimes," I confirmed, continuing to write.

"Exactly. Valet to the viscount—a big chap—also comes and

goes on errands, but he don't leave the house for long. Every-one else stays put."

"Including Daniel?"

"Including Dad, yeah. Who *would* pull me limb from limb if he saw me, so I don't get too close, no matter what you say."

I paused in my note-taking. "Do you think he might have spied you talking to the scullery maid?"

"Nah, because the kitchens are well to the back of the house, which opens into the mews. The windows above don't overlook the door, which you come to through a little side pas-sageway. I don't like that passageway, because anyone could sneak down it without those in the house knowing."

I decided I didn't like it either. If James had found a hidden back way in, a villain could as well. "I am glad you are keeping an eye on the house, then."

"When I can. Dad has me doing his routes, I suspect not only so I can earn some coin and keep his clients from turning to others, but to keep me out of his business."

"Yes, I imagine he thought of that," I said in commiseration.

"There is one change in the household," James said as New-gate Street merged into Cheapside. "They have a new maid. She started on Saturday afternoon. Never seen her before, not there or in any of the other houses Dad delivers to."

He wouldn't have, of course. "Tell me about her." I dutifully made a note of this new maid.

James shrugged. "Ordinary. Quiet-looking, dark hair, a bit lofty, I think. I've watched her talk to the scullery maid who was scrubbing the front step. Stern and la-di-da."

James was an observant lad, but Hannah projected what she wanted everyone to see.

"Does she look like an anarchist at all?" I asked.

James chortled. "Not her. Probably they need more help since the viscount is stuck in his wheeled chair. He's gone out a few times, carried into his carriage by the big valet. Comes home soon, drooping as he's taken back inside." He let out an exasperated sigh. "If not for Dad being there for police business, I'd say it was an ordinary toff's house, same as any other in Belgravia."

I had no doubt James's description was apt. Why, then, was Mr. Monaghan so certain there were bad goings-on in the viscount's home? I itched to talk to Hannah but knew I'd have to wait.

The hansom slowed as it rolled along Cheapside. The busy road was as crowded as ever, a large knot of people gathering halfway along to observe Mr. Bennett's clock perched above his watch shop. On the hour, the ancient gods of Gog and Magog would raise hammers and strike and restrike a bell, sounding out the time. This entertaining spectacle drew hordes despite police efforts to limit their numbers. Nothing could keep Londoners from their pleasures.

Clover Lane was west of the clock, so the hansom could pull to the side of the street relatively unencumbered to let me alight.

I invited James to join me, as Grace and Joanna and family adored James, but he declined.

"Too many things to do," he said as he assisted me down. "I'm a working gent now, Mrs. Holloway."

I was happy James was earning his bread, though I hoped he could someday find a more lucrative trade.

I forestalled him leaping back into the cab. "Before you rush away, James, will you try to find Mr. Grimes for me? I'd like to speak to him."

Zachariah Grimes, who sometimes helped Daniel, unofficially, in his cases, looked like the most dangerous bone breaker one could meet, but he had a warm heart, and he was very fond of Daniel. I wished to confer with him on a thing or two.

Asking anyone to scour the masses in London for one man would be daunting for any other person, but James didn't flinch.

"Right you are, Mrs. H. I'll send him your way." James sketched me a salute and dove back into the hansom, which turned swiftly and rolled back toward St. Paul's.

I left the crush of Cheapside for the quiet of Clover Lane and the small house near its end.

Grace greeted me with enthusiasm that hadn't dimmed over the years. My heart ached as I held her in the vestibule of Joanna's cozy home.

My dream of running a tea shop while Grace played in the back room would soon be beyond reach if she kept growing up. I might be in the tea shop, but she'd be gone, off in her own life, with a family of her own. Perhaps she'd sometimes spare a thought or two for her old mum.

Until then, I intended to extract as much pleasure from our visits as I could.

Grace gushed over the little trinket box I'd brought her, and we took some time to find the best place to display it in the bedchamber she shared with Jane, Joanna's oldest daughter. Grace thanked me as profusely as if I'd brought her a string of diamonds.

"Where shall we go today, Mum?" Grace asked me when we went back downstairs to prepare for our walk.

"It is such a fine day," I said. "Hyde Park?"

There were closer green areas, like Lincoln's Inn Fields or the Victoria Embankment, with its gardens along the Thames.

When I'd been a babe in arms, the Thames had been foul, my mother had told me, with all means of offal and filth floating in it, so that one could not go near its sickening stench.

A new brick-lined sewage system, which apparently was a wonder of the world, had drained the horrors from our river. The embankments on either side of the Thames now both prevented flooding and provided a fine place to walk on a spring day.

Grace looked puzzled with my choice of Hyde Park—we usually did not go so far on my half days, but then she smiled. She suspected what I was up to.

Joanna insisted on helping Grace into her coat, as attentive as any mother, and she sent us off with a wave and a smile.

"I am lucky to have such a friend," I said as we walked back to Cheapside so I could seek yet another hansom.

"Aunt Joanna is lovely," Grace said. "I do love her. I hope you don't mind."

I regarded her in surprise. "Why on earth should I mind?"

I supposed I ought to be jealous of Joanna for being able to spend more time with my daughter than I could. I *was* envious, because I wanted to be the one to tuck Grace into bed and kiss her good night. But Joanna, my dearest friend in life, would never, ever think to usurp my place.

At one time, she and Sam had offered to adopt Grace, the too-good people believing they'd do me a favor, and I'd wept for days over such an agonizing choice. In the end, I'd refused, and Joanna had understood exactly why.

I did not have the skill to simply summon a cab as James did, so we walked through St. Paul's Churchyard to a hansom stand in Ludgate Hill. The cab we embarked took us along Fleet Street and then to the Strand, which was as thronged as

Cheapside. The cabbie turned through the West End's theater district, and soon we emerged into Piccadilly and Mayfair.

I'd swept as many coins as I could into my purse today, in anticipation of this journey, so I had no trouble paying over the shillings when we descended at Hyde Park Corner.

We chose a path that reached out to entice us into wide swaths of green. Hyde Park was open to anyone in London, and a cook and her daughter could stroll there with impunity, though mostly we saw ladies with parasols and fine feathered hats or nannies pushing children in their tiny carriages.

I kept busy Knightsbridge in our sights, and Grace, an intelligent girl, pointed toward it. "What's on the other side of that road, Mum? Should we go look at the pretty houses there?"

I paused and wrinkled my forehead as though I hadn't considered this every day since Daniel had locked himself into Viscount Peyton's home in Belgrave Square. "I suppose we could," I said, trying to sound doubtful. "It isn't far, is it?"

We returned to Knightsbridge, waited for a clearing in traffic, then plunged across the road, hand in hand, sealing our fate.

6

Grace and I peered into a few shop windows in Knightsbridge, pretending idle curiosity, then we turned down Wilton Place to Wilton Crescent, as though simply wandering along. We admired the elegant rows of homes we passed and soon found ourselves approaching the elite quadrangle that was Belgrave Square.

Lord Peyton leased number 38. Daniel had told me only that the house was on the south side of the square, but it hadn't taken much inquiry to discover its number. I'd needed to, in order to send Hannah to the correct house. Daniel hadn't given James a more specific address than he'd given me, but James had discovered it easily enough too.

The fact that Daniel wanted his son and me to know his exact whereabouts—he'd never have told us as much as he did if not—meant he feared what might happen to him in that abode. If he hadn't, he'd have said nothing at all.

I kept us to the north side of the square, worried that a

sharp-eyed Daniel would spy us if we drew too close. Grand houses in pale shades of yellow, ivory, and pink lined the roads, surrounding a lushly wooded park behind an iron fence.

Each home rose four floors from the street with an attic above and had flat-roofed porticoes over the front entrances supported by Greek-style columns. A pediment ran above most second floors, lending interest to the otherwise flat façade, and railings shut off the stairs that led down to the kitchens and servants' domains.

The entire street had a classical appearance, which had been popular much earlier this century, unlike the red bricks and black shutters of the older homes in Mayfair.

The entire area was luxurious but rather forbidding to those not wealthy enough to live here. One had to be invited into these places, with no cheery welcome as I would receive knocking on the door of Joanna's house.

I led Grace across the street to walk along the west side of the square, keeping carriages and delivery vans between us and the park side of the road. Grace traipsed along beside me, subdued, as though she had no interest in the beautiful homes around her.

I continued south, well past the square, the road changing to one called Belgrave Place. Not far along, I found the narrow artery that was the mews James had mentioned.

This lane, which ran behind the large homes on the south end of the square, contained coach houses and stables for horses and carriages, plus quarters for the grooms and coachmen who worked for the families. It was a typical mews, with horses being groomed under the open sky, men tinkering with vehicles their masters would soon require, and grooms and stable boys lounging against the walls, passing the time of day when they weren't harried to another chore.

I spied the back of number 38, having found its exact location on a map I'd been studying in my chamber for the past few nights.

James had been right about the passageway to the kitchen door. I edged into the mews as far as I dared, and saw that the small corridor ran between the wall of the house next door and whatever room jutted from the house it was in. I glimpsed a solid door, shut, at the end of the passageway.

The house's ground floor had no windows in back, possibly so the inhabitants wouldn't have to view the horses, who left dung everywhere, and the stable boys with brooms who swept the refuse away. The higher floors did have windows, which fortunately for me were muffled by heavy curtains.

I gazed at the door, probably meant for deliveries, which likely opened to a set of wooden stairs leading to the kitchens. Behind those windows above me, Daniel was no doubt attending to whatever business a secretary to a viscount would do.

He might also be ill, hurt, held captive, even dead. I could not know, and Mr. Monaghan probably wouldn't bother to tell me if so.

Would the others at Scotland Yard give James or me the awful news if the worst happened? Or did Inspector McGregor and other detectives even know what Daniel and Monaghan were up to? Would they realize if Daniel had been killed or simply wonder why he'd ceased turning up?

My careening thoughts threatened to land me in a panic. I told myself that Hannah was inside that house, and there wasn't much that frightened her. She'd look after Daniel, which was one reason I'd immediately thought of her for this covert task.

One of the grooms noticed us lingering and started toward us. I turned Grace, gave the groom a little smile and nod, and walked on. We were simply two ladies who'd stopped to admire the fine homes and the carriage houses that went with them.

The groom nodded courteously back, but he watched until we were out of sight.

G race and I returned to wander through Hyde Park, as we'd come all this way, but we were both distracted.

"When will Uncle Daniel be able to come home?" Grace asked. "It must be awful to be a police detective."

I agreed, though I'd always wondered what sort of role Daniel actually played at Scotland Yard. He certainly did not sit behind a desk with his name on a placard as did the sergeants and inspectors I'd met there.

"I wish I knew," I told Grace. "It is devilish worrying."

"James wants to be in the police," Grace announced. "He says then he could be paid for running about nosing into things, which he does anyway."

"Does he?" Time was marching on, so I led us out of the peaceful park and its vast stretches of green back to the road. We passed the gate to the splendid Apsley House and entered Piccadilly. "When did he tell you this?" I hadn't heard James mention his future much when he'd joined us on our outings.

"A few weeks ago. James comes to the house to visit sometimes. He's a nice lad."

I had not known of this. James was nearly a grown man and could visit whomever he liked, but I didn't realize he was a regular guest at Joanna's.

Grace was growing more lovely every day. She was a bit younger than James, but ...

Oh dear.

My heart beat swiftly as I hurried toward a hansom stand and a cabbie waiting there.

Grace and James? It was natural that they would become friends, as Daniel and I were growing so close. Grace was still a girl, but the five-year difference in age between her and James would become less important in time.

Nonsense, I told myself. Grace was still far too young to attract the attention of a lad like James. Joanna's daughter Jane was turning into a pretty young lady. Perhaps James's interest lay there.

This relieved me somewhat, but not entirely. I could think of no finer young man than James McAdam to court my daughter, but gracious, it was far too soon to be worrying about *that.*

Once we were in the hansom, I determinedly turned our conversation to everyday things, such as what Grace was learning under Joanna's tutelage and how Joanna and Sam's oldest son, Matthew, was now in a good grammar school, thanks to Sam's hard work and a scholarship Matthew had earned for his diligence.

Sam was employed again, thank heaven, after his firm in the City had tried to have him blamed for all sorts last year. He now was a clerk in a quiet solicitor's office near Gray's Inn, earning a decent salary helping his solicitor sort through lawsuits. Not anything I would understand, but Sam was happy enough.

So chatting, we wended our way across the metropolis and into the City to alight in Cheapside.

Saying good-bye to Grace grew more difficult each time. I was missing her growing-up years, and one day soon, I feared she'd want our little outings to cease altogether.

I held Grace as long as I could, liking that she held me back as tightly.

Our excursion had taken enough time that I could not stay for tea. Instead I'd return to Mount Street and make tea for others. That was what I was paid to do, I reminded myself. If I ceased making a living, I'd not be able to provide what little I could for my beloved girl.

Both Grace and Joanna waved at me cheerfully as I departed, but I wiped my eyes as I emerged into Cheapside.

Because my quick tears had blurred the crowds, I did not see the man in spectacles who cut across the street until he stepped in front of me.

"Mrs. Holloway," he said in his expressionless voice.

I knew two gentlemen who wore spectacles. One was the congenial Mr. Thanos, who didn't like to be seen in his, though he squinted at everything without them.

The other was the gray-haired, cold-eyed Mr. Monaghan, who commanded Daniel's life and held his fist around his soul.

I stopped short, my heart in my throat, but I refused to allow this man to know how much he unnerved me. I lifted my chin and met his cool gaze with one of my own.

"Mr. Monaghan, I believe I told you not to come anywhere near my daughter."

"I waited until you'd seen her home," Monaghan said, as though his behavior was entirely reasonable. "I will speak to you."

Not *I would like to* or *please, may I?* Monaghan was so used to commanding people he did not know how to cease.

"I must return to Mayfair, or I will be late." I started to move around him, but he caught my arm in a surprisingly strong grip and jerked me back.

I considered screaming and flailing, shouting at passersby that I was being robbed. The mob could quickly be stirred against a miscreant.

Monaghan did not hold me roughly, but his grasp was firm. I kept my silence only because I feared he'd retaliate against Daniel if I was uncooperative. Or he might simply haul me to the nearest police station and request they lock me in.

"If it is that important you must walk along with me," I said, pretending I wasn't rattled. "I really must reach my kitchen soon or be out of a job. Then I *will* go to Scotland Yard and blame you. Inspector McGregor will take my complaint."

Monaghan's lips thinned. I had no idea if Inspector Mc-Gregor, who disliked Monaghan intensely, could have any effect on the man's employment, but Monaghan was not happy that I'd mentioned his name.

"Let us walk, then." He released me but stayed close beside me, his longer stride propelling me along.

I said nothing, waiting for him to begin. I'd learned at an early age to never let the police know more than they needed. Even an honest woman could find herself arrested on the merest pretense if she said the wrong thing at the wrong time.

Not until we'd passed through St. Paul's Churchyard and emerged into Ludgate Hill did he speak. I'd steered us in that direction, not wishing to take the northerly route from Cheapside, which would pass too near Newgate Prison for my comfort.

"Stay away from Belgrave Square," Monaghan stated. "If you go near it again, I will have you arrested."

My mouth went dry. "You've been following me about?" I tried to make my voice light. "A free subject like myself? I believe I *shall* lodge that complaint at Scotland Yard."

"The house is watched. Anyone who passes it is reported to me. You stay away. Tell the boy to as well."

James was hardly a boy any longer, but I knew whom he meant. I waited for Monaghan to mention Hannah, but he did not, to my relief. His watchers must believe she truly was a maid and nothing more.

"You have placed Daniel into grave danger, haven't you?" I asked. "No, he did not explain his mission, but I know that any assignment from you is fraught with peril. It is only natural that I am concerned."

"Your concern could kill him." Monaghan's lips were flat. "I will drop you into the deepest hole I can find and close the grate if my men see you walk past Belgrave Square again. With or without your little girl."

Any mention of Grace banished fears for myself and awoke my anger. "If you touch her, Mr. Monaghan, you will understand what a mother's wrath can be."

His expression did not change. "Keep her home and safe, and you should have no worry for her."

While he was right about that, damn the man, I knew that Monaghan could have Joanna and Sam and their entire family, including Grace, arrested on a false charge to make me behave. I hated that such a person had this kind of power.

"She will go nowhere near the entire area of Belgravia again," I promised. "In fact, I will not let her past Regent Street until the case is concluded and Mr. McAdam is safely home."

Monaghan did not comment on the fact that I hadn't included myself in this restriction from Belgravia, but his eyes flickered, and his voice grew icier than ever.

"It might take some time. Months, or longer. McAdam will stay put and do my bidding until I say otherwise. These are dangerous people, and I will have them."

I halted to face him. We were in Fleet Street, the bastion of the newspapers, and curious journalists could be swirling about us even now.

"Mr. McAdam has done enough for you. You keep at him and at him and will until he is dead, won't you? I am sorry your friend was killed in that incident years ago, but Mr. McAdam was not the only one involved in the catastrophe. I believe *you* were there as well. Blame yourself, Mr. Monaghan, for your own shortcomings, and leave the rest of us be."

I heard myself say far too much, but the words wouldn't cease once they welled up inside me.

Hot rage sparked in the man's eyes, for once breaking his cold barrier.

"I have blamed myself, believe me," he said in a hard voice. "Many times. I used to be a very dangerous man, until I turned to the side of the law. And because of that, a man who was truly good died. Yes, McAdam will pay for it. He'll pay for every ounce of pain, just as I have paid for it. If McAdam is killed in that house, then justice will have been done."

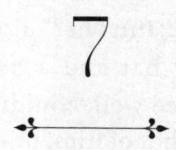

7

The ice-cold fear that washed through me at his words paralyzed me a moment. He'd sent Daniel to an almost-certain death, he meant, and he didn't care.

The fear turned to blinding fury. "You bloody, self-righteous bastard," I cried. "People depend on Daniel, not only myself. If he is harmed in any way, you will have an enemy in me, and believe me, Mr. Monaghan, you do not want this. Nothing can stop me when I decide to act."

Mr. Monaghan regarded me with predictable outrage. I knew I'd gone too far, he'd arrest me on the spot, and I'd have no recourse.

For a brief instant I thought I glimpsed understanding in his eyes. He hid this quickly, so I could not be certain.

He tucked his anger behind his cold mask once more. "Do not make the mistake of creating an enemy in *me*, Mrs. Holloway." He spoke almost calmly, as though he was inured to people threatening him. "Stay far from Belgrave Square and McAdam. This is my only warning."

Monaghan turned on his heel and walked away, his lean form making swift headway through the traffic in the Strand.

"Well, he's a rude one, inn't he?" a ruddy-faced woman in a drooping brown straw hat and a basket on her arm proclaimed. "Not a fare-thee-well, couldn't even be bothered to tip his hat. You're well shot of him, missus."

"He certainly ain't a friend," I agreed, easily falling into the speech patterns of my youth. "Happy to see the back of him, I am. Good morning to ye."

We nodded to each other, two strangers practicing more courtesy than Mr. Monaghan did with anyone he knew. My mother would have had plenty of opinions about *him*.

"I wish you were here, Mum," I whispered to myself as I trudged along the Strand. "You could tell me what to do. I miss you so."

My mother would have loved Grace and done everything she could to help look after her. I blinked away my sadness as I reached Charing Cross and turned my steps toward Mayfair and a house that would never be my home.

I spent Tuesday and Wednesday doing nothing but my job as cook. I did not see Mr. Grimes, and decided either that James couldn't find him or Mr. Grimes was too busy with whatever he did in South London to make the journey across the Thames.

Tess and I made another star bread—the dough was so easy to handle that I created four more, two sweet and two savory—and plenty of tarts. Strawberries were just coming into season, and I bought basketfuls of ripe ones from girls who sold them on the streets. Strawberry tarts were best when kept simple, with plenty of strawberries nestled in a bit of crème anglaise on a thin, buttery crust.

Mrs. Bywater fortunately had no guests in the middle of this week, and so the suppers Tess and I cooked were relatively simple, to Mr. Bywater's joy. A good chop, roasted potatoes, and a bit of carrots for a side dish were all he needed, Mr. Bywater often declared. With my distractions, I was happy to please him.

Thursday could not arrive quickly enough for me. I brushed my best frock in the morning after breakfast, realizing that I could no longer delay replacing it. I'd kept it mended as much as I could, but a few of the seams were now frayed beyond repair. If I took up the hem many more times, as I did when it became too bedraggled from London's streets, the skirt would soon be halfway up my calves.

I'd have to dig into my meager funds to either find a decent secondhand dress or cloth to make my own. If the latter, Joanna would have to make it for me. My needlework skills were far less competent than hers, and I had very little time to cut and sew a frock.

I decided to don my second best today. Ironically, the brown broadcloth with black piping was not as worn out as my best gown. Thus attired, I set my dark brown hat on my head and went downstairs.

Mr. Davis was gliding toward the butler's pantry when I reached the kitchen level. "Enjoy your day out, Mrs. Holloway," he said.

"Thank you, Mr. Davis."

He halted directly in front of me. I was in a hurry, but I could hardly push rudely past him.

"Is anything the matter with Lady Cynthia?" he asked in puzzlement. "Is it something I can help with?"

Mr. Davis was quite fond of Cynthia, which I found pleasing, though at the moment I had no time for a long discussion.

"She's in good health," I answered evasively. The letter meant for Lady Rankin had renewed some of Cynthia's distress over her sister, but she seemed more excited about catching the writer and wringing his neck.

"She watches me like a hawk," Mr. Davis said. "Especially when I bring in the post. As soon as I sort through it and leave it on the hall table, she pounces on it. If she is waiting for a letter, she only has to ask me to keep an eye out." He sounded hurt.

"I did bid her to look for any letters to me," I extemporized. Cynthia had told me only this morning that no further poisoned-pen missives had appeared. "I apologize for upsetting you."

Mr. Davis's aggrieved expression increased. "I would always bring any post down to you immediately. In any case, you should receive your letters through your agency."

I did have the agency as my official address, though I got few letters but the confirmation receipts from the building society where Mr. Davis had persuaded me to deposit my extra funds.

"That is true, but I don't always trust those at the agency not to have a peek."

Mr. Davis considered this and nodded. "It is a pity, but sometimes we can't depend on those we ought. Please tell Lady Cynthia I will bring you any correspondence right away. She does not have to intercept it before her aunt sees it."

"Thank you very much, Mr. Davis." I paused, considering bringing him into my confidence, but hesitated. Cynthia hadn't minded Tess knowing, but if she wanted Mr. Davis to learn of the blackmailing letter, she ought to be the one to tell him. Also, Mr. Davis was a man, of course, and Cynthia might not wish him to know what sorts of scurrilous accusations had been made against her sister.

Deciding it was Cynthia's decision who knew about the letter, I said nothing more to Mr. Davis. I bade him good morning and continued around him to the kitchen.

After instructing Tess to marinate the roast in plenty of wine with the herbs and pepper I'd left out for her, I sailed out into the world.

The weather, being fickle in spring, had turned colder again, with a chill wind blowing light rain into my face. I didn't mind at all, as at the end of a brisk walk would be an entire glorious day with my daughter.

I knew Monaghan had eyes on me. The past few evenings, when I'd gone out to distribute food scraps to the less fortunate, I'd seen a scruffy man trying to be inconspicuous across the road. He'd lounged like the beggars but wasn't interested in coming forward for his share of food. Also, his coat and hat weren't as ragged as the others', and he remained even after the beggars had gone.

I'd pretended not to notice, but I could have given him a few instructions on how to be less obvious.

Another man, similarly garbed, followed me now. I allowed it, as I was going nowhere but Clover Lane, though if he did anything to frighten my daughter, he'd gain an earful from me.

I had no intention of returning to Belgrave Square today. Mr. Monaghan's warning had rattled me and also convinced me that I had been foolish. I would heed the warning, not because Monaghan had frightened me with his threats, but because I had no wish to expose Daniel or endanger him.

I missed him, and I feared for him, but I'd done all I could for now. I'd have to trust Daniel to take care of himself.

Grace and I spent a lively day together, while I put aside my fears to focus on her. I'd learned that absorbing oneself in a pleasurable thing for a few hours leaves one refreshed enough to meet one's troubles later. Fretting without pause generally did more harm than good.

Today we walked through the City to the Tower of London, that place that had seen the triumphs and tragedies of England's kings and queens. The blue- and red-garbed Yeomen of the Guard strolled about, relating lurid tales of the famous prisoners here and giving a history of the crown jewels, which lay within.

Both Mr. Davis and Daniel had told me tales of how those jewels had been pawned and recovered over and over down the centuries to fund wars and other ventures for the kings and queens.

Being of a suspicious nature, I wondered if the jewels in the Tower now were the true ones. So many wealthy people sold their jewels to pay off debts and replaced them with very good replicas. Why should not the ancient royals have done the same? I doubted I'd ever know the truth, of course.

We ambled from the Tower and west along the Thames to the Strand, where we admired the little church of St. Mary le Strand. The original church had been pulled down so that Somerset House could be constructed for the first duke of that name in the 1500s and not replaced until the past century. It had been designed by James Gibbs, so said the plaque I read all this information on, part of a project to build multiple churches across London. I liked little St. Mary's, on its island in the Strand, with arched clear-glass windows and a simple porticoed porch.

Turning from here down a side street, we passed the colossus of Somerset House that St. Mary's had been sacrificed for, and emerged onto the Embankment for a walk there.

The rain had petered out as we'd emerged from the grounds of the Tower, and now clouds rolled back, bathing us in sweet sunshine. If Daniel had been with us, the day would have been perfect.

Once we returned to Cheapside, I took Grace to tea in our favorite shop there, and reluctantly took her back to Joanna's. I knew we'd been followed by some poor constable assigned the duty the entire day, and I hoped he'd enjoyed the pretty sites.

To distract myself from the ache of leaving Grace, I turned from my route home to Covent Garden to find what remnants I could in the market. Some of the vendors who knew me would keep back good bits and give me a discount to rid themselves of their excess produce at the end of the day.

I was tucking some bright green asparagus into the small basket I always made certain I had with me, when someone collided hard into my back.

I rocked on my feet, grabbing at the edge of the greengrocer's stall to steady myself. My basket slipped, and I frantically righted it before the asparagus could be tumbled all over the ground.

"Here, you," the greengrocer I'd purchased the asparagus from snapped to whoever was behind me. "Watch what you're about."

I swung around to find a personage with grimy red hair under a battered hat standing very close to me. She had a ruddy face with sparkling blue eyes, her grin betraying crooked teeth. She shoved a wrinkled pear at me.

"Buy me fruit, missus. They're ever so sweet, and I can't go back home with 'em and no money."

8

As I gaped at this bizarre personage, my heart speeding, the greengrocer scowled at her. "Clear off," he barked.

I raised a soothing hand to him. "It is all right. She didn't hurt me. Now, I sympathize with you, my dear, but those are sorry specimens. I'd throw them into the gutter were I you."

The woman seized my arm. "But I've got so much better. Come on with me, love. I've a basket full of 'em just over yonder."

The greengrocer continued to scowl, I suspected not so much because the young woman might be towing me off to rob me, but because she was poaching on his territory. I sent him a conciliatory nod and let the woman lead me off.

"I do need some good fruit for tarts," I said loudly enough so anyone following would hear. "They had better be worthwhile, or I am buying nothing."

"They'll do for ya, missus. I promise. Here we are."

She led me around to the steps of the Covent Garden opera house, where she pulled a basket out from behind one of the porticoes. It was indeed heaped with bright pears, apples, and grapes. Where she'd found such nice ones out of season, I couldn't say, but this woman was ever resourceful.

She plopped herself down on the steps in full view of anyone passing, but the place she'd chosen was nearly deserted, as the market was winding down for the day. We'd see anyone who came close enough to listen to us in time to change our conversation.

I tucked up my skirts and sat on the steps, her basket between us. As I bent to examine the produce, Hannah whispered to me.

"Sorry I didn't send word. Didn't want none to intercept it."

My heart beat thick and fast, both wanting to hear what she had to say and fearing the information. "That is perfectly all right."

Hannah today looked nothing like the free and easy woman I'd spoken to on the Portobello Road. She hunched herself up, her fingers crabbed as she picked over the fruit. I had to wonder where she'd obtained the very realistic red wig. She'd hardly have time to dye her hair and then dye it back again before she returned to Belgrave Square.

"It's been an interesting week," Hannah said in a soft voice as we appeared to haggle over the pears. "An interesting household. What'cha want to know?"

"Everything. But I suppose you should relay it in some order. First, is Daniel—Mr. McAdam—well?"

"Aw, he's a right one, inn't he?" Hannah grinned, and I immediately felt better. If Daniel was busily charming all those around him, then he was in good health. "He don't trust me one whit. I know that, because he asks me all sorts of questions about where I worked in the past. I have to dance to keep my secrets, but I'd worked out a story before I went, so I feed him bits of it at a time. I think he's starting to believe me."

"What about the others in the household? Do they believe you?"

"They do. Your McAdam is far more suspicious than them, which is good for me, and for him. He ain't calling himself McAdam, you know. He's Thomas Delamarre. Frenchy ancestry." Dimples showed in Hannah's cheeks.

I'd not heard the name before, but it made sense for Daniel to take a new alias for this assignment. No doubt Monaghan and others had made certain his background tale was impeccable.

"What happened to the other secretary?" I asked. "The man Mr. McAdam replaced?"

"No idea," Hannah said. "Housekeeper says his name was Mr. Howard. A soft-spoken, polite man, she said, but one day, he packed his bags and went. There the night before—gone in the morning."

"Sacked?"

Hannah shrugged. "Housekeeper don't know. A few days later, in comes Mr. McAdam. Housekeeper likes *him*."

I was not surprised about that. I wondered if Monaghan had removed the secretary, by whatever underhanded means he'd employed, in order to have the way clear for Daniel.

"Is Viscount Peyton truly an invalid?" I asked.

Hannah nodded. "Can't walk more than a step, sleeps half the time. I've charged into a sitting room unexpectedly, meaning to catch him walking around on his own, but I think his ailment is true. When he has to leave his chair, he's carried about by his big brute of a valet, name of John Fagan. Fagan never has much to say, and I can't decide if he's shy or surly. He's devoted to his lordship, by all I can see."

I longed to write this down, but I'd have to wait. I'd be too obvious whipping out my notebook and scribbling like mad.

"Tell me about the household," I said. "You mentioned the housekeeper."

"Mrs. Proctor. She's not a bad sort but a stickler for keeping every room in that great mansion neat. I'm wearing out me fingers putting everything in order." Hannah showed me reddened fingertips poking from worn gloves. "Two downstairs maids who live in fear of Mrs. Proctor. I'm the upstairs maid, taking over from a lass who went off to get married. No one speaks of her."

"Why not?" I asked. Disappearing maids and secretaries caught my interest.

"Mrs. Proctor says stiffly that she deserted the master and is best forgotten. Lord Peyton walks on water, according to the staff—if he could walk, that is. In the kitchens is Mrs. McGuire, the cook, and Millie the kitchen maid. No footmen or butler. Fagan does all those jobs, in addition to valeting. Mrs. Proctor says because it saves on expense."

Male servants were subject to an extra tax, because they were considered a luxury while female servants were deemed a necessity. The only reason the Mount Street house had footmen and Mr. Davis was because the bills were paid by Lord Rankin. If Mrs. Bywater ran the place, she'd have a maid of all work upstairs and one poor soul slaving in the kitchen to produce lavish meals on pennies.

"Anyone sinister among these servants?" I asked.

"No." Hannah shook her head. "Everyone seems to be what they claim."

"Does anyone else come to the house?" I asked. "Family, friends, hangers-on?"

"Yes, indeed. Lord Peyton's well-liked. For family, he has a sister called Lady Fontaine. Christian name, Mary. She arrived two days ago, come to stay for a time. His lordship was not best pleased to see her, I can tell you. A widow, she is, and apparently remains for months at a time, whenever it suits her. Or, as Mrs. Proctor says, when she runs short of funds and decides it's time to live off her brother."

A family member appearing hard on the heels of a new secretary and new maid was a coincidence worth noting. "What is she like?" I asked.

"Reminds me a bit of Lady Mortimer—you know, the one who pinched the spoons and left me to take the blame. I unpacked Lady Fontaine's things, and she had many little trinkets tucked throughout her trunk and other bags. She told me they were bits and bobs she liked and didn't want to leave behind, but they're odd things. Some very costly. Others sparkly junk—little boxes and such that have been decorated to look rich but ain't. I should know."

"It is possible they're presents given to her by people she's fond of," I mused. "Children, grandchildren, nieces and nephews."

"I shouldn't think she's the sort children would be fond enough of to give gifts to," Hannah said. "She has a pinched-up face and a harsh tongue. Lady Mortimer was a sweet old thing—Lady Fontaine will never be."

"You say she and Lord Peyton do not get on?"

"Not a bit of it. He called her into his study the night of her arrival, and such shouting there was." Hannah shook her head. "Toffs can be nastier to each other than the likes of us ever will be. He wanted her to go at once, but she refused."

Interesting. Was Lord Peyton angry because his sister would disrupt his nefarious plans? Or were they simply a brother and sister at odds?

"Is that all of the household?" I asked.

"Aye, that's the lot. They're quite demanding. I might have to ask for a rise in wages." Her dimples showed again.

"What about his other visitors?" I hoped for groups of conspirators crowding the drawing room, so loudly plotting the government's demise that Daniel would have plenty to tell Monaghan.

"As I say, he's well-liked, but visitors don't come in clumps or stay long, because of Lord Peyton's poor health. His most frequent visitor is the Earl of Pelsham. He spends a few hours there and then goes off. He's been there several times already since I've been there, and I gather he and Lord Peyton are boyhood friends. There have been a couple other callers, one a lady and gent called Lofthouse, the other, his doctor, Mr. Hampton. Mr. Hampton's already come twice. Most of the time, though, it's quiet. Course, I've only been there a week."

No hordes of angry gentlemen ready to assassinate the queen or Mr. Gladstone, I concluded. "At this rate, Daniel will never come home," I said glumly.

Hannah sent me a look of sympathy. "He's playing a long game, I can tell. Those can take months, sometimes years. I'm sorry, pet."

"It won't be years," I said with a confidence I did not feel. "Daniel is clever. He'll quickly discover whether anyone in the house needs to be arrested. Even Lady Fontaine, if only for being disagreeable."

Hannah chuckled. "She'd be the first to go, if that were the only reason." She sobered. "If your man does start making arrests, I'm in the wind. I don't need to see the inside of a nick. Not again."

I gave her a warm smile. "As long as you don't steal the silver, Mr. McAdam will know you have nothing to do with anything."

Hannah looked aggrieved. "I keep saying, I never touched them spoons. I'll confess to the cash that was in our mistress's desk. She was always boasting about how she kept fivers in there. Easy to take a few."

"Well, don't pinch any fivers from the viscount, please."

"No fear. I'm there to watch, right? As a favor to you." Hannah's friendly grin widened. "You must fancy him something fierce, your Daniel. You keep slipping and calling him by his given name, plus you wouldn't go to all this trouble if he meant nothing to you."

"He is a dear friend," I said stiffly.

"Not what your eyes tell me, Katie, me darling." She continued in a louder voice. "Now, missus, you gonna buy this lot or not? I have others I can flog them to."

"Very well, give me a dozen pears and six apples."

"Right you are, love. I'll toss in the grapes for nothing. Two shillings for the lot."

"Two shillings?" I cried in true outrage. "You are mad. One and we are finished."

Hannah let out a long sigh as she jumped to her feet. "Only because I'm in a hurry. Robbing me, that's what you are."

I counted over the coins and transferred the fruit from her basket to mine. Hannah flounced away, as a disgruntled seller would, quickly disappearing into the gathering shadows.

I climbed down the steps of the opera house with my now-laden basket, and immediately banged into a slim man with a neatly trimmed beard in a dark suit topped by the pale smudge of a dog collar.

"My dear Mrs. Holloway," the man said in a quiet voice as I apologized profusely. "You do know you're being followed, do you not?"

9

"I do indeed, Mr. Fielding," I said. "Please do not draw attention to the fact."

Mr. Fielding raised his low-crowned hat, for all the world a solicitous vicar concerned about a lady. "Then forgive my intrusion. It will be dark soon. Might I escort you to a more salubrious part of the metropolis?"

"The daylight lingers well past eight o'clock these days," I pointed out. "But if you must."

I took his offered arm, happy in truth that he could lead me past the watchers. They might all be constables under the thumb of Mr. Monaghan, but then again, they might not. In addition, Mr. Monaghan sometimes employed ruffians to assist him, Daniel had told me, including those Daniel did not trust.

We strolled back through the market and down Southampton Street. I tried not to glance at the house where Daniel lodged as we passed it.

The Strand was more crowded than ever, especially as we approached the huge Charing Cross railway station. Mr. Fielding and I both knew London well enough that we turned without discussion down a side street to avoid the throng, emerging into St. Martin's Lane and Trafalgar Square.

"My dear brother asked me to look in on you," Mr. Fielding said as we reached an open space in the middle of the square.

His "dear brother" was Daniel. Errol Fielding and Daniel had been looked after as lads by a Mr. Carter, a criminal himself but apparently one who had been good to both boys. They were foster brothers rather than related by blood, and they cared about each other, though both nearly had to be threatened with torture to admit it.

"Did he?" I inquired in some irritation.

"He did," Mr. Fielding said. "I was happy to comply."

My tone remained testy. "Daniel has been absent more than a week. What has kept you away?"

Mr. Fielding chuckled. "Nothing, dear lady. I have been keeping you in my sights all this time. I am simply much better at hiding it than the clumping dolts following you about town."

I could not be surprised. Mr. Fielding, though he was truly a vicar now, had long been a confidence trickster with much knowledge on how to dissemble.

"Do you not have a flock to attend in the East End?" I asked him.

"I do, but I also have lads in my parish who do not mind earning a bob or two letting me know how you fare."

I recalled the more youthful of the beggars I'd been distributing food to this week. "Does one have thick brown hair and a broken front tooth? The other from the Punjab?"

To my satisfaction, Mr. Fielding started. "You are an observant one, Mrs. Holloway. The Punjabi lad is as much a Londoner as you or I, born and raised here. Both know the streets well and, as I say, don't say no to a bob or two. Also, I trust them. They're loyal to me, and they are quite taken with you."

"I ought to have thought of you when they suddenly turned up." I studied the worn base of Nelson's Column beside us. "Give them my best wishes, and tell them it is not necessary to watch over me every moment."

"It *is* necessary." Mr. Fielding sobered. "Daniel is in this business up to his neck, and it might endanger you, I am sorry to relate. My watchers stay."

I ceased arguing, knowing it would do no good. As long as Mr. Fielding's lads did not impede me, I'd not object. I might even make some use of them.

"I suppose you are observing Daniel as well?" I asked. "Though he pleaded for us both not to?"

"Of course." Mr. Fielding gave me his perfected innocent expression. "Not that Daniel pleads, ma'am. Don't exaggerate. He states his wishes quite firmly and grows exasperated when we don't comply. I have stationed others near the house, who saw you wander there on Monday."

"Is one a groom?" I thought of the man who'd started to move toward me as I'd peeked into the mews.

Mr. Fielding heaved an exaggerated sigh. "Of course, you spotted him too. He is. I installed him to work for the lordship next door to the viscount. He said he meant to warn you away, but you took the hint and disappeared."

I was happy to learn that the groom had worked for a friend, not an enemy. I was also glad Mr. Fielding had stationed people near, even if he inferred that I disapproved.

"What does the lordship next door think about Viscount Peyton?" I asked.

Mr. Fielding ran slim, gloved fingers over his neat beard. "Feels sorry for the viscount, being unable to get around by himself. Lord Downes declares that a man in that state might as well be dead. Very hearty sort, is Lord Downes."

"Mm, he sounds it."

"Acknowledges that Peyton has a good mind though. Brilliant at chess—at least, he bests Lord Downes every time, which, according to the groom, must not be difficult. Viscount Peyton has a finger in many governmental pies, always pushing for reform. Is sympathetic to foreigners, supports Irish Home Rule. All the traits Downes despises. Gents like Peyton will ruin Britain, and so forth, says Lord Downes."

I'd overheard many a gent in London state similar opinions. Ladies too.

The Irish question had figured prominently in other cases Daniel had taken, dangerous ones that had nearly hastened his death.

Irish Home Rule was a volatile subject these days. The newspapers harangued about it on both sides of the question. I had compassion for the Irishmen who wished to govern themselves after centuries of subjugation and impoverishment, but I could not condone those who tossed incendiary devices onto railway platforms or into streets, injuring or killing innocent children. It might be *my* daughter who inadvertently stepped in their way.

"Is Lord Peyton involved with Fenians?" I named the group, begun in America and funded by Americans who supported the Irish. Many American Fenians had family in Ireland and had themselves emigrated to Boston or New York to find employment. While those who worked for Irish Home Rule had a common cause with them, the Fenians were the ones who advocated using violence, including the bombings, to obtain their goals.

Mr. Fielding shrugged. "It's uncertain, though likely. Peyton is in a circle that fuses highborn and low, striving for the freedom of Ireland by any means necessary. No one can prove Peyton's connection to Fenians, hence Daniel. I imagine our Danny's looking for any evidence that can implicate Peyton in working to destroy the government, or else information to expose the entire ring."

The qualms that had fluttered through me since Daniel had gone now returned as watery fear. "Daniel could not have told you all this."

"I have my own sources. Peyton's connections are dangerous, Mrs. Holloway. I am certain you understand that if Daniel is caught, they will not hesitate to dispatch him."

I believed him. I'd encountered such people before in Daniel's work, from those who tried to blow up railroad bridges to a duke ready to eliminate the cabinet from within.

"And Daniel is sitting in the midst of them." I clenched the handle of my basket. I'd sent Hannah into the midst of them too. Peyton and his followers wouldn't hesitate to rid the world of her as well. "What are we to do? I can't know what is going on in the house every minute, and it seems very quiet there." Indeed, the silence was unnerving.

"I have my spies, and no doubt you have yours." Mr. Fielding's steady look told me he knew I'd not have stayed idly in my kitchen.

"Spies who themselves can be in danger."

"But you and I choose carefully," Mr. Fielding said with assurance. "We'd not have asked those who would be easily found out or who'd do anything foolish."

That was true in my case, and I knew Mr. Fielding was canny enough to send people who'd never be looked at or questioned. I'd had no suspicion of the groom until Mr. Fielding had told me he had a man in place today, and I'd put things together.

"It is difficult to wait for reports," I said.

"But wait we must." Mr. Fielding cast a glance at those hastening around us. "I will not tell my watchers who your watchers are in case they are caught trying to confer. Ignorance is best in this situation."

"Perhaps." My jaw hurt from being so tight. "Then again, if each knows there is help nearby, they can reach it if necessary."

"I will think on it. In the meantime, please keep my men's identities to yourself. I don't wish them to be exposed."

As I could speak to Hannah only whenever she extricated herself from the house, it was easy to agree.

"I hope nothing happens at all," I said. "Then it won't be necessary to have reports or other actions from any of them."

"That would be ideal," Mr. Fielding answered. "But I am not optimistic. There is unrest and impatience. Gladstone is the best hope for introducing a bill for Home Rule, but the going is slow. Violence is so much quicker."

"Why does Daniel have to be in the thick of it?" I burst out in vexation. "He is neither causing the violence nor working to keep Ireland under Britain's thumb. What has all this to do with him?"

"The paths we walk are never the ones we start down." Mr. Fielding raised a hand as I began to splutter my frustration. "I know, philosophical aphorisms right now are not helpful.

Daniel is paying for a mistake—he told me the tale once—which is not fair to him. I long to pull him out of the fire, but I can't fight the entirety of Scotland Yard any more than I can call out the Fenians who have infiltrated this country."

I strove to calm myself. "I do realize this is a problem Daniel must solve on his own," I said grudgingly.

"With us to watch him and catch him when he is in peril." Mr. Fielding sent me a comforting smile. "Fear not, Mrs. Holloway. We'll pluck him away and keep him safe. Damn the man for making me worry about him so much."

I was pleased, actually, to see his concern. When I'd first met Mr. Fielding, he'd showed annoyance that he'd had to ask for Daniel's help and resentment toward Daniel for what Mr. Fielding had perceived was his soft life. They'd lost touch with each other in the aftermath of their foster father's death, both clawing their way up from the streets and both believing the other had had an easier time of it.

"I must ask you another question," I said before Mr. Fielding could suggest we move on. "In your experience of swindlers, what can you tell me about blackmailers? Particularly those who claim to know one's nastier secrets?"

Mr. Fielding regarded me in surprise. "Surely, no one is trying to blackmail *you*, my dear Kat—I mean, my dear Mrs. Holloway. You lead a blameless life."

I had not in the past, and he knew it. "No, not me. Ladies of quality, shall we say. What sort of person writes scurrilous letters threatening to reveal all unless one pays? Is it a trickster trying his luck? If he or she sends out enough letters, they'll come upon someone willing to settle up? Or is it a madwoman? Or madman?"

Mr. Fielding shook his head in distaste. "An accomplished confidence man doesn't need to use sordid letters and threats.

They can convince a mark to hand over the cash while buttering them up without penitence. The mark usually doesn't even know they've been had until too late. Blackmailers, on the other hand, are repugnant creatures. They play upon people's weaknesses and fears. A good trickster plays upon one's deepest desires, not one's deepest dread."

"Well, I am very glad there are fraudsters in the world with clear consciences," I said with some impatience. "Putting aside your revulsion, would it be more likely to be someone seeing blackmail as a business venture? Or a miserable wretch who wants to cause as much misery as they feel themselves?"

"I could not venture my opinion until I saw the letters," Mr. Fielding said. "A good idea is to compare several of them—is the handwriting neat and even? Or scrawled in rage? Are they rambling? Or precise in their accusations?"

"The two I have seen look much alike. The handwriting is clear, but I could not say if it is a man's or a woman's. The letters indicate another will come with instructions as to where to leave the money, but so far, none have."

"Curious." Mr. Fielding tilted his head back to study Admiral Nelson, who calmly surveyed Charing Cross and on into Whitehall, pigeons perched happily on his shoulders. "It could be someone wanting to foment trouble for the sake of it. There are some who enjoy that. Or they are waiting for their moment. The most dangerous time for a blackmailer is the exchange of money for the goods. The victim might bring the police. Or a pistol." Mr. Fielding pulled his gaze to me again. "Is there any chance I could have a look at them? I might be able to advise you better."

"I will have to ask. The letters are not mine, you understand, and the ladies might object to a vicar reading about their sins."

Mr. Fielding barked a laugh. "There are plenty corrupt members of the clergy in the world, I assure you. Compared to many of them, I am a saint. But I take your point. I can offer complete discretion, if they will trust me. I am only interested in uncovering a quivering, cowardly blackmailer, not exposing the ladies' secrets." He paused. "Do not say that dear Lady Cynthia, the trouser-wearing, splendid young woman, has received one?"

"She has not," I could answer. "Nor has her friend Lady Roberta."

"No? That is interesting. But a relief. Lady Cynthia's book-learned genius young man might try to defend her honor in some fashion and come to grief. Not Lady Roberta, you say? No letters to her brother threatening to shame him for his sister's behavior? Not that Lady Roberta is very secretive about her life. I admire her for that." Mr. Fielding beamed his approval.

"Her brother and sister-in-law have not received any, as far as I know," I answered. "Miss Townsend has, but her letter did not mention Lady Roberta. Miss Townsend regarded the letter she received as a tasteless joke."

"Ah, the formidable Miss Townsend. I ever pity she has no interest in the male of the species, or I'd be tempted to offer her the position as vicar's wife. Not that she'd hasten to trade her luxurious home in Mayfair for a cramped vicarage in the East End."

"Quite so," I agreed. "The letter was horrible, but Miss Townsend took it in her stride. I'll wager, as she lives unconventionally, that she is not a stranger to them, which is sad. Several of her friends have had letters—I can ask Lady Cynthia if they'd be willing to let us compare them."

Mr. Fielding looked thoughtful. "We must ask ourselves why Lady Cynthia and Lady Roberta have not been threatened. What do the other ladies have in common that those two do not share?"

"I have been wondering about that." I'd made lists in my notebook, but again, I could hardly consult it here. "Miss Townsend and the other two are connected to important men, either by marriage or other relation. Lady Roberta's father is an earl but doesn't do much in the way of politics. Her brother has his own circle, but no real power, according to Lady Cynthia. Cynthia's father won't go near the House of Lords—he finds it appallingly dull. That does not explain though why her sister was sent one."

Mr. Fielding stared at me in some shock. "The deceased sister?"

"Yes, it is most strange."

"I'd say that was the strangest fact of all." Mr. Fielding shot Lord Nelson another assessing look, then took my arm again. "We have stood here too long. Let us get you home. You quiz Lady Cynthia on whether I can have a butcher's at a few of the letters. If it's a scheme hatched by a confidence trickster I know, I can have a word with the bastard."

I did not like to ponder about what state the blackmailer would be in once Mr. Fielding was finished with him.

"I will welcome your help, Mr. Fielding," I said warmly. "But please do not get yourself arrested."

Mr. Fielding's laughter was filled with true mirth. "I never do, my dear Mrs. Holloway. I never do."

I entered the kitchen of Mount Street not long later, in time to help Tess finish the supper for the Bywaters and Cynthia. Later, when Lady Cynthia breezed out through the below-stairs entrance to join her friends, I asked whether she'd have a word with Miss Townsend about showing Mr. Fielding some of the letters.

"Fielding, eh?" Cynthia had already adopted the masculine mannerisms she'd use throughout the night. "Excellent idea—he might know a thing or two. I'll ask Judes. Good night. Don't wait up."

She grinned as she swept past, her eyes alight.

"Wish I could rush about so free and easy," Tess said as we stacked used pots in a pile in order to scrub off the work table. "I hope she won't be too reckless."

"We do not need Lady Cynthia in trouble with the law, no," I agreed. "Let us set up the bread and prepare for tomorrow. I have a new dish for us to try. I found ever so many pears and apples. You will see."

I set the fruit I'd bought from Hannah—who knew how she'd obtained it—on the dresser then collected peppers and onions in the larder and left them in a bowl for chopping the next day. Tess and I continued our labors, then I sent her up early, as she'd been working hard today on her own.

Once alone, I retrieved my notebook and opened it to my notes on Daniel's case. I wrote the names Hannah had given me, making neat lines between them.

I jotted down Hannah's observations, and also Mr. Fielding's, but I would need more information.

This did not worry me. I'd lived in Mount Street for a few years now, and I'd come to know who lived in nearly every house in Mayfair, as well as north across Oxford Street and south into Belgravia.

I also knew what cooks and maids worked in which house. They'd know what went on above stairs—who visited whom, and their views on every issue in the land. Mr. Davis was acquainted with most of the butlers and other manservants, and

I could recruit him to tell me a few things if I could not find out via the kitchens.

The servants' gossip network in London could outdo spies for the queen any day.

I made more notes on the pages where I'd listed whom had received blackmail letters—Miss Townsend, her friends Delia and Viola, and Lady Rankin—with a query to find out more about what the victims had in common. So far, with the exception of Lady Rankin, they all belonged to Miss Townsend's set. However, others in Mayfair might have received them as well, unbeknownst to Miss Townsend. Letters like these were not ones a lady boasted to her acquaintances about.

I also wondered whether any gentlemen, who'd be even more reluctant to speak, had been gifted with such letters. Mr. Fielding, in his role of ingenuous but kindly vicar, might be of help in that regard.

Satisfied I'd done all I could for the day, I tucked my notebook into my pocket and climbed the many stairs to my chamber in the attic. I fell into bed, exhausted, but dreamed of Mr. Monaghan pursuing Grace, Daniel, and me through narrow London streets, while incendiaries rained upon us.

I woke too early, rattled, and rushed through my ablutions to return to the kitchen, hoping that hard work would take my mind off things.

As I was pinning on my cap, a knock sounded on the back door. I answered it, as I was the first one into the kitchen this morning.

The lad who'd delivered the note from Hannah last week stood on the threshold. He handed me a new note and stuck out his soot-streaked palm for a reward. When I gave him another ha'penny, he frowned his disappointment and stamped back up the stairs.

The missive was short, as Hannah's last one had been.

It weren't him.

That was all. I turned the paper over, but nothing was on the back. I even held it up to the gaslit sconce to see if she'd written something else faintly on it, but no.

I crumpled the paper into my pocket, wondering what on earth she meant.

It wasn't who? Lord Peyton? Daniel? Lord Peyton's giant manservant? And what hadn't they done? If anything at all?

I puzzled over this as Tess and I made omelets, bread toasted on the rack and slathered with butter, sausages with a bit of cheese, and a chutney from part of the apples and pears I'd set out.

Mr. Davis came down after serving breakfast to sit at my table and relax, as he often did, before he took up his other duties. He spread out a newspaper, which contained the lurid headline *Body in the Thames*.

Drownings, whether accidental or deliberate, sometimes tragically did happen. I usually took a moment to feel sorry for the man or woman and their families and then carried on with my drudging.

Today, I laid down my knife and walked around the table where I could better see the paper. "What is that about, Mr. Davis?" I asked, my voice cracking.

"A lurid murder," Mr. Davis said easily, then he read:

> A waterman was startled in the small hours of the
> morning to find in the nets he leaves out for flotsam
> the dead body of a man. His throat had been cut,
> and he had several bruises and other cuts along his

body. He wore a tailored suit, and the one shoe that had remained on his foot was from a firm in Bond Street. By this, one can say that the man was a gentleman. His name was not revealed to us, but the police have put into their report that he was the secretary to a lordship in Belgravia. We have made inquiries—

Whatever else Mr. Davis said was lost to me. I found myself sitting on the floor at his feet with a worried Tess peering down at me.

10

"M rs. Holloway?" Tess chafed my wrists, her voice full of fear, while Mr. Davis wafted a handkerchief in front of my face.

I was folded up so that my stays cut into my abdomen, preventing me from drawing a long breath, or so I supposed. There should be no other reason I was gasping.

Daniel had a nicely tailored suit and shoes from Bond Street, which he used when he portrayed an upper-class gent. He had new ensembles made each season so he'd always be in the height of fashion, no matter how subtle the changes in men's dress were that year.

Had they found Daniel out? Taken him aside to kill him and heaved his body into the river?

"You've had a turn, Mrs. Holloway," Mr. Davis was saying. "Was it the gruesome tale? Or was the chutney bad? Pears out of season can be unhealthy, I always say."

"It was not the pears," I wheezed. "Help me stand, please."

Tess and Mr. Davis each gripped me under an arm and hauled me to my feet. My knees buckled as soon as they let me go, and I quickly found a chair to collapse into. My hands fell to my sides, black spots dancing before my eyes.

The memory rose of me sitting here in the dark of night only a week ago, with Daniel across from me as he shoveled down my meal and smiled at me.

Dear God, he could not be gone. Once before in my life, I'd thought Daniel dead, and only a visit to the morgue had confirmed he'd not been the victim. Would I have to repeat that awful journey, with a different result this time?

It weren't him.

The words of Hannah's note floated through my agitated thoughts.

Was this what she'd meant? Hannah would have been present when news of the death was brought to Viscount Peyton—if he was indeed the lordship referred to in the rather flippant newspaper story.

She'd realize that I'd hear the tale or read of the murder myself. Hence the hastily sent note with her messenger, which would mean nothing to anyone who intercepted it.

Had she been reassuring me that Daniel was alive and well? Or was I wildly misinterpreting Hannah's purpose? I'd like to have both her and Daniel here before me, so I could shout at them and relieve my anxiousness.

Mr. Davis and Tess had drawn back in some relief, so my color must have returned to normal.

"I beg your pardon," I said, trying to calm my breathing. "I did not sleep well."

By their expressions, neither Tess nor Mr. Davis believed this explanation, but they didn't press me.

"You sit still, Mrs. H.," Tess said. "I'll fetch you a cuppa."

"That would be kind, thank you." My words still didn't sound right, but Tess trotted away without question. "Carry on with the story, Mr. Davis. How did they know the poor man was someone's secretary?"

Mr. Davis sent me another skeptical look but returned to his chair and the newspaper. He ran his finger over the lines he'd already read until he reached the place he'd left off.

> We have made inquiries, but the police are content to say very little about this poor soul. He washed up near Blackfriars Bridge after a journey in the water of some days. We suppose the physicians and detectives of Scotland Yard will draw conclusions of where he went in and how long ago from the wetness of his clothes and the condition of the body and so forth. We can only send our sympathies to his family, whoever they are.

"His family will not thank the journalists for that disrespectful description," I said in disapproval.

"The more impertinent a story, the more likely it will be read," Mr. Davis said. "Especially in a rag like this." He turned to the front page, whose banner was from one of the many newspapers sold cheaply on any street. "Probably why the master only reads the financial and sporting news."

From the article, I concluded that the police had decided not to release the dead man's name. I wondered why they were being cryptic. Had Lord Peyton asked them to be?

Tess returned to me with my cup of tea. She'd added a piece

of lemon shortbread, which I really did not need, but I munched it anyway. The repast did make me feel better.

Hannah had said that the former secretary had been a Mr. Howard. This gent had packed his bags one morning and disappeared.

Had he actually walked out of his own accord? Or had he already been dead, the housekeeper instructed to send his bags on somewhere? I itched to make a note of all of this.

Even more, I longed to see Daniel in the flesh. To touch his face and make certain that I wasn't terribly wrong about Hannah's note.

I knew of someone who could tell me everything, a person I would not need to be surreptitious in order to approach. I was certain he'd not want to see me, but he would answer my questions or face my wrath.

Thinking of that scenario returned my spirits to me. I finished the tea and biscuit, rose from my seat, and continued the luncheon preparations with some of my usual robustness.

I could not leave the house that day to rush about London asking questions, so I put my own resources to work.

Errand boys went everywhere, saw everything, and were willing to share their knowledge for a few coins. Hannah had given me the names of Lord Peyton's most frequent visitors: Lord Pelsham, Mr. and Mrs. Lofthouse, and Dr. Hampton.

Lord Pelsham, an earl, lived in Hill Street, which ran west from Berkeley Square. If Hannah meant that the doctor was one Graham Hampton, he had a home in Berkeley Square, which proclaimed how grand he was. I had not heard of the Lofthouses, but I asked the lads who carried out tasks for me to look out for anyone of that name. They were also to skulk about the homes of the other two, perhaps asking to do odd jobs, and tell me of anyone who came and went or any unusual behavior of the household.

Once I'd dispatched the boys, I returned to the kitchen. Mr. Davis had resumed his duties, which by the sound of it, meant haranguing the footmen for the terrible job they'd done cleaning the silver.

Tess glanced up from her chopping board when I came in. "Want me to ask Caleb about the murdered man?"

I had been about to suggest she discover if he knew anything about the case. I smoothed my apron and took up my knife. "Only if he happens to know and does *not* poke about in papers he has no business touching or ask too many questions."

Tess brightened. "He's become ever so good at finding things out without anyone knowing. He'll make detective soon, I'm sure."

"Unless they sack him first," I said warningly.

I was very protective of Constable Greene, not only for Tess's sake. He was an amiable soul, and he adored her. On the awful day Tess would announce she was leaving me to marry him, I would be comforted by the fact that Caleb was a kind, hardworking young man who would do well by her.

"I'll ask him," Tess said, undaunted. "You worried the bloke in the river were Mr. McAdam, didn't you?"

I pulled an onion to me Tess had peeled and sliced off one end. "For a moment, yes. But Daniel is resilient and a bonny fighter. I've watched him dispatch those who tried to hurt him in the past." I bolstered my doubts with this recollection. "There would have been many ruffians lying about, bruised and bleeding, if it had been Daniel who went into the river."

"That's a mercy," Tess said. "Though not for the poor sod who actually died."

I kept to myself my theories about who the murdered man was, but I puzzled over them.

Why should Lord Peyton's former secretary have been killed? Had he discovered too much? Or had he simply been the victim of a robbery? London was rife with thieves who didn't mind cutting a gent to take all he had. Perhaps one had done so to Mr. Howard and tossed him into the river to be rid of him.

Unhappily, at the moment, I could not rush to Scotland Yard and demand answers. I was a cook, and cook I must.

I brought out my newly bought apples and turned my mind to the task at hand.

"I need a pint of cream from the larder," I instructed Tess. "There should also be some preserved lemons leftover from Christmas—grate the rinds into the cream and also add a cinnamon stick. Put that to simmer at the back of the stove, and meanwhile, we'll peel and chop the apples."

Tess wiped her hands from the sweet peppers she'd been slicing and obediently trotted to the larder. When she returned, she uncomplainingly began to peel the apples and cut them as I instructed.

"Me mouth is watering already," she said. "Can we have any of this?"

I did not look up from the apple I was paring. "We'll have to taste a good portion to make certain it is fit to serve at table, of course."

Tess winked at me. "Right you are, Mrs. H."

I'd ceased bothering trying to prevent my friends from addressing me as *Mrs. H.*, which hardly painted the respectability I wanted to portray. I now took it as a sign of affection and said no more.

After the cream had simmered a bit, I moved it to a hotter

burner and added a smidgen of flour to thicken it, stirring it well. Next went in a few eggs Tess had broken into a small bowl for me. Once the mixture was custardy, I set it aside to cool.

The dish I meant to prepare was called apples à la frangipane, from a recipe a cook in Brook Street had shared with me, though that name could not be accurate. *Frangipane* referred to an almond paste or cream, and this had no almonds at all in it. But the cook had inherited the recipe from her mother, who'd sworn it had been made in the court of Queen Caroline, wife of the second King George, long ago.

As Tess and I sliced apples to place in a ceramic dish I'd buttered, one of my errand boys came to find me.

The lad would not say a word until I put fivepence in his hand. We stood near the railings outside, while a warming May breeze wafted over us. I did not try to be secretive, as a cook paying a boy who'd taken a message or brought her some greens was not an unusual sight in Mayfair.

"Found the mister and missus you was looking for," the little chap, who had very blue eyes, said.

"Well done, Albie," I told him. "Are you certain you had the correct people?"

"The Lofthouses, yeah." He gave me a confident nod. "Funny name, that. They lease a house on Portman Square. North side, close to Upper Berkeley Street. Blue drapes in the ground-floor windows, black door. Gent has a coach with matched bays and a coachman who let me help him brush the beasts. The lady and gent go out all the time, and came out when I was there. When the coachman drove them away, another groom said they spend money like water except to their own staff, where they're mean as anything. Never drop a tip in your hand, the misers, says he."

I had the feeling they also hadn't given Albie a coin today, even though he'd helped curry their horses. "Do you know where they were going?" I asked.

"Museum in Bloomsbury. The big one."

"The British Museum?" I asked in surprise.

"That's the place. Groom says they meet their highbrow friends there and talk about all sorts."

The museum had a reading room only scholars were allowed into, but I supposed they had other areas where people of like minds could speak to each other. Or perhaps they met in a nearby pub, as Lady Cynthia and Mr. Thanos did with their acquaintances. In the upstairs rooms of that pub, bluestockings and other intellectuals discussed everything from suffrage for women to the properties of electricity.

"Do the Lofthouses have many friends visit?" I asked.

Albie nodded. "House can be lively, groom says. Mostly toffs from around Mayfair, but sometimes Americans come to stay." Albie wrinkled his nose at the dubious social position of Americans.

"Anything else unusual?"

"Not really." Albie sounded disappointed. "They sometimes send for the carriage in the middle of the night and rush off, but that's not strange for a toff, is it? They run around to other fancy houses, some so close anybody else would walk to them."

"Perhaps they worry about thieves," I suggested, though I didn't really believe that. "Even in Mayfair, wandering along in the dark can be dangerous, can't it?" I pulled another penny from my pocket. "You've done excellently well, Albie. Thank you."

Albie studied the copper coin as though hoping it would morph into a shilling, but I resisted his silent wish. I'd already given him fivepence, which would buy a small boy much sustenance if he was frugal.

"If you discover anything else, come directly to me," I instructed him. "Of course I will reward you."

Albie grew abruptly more cheerful. He tipped his cap, grinned, and rushed off down the street, earning a curse from a coachman he darted in front of.

I recognized the carriage that had to swerve to miss Albie, having ridden inside it myself. It belonged to Miss Townsend, and the annoyed coachman was called Dunstan.

One of our footmen rushed from the front door to let down the step of the coach and open its door, his sturdy hand out to help Miss Townsend alight. Unlike the apparently stingy Mr. and Mrs. Lofthouse, Miss Townsend pressed a glittering silver coin into the footman's gloved palm.

Miss Townsend spied me lingering beside the railings and turned her steps to me, to the consternation of the footman.

"Mrs. Holloway, how fortunate I've caught you." Miss Townsend slid her hand into the pocket of her light spring jacket and handed me an envelope, her eyes alight with excitement. "The next letter came," she said, sotto voce. "Look that over and tell me what you think. I'll be upstairs having a sedate tea with Cynthia and her aunt. We'll confer when I am ready to depart."

I had no time to answer before Miss Townsend sailed back toward the house's front door. "Not to worry, dear boy. Here I am." She let the footman, who doubtless hoped for another gratuity, lead her under the square portico and through the open door into the house.

I kept the letter crumpled in my hand as I hastened down the stairs to the kitchen. Once inside I shoved aside the bowl of sliced apples—in cold water so they wouldn't brown—and unfolded what Miss Townsend had given me.

The letter was in its envelope, addressed to Miss Townsend of Upper Brook Street in a clear hand. I stared down at the envelope, my hand drifting to my parted lips as a coldness stole through me.

"Mrs. H.?" Tess asked in concern. "What is it? Not more bad news?"

It was no news at all. But I recognized the handwriting that blared up at me. I'd seen it in notes addressed to me, passed to me by James, and also from careful entries he'd made about our inquiries into my own notebook.

I knew without any sort of doubt that Daniel McAdam had written the direction on this missive.

11

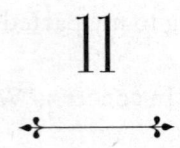

I remained still for so long that Tess put a hand onto my shoulder, startling me.

"Is it one of them nasty letters?" she asked. "That's not your name though."

I made myself look up from the envelope, but I was all amazed. How on earth had Daniel come to be involved in this blackmailing scheme? It had not been his hand on the previous letters, so why had he written *this* particular envelope?

"No." My mouth was so dry I could scarcely form the word. "It came to Miss Townsend."

"Are you going to open it? Be easier to read, then, wouldn't it?"

Tess obviously did not recognize Daniel's writing, but she had no reason to. She had a point, however, so I parted the envelope where Miss Townsend had slit it and withdrew the single page.

Daniel had not penned the letter itself. I didn't realize I had been holding my breath as I unfolded it, until my exhale rattled the paper.

The message inside had been written in the same slanting hand as the first and began with a few vitriolic words about Miss Townsend's character. Once the invective was over, the person stated:

I have decided to be kind and not demand the cash you were fearing. Much easier for you to do me a favor instead.

Speak to your father about the formation of the secret police. He will know what I mean. They would do well to dissolve it before someone is hurt.

It is disgusting that a free land has resorted to men spying on other free men, taking notes on what they do. Tell him to have it stopped.

He will listen to you, no matter what sickening tricks you get up to in your bedroom. Urge him to end it or your high jinks will be touted to all and sundry, in exquisite detail. Perhaps photographs will be involved.

The letter wandered off into more vituperation, which I had no desire to peruse.

I reread the demands, becoming more puzzled each time. What did they mean by a secret police? I'd never heard of such a thing, though I suppose the term *secret* would cover that contingency.

Miss Townsend's father was something in the Home Office, which oversaw the Metropolitan Police and other domestic measures in Britain. If anyone would know what the police were up to, it would be Mr. Townsend and his colleagues.

The larger question was, why had *Daniel* addressed the

envelope of a letter threatening Miss Townsend and mentioning a secret police service?

I folded the paper and slid it back into the envelope. Like the first letters, this had come through the post, with a proper stamp, which had been cancelled with today's date, which meant it had been posted this morning.

Daniel at the moment was inside a house in Belgrave Square—if it hadn't been his body pulled from the river, I reminded myself with a wrench—watching over a viscount who might or might not be a miscreant.

Were the letters—at least this one—originating from the Belgrave Square house, where Daniel was busily purporting to be a secretary?

I could not imagine Daniel letting such a nasty thing, with mention of the police, which he was very much a part of, slip through his fingers. He'd have found some way to purloin the letter, especially as he was acquainted with its recipient. I could, however, picture the writer sealing up the envelope and passing it to Daniel, telling him to address and post it as part of his duties.

Would Daniel risk sending Miss Townsend, a person he knew, a surreptitious message using this correspondence? I removed the letter again and scoured the envelope for writing or a hidden slip of paper or some such, but found nothing. Likewise, the letter contained nothing but the malicious threats, no extra sentence from Daniel or other cryptic marks.

Most frustrating of all was that I could not stand in front of Daniel and demand to know what this strange business was all about.

I could only hope that Hannah would find a way to communicate with me again soon. A greater hope was that Daniel would find evidence on whatever culprits he needed to and go home, ending his obligation to Mr. Monaghan.

I tucked the letter into my apron pocket so I could return it to Miss Townsend, and made myself concentrate on finishing up the apple dish.

We laid our apple slices into the baking pan and dotted them with butter. Next came a spread of apricot jam, then the custard cream, then another layer of apples. We continued to pile the apples, jam, and cream into the dish until it reached the top.

So intently did we focus on our task that we spoke about nothing but the dessert until I carried the whole thing carefully to the oven and slid it inside.

"Everything all right?" Tess asked me as we turned to preparing scones for afternoon tea for the upstairs. "You were pale as a ghost reading over that letter. Am I right it was another of the foul ones?"

"Indeed." The letter felt heavy in my pocket. "Miss Townsend passed it to me on her way inside."

"Awful what people spew at a lady just because she's rich and pretty," Tess said as she cut chunks of butter into a bowl of flour. "Of course, the poor get the same sort of venom. You should hear what some have said about my brother."

Her words pulled me from my own troubles. "Oh, Tess, I am sorry. They have no call to hurt you two like that."

Tess squared her shoulders. "We're used to it. Besides, since I'm not a proper lady, I can give them a punch in the nose."

I hid my surge of pride in her. "Indeed, having to smile and nod at the world when they are taunting you is a drawback of being a well-bred lady. It's no wonder Lady Cynthia puts on trousers and smokes cheroots. Her armor against the world, I suppose."

"Suppose," Tess said dubiously. She finished with the butter and stirred in the cream. "I don't need to don my brother's clothes to defend him though. I've taught plenty to be scared of me fists."

"Good for you, Tess. Now, do not mix currants into all of the scone batter. Miss Townsend prefers them without, so we'll make a plain batch for her."

Once Tess had finished mixing up the dough, I gently rolled it out, and then we used a round cutter to form the scones. These went into the oven to bake beside the apple-cream dish.

I always kept a selection of small pastries on hand, or ordered them from the nearest confectionery, for when Mrs. Bywater took it into her head to host an afternoon tea, the sort made popular by the Duchess of Bedford, lady-in-waiting to the queen some forty years ago.

That kind of tea is quite different from what is known as high tea, which is a cooked meal taken in the early evening, usually by working-class men and women. The dainty delicacies that wouldn't keep a fly satisfied were for the gentry.

We prepared trays of little sandwiches, the scones, and the tiny pastries along with bowls of lemon curd and Devonshire cream. These went up the dumbwaiter for Mr. Davis to set out for the ladies. The apple dish would be served later, at supper.

I never enjoyed fixing the tea that Mrs. Bywater used to impress her friends, because it cut into time I needed for the evening meal. Mrs. Bywater always expected me to serve a substantial supper by eight, even after she'd stuffed herself with scones at four o'clock.

As Tess and I threw ourselves into our tasks, the letter and Daniel's involvement in it continued to push itself to the front of my mind.

What had the letter writer meant by *men spying on other free men, taking notes on what they do*?

Daniel often disguised himself to spy on people, but always to make certain they didn't hurt others. I did not consider that to be the same thing as simply making notes on someone at random. I myself had been busy sending out lads to tell me about people I'd never met, but this was to make certain Daniel was not endangered by them.

However, I could well imagine Mr. Monaghan heading up a secret body of policemen and intruding on the rest of us without compunction. I could also believe him coercing Daniel into this body of spies and forcing him to do his deplorable work.

I most definitely would have to speak to Mr. Monaghan.

At about five o'clock, Maggie, one of the downstairs maids, came to tell me Miss Townsend wished to speak to me. "To heap praise on ya, Mrs. H.," Maggie said with a mocking smile. "She said to meet you outside the front door."

"Thank you, Maggie." I would not return her jeering with unkindness, so I added, "There are extra scones in the servants' hall for us all. Jam too."

Maggie's sneer turned to eagerness, and she hastened into the servants' room, where I'd laid out sandwiches and currant scones.

I made certain the letter was secure in my apron pocket and departed through the scullery to climb the outside stairs to the street. Miss Townsend made a show of adjusting her gloves while our footman rather impatiently held her coach door for her.

"Mrs. Holloway," Miss Townsend said brightly, as though happy to chance upon me once again. "Thank you for the lovely scones." She lifted her hand toward me, a crown coin between her fingertips.

"No need for that," I said hastily. "They were naught but butter and flour, held together with a bit of cream."

"And ingenuity," Miss Townsend assured me.

I pretended to take the coin but slid the letter into her hand instead. The crown fell to the pavement. I picked it up and firmly handed it back to her.

I debated whether to tell her the handwriting was Daniel's and decided against it, for now, with the footman too near.

"The letter writer knows exactly what role your father plays at the Home Office," I whispered to her. "What did they mean by a secret police?"

Miss Townsend shrugged. "I have no idea. People get notions into their heads. In any case, my father is not going to reform the Metropolitan Police because his daughter begs him to."

I didn't quite believe that Miss Townsend did not know what the letter referred to. She too quickly moved her gaze to rest on the railings beside us, her smile becoming fixed.

I continued. "It was written neatly, not scrawled in anger. As though they worked out what they would say first and then copied it out onto a clean sheet. There is no hesitation, only very even spaces between the words."

Miss Townsend flicked her eyes to me again. "That is very cleverly thought, Mrs. Holloway. You ought to be an expert in handwriting for Scotland Yard."

I nodded modestly, though I thought it was silly praise. As though Scotland Yard would listen to the likes of me.

Miss Townsend gave me another smile and continued in a louder voice. "I truly thank you for the tea. It was the best I've had."

I curtsied, so anyone watching would believe I merely accepted the compliment. At least Miss Townsend did not try to give me the crown again.

We said our farewells, and Miss Townsend returned to the coach. The thoughtful glance she shot me as she entered the carriage had me running through our conversation once more, wondering what she was refusing to tell me.

T ess and I finished supper and sent it up along with the apples à la frangipane. The plate it had rested on contained only a smear of cream when the footmen cranked the dirty dishes back to us.

When I'd put some of the apple dish aside for Tess and me to enjoy I'd automatically begun to add a helping for Daniel, before remembering he wouldn't be visiting, for who knew how long.

I stilled in the larder, where I'd gone to tuck away leftovers, indulging myself in a few moments of despair. If I lost Daniel, it would leave an emptiness in my life that nothing could fill.

When I returned to the kitchen I had an even greater determination to see Daniel returned home safely. It was quite important to stop people setting off bombs and hurting innocents, but I wanted the task to be accomplished without Daniel losing his life.

I held to the idea that Daniel had been given sealed envelopes to deliver, without the writer letting him see what was inside. Though knowing Daniel, he would have made a valiant attempt to find out what it was he posted.

But there was another possibility. Daniel might have addressed the envelopes during a previous job—he'd pretended to be a young and impoverished gentleman secretary before—that had nothing to do with Lord Peyton or his household. The blackmailer could have hoarded the envelopes and then used them later, once Daniel was well away.

This might account for Lady Rankin being sent a letter—the blackmailer had waited so long that Lady Rankin had died in the meantime. Perhaps he'd simply sent out the entire batch without remembering to pull hers from it. Or he'd decided that the current lady of the house might have as many guilty secrets as the former.

This did not explain why the first batch of letters was addressed in a different hand, but I was fumbling to understand what was happening.

I made myself get on with my tasks, then I carried my basket of scraps upstairs to greet those who gathered around me.

Mr. Fielding's two young spies were there. I gave them less than I did the others, knowing Mr. Fielding was making certain their bellies were full.

A giant of a man surged from the back of the crowd once I'd handed out my last bit of bread and leftover apples. The others faded before him, pretending not to fear the huge specimen who brushed them aside like a rolling boulder.

The man seized my hands in a massive grip. "Mrs. Holloway," he boomed. "I'm that pleased to see you. It has been too long a time, hasn't it?"

12

Zachariah Grimes beamed at me from his great height, his blue eyes in his rather squashed face filled with unfeigned delight.

He wrung my hands, jiggling my now-empty basket, and I gasped for breath. "I am happy to see you as well, Mr. Grimes," I managed. "Your grip is rather tight."

Instantly, Mr. Grimes released me. "Beg pardon, missus. I forget me own strength when I'm chuffed. You look well. Danny's worried about you, but you're as hearty as ever."

In fashionable society, a lady's beauty depended on how delicate she was, and calling a woman hearty would be seen as an insult. I often thanked the Lord I wasn't a fashionable lady— I'd be useless if I reclined on a chaise pretending I couldn't lift a teacup on my own.

The beggars had dispersed, and I felt able to speak freely. "I am quite well, Mr. Grimes. It is Daniel I'm worried about."

"Aye, that's why I've come. I hear it's in the newspapers that a secretary to the toff in Belgrave Square was done over, and I wanted to tell you it weren't our Danny. Rest assured. I saw him this morning."

I sagged, thankful the house's railings were behind me. Mr. Grimes was quickly beside me, his strong hand under my elbow.

I'd already concluded from Hannah's note and the lack of a grief-stricken James on my doorstep that the murdered man could not be Daniel. Also Constable Greene would by now have told me, or at least Tess, if the body had been Daniel's.

But reasoning and believing were not the same as knowing.

"Thank you, Mr. Grimes," I said, my voice faint. "I had deduced this."

Mr. Grimes nodded at me. "You're a sharp one, you are. But I thought I'd reassure you. Newspapers say all sorts."

He did not release my elbow, bless the man. He was a large, frightening, South London tough, but I'd come to learn he had a warm heart and would do anything for a friend.

"You say you saw Daniel this morning?" I longed for news of him, longed for a sight of him.

"Aye. He goes out on occasion, and he told me to be nigh, in case he needed me. He went to a newsagents on the Brompton Road, and I pretended to happen to be there looking for a newspaper. Not that I could read it." He guffawed. "Danny didn't give me no particulars on what he was doing in that house. He just told me to tell you he was well, and to look after you."

"I am glad." I'd wondered why Mr. Grimes hadn't come to me after I'd asked James to look out for him, but if he was hanging about waiting to see if Daniel needed him, I understood. I was happy now for the wait. "I am grateful to you for guarding him, as much as you can," I said in all sincerity.

"I can't get as near as I'd wish, in that part of London," Mr. Grimes answered. "A constable is always ready to run off the likes of me. But if Danny needs me, I'm there with me fists. Let anyone try to hurt 'im." He released me to pound one meaty hand into an open palm.

"I do feel better, knowing you are prowling," I assured him.

Mr. Grimes boomed his big laugh, the sound cheering. "Not many would, would they? Oh, Danny also told me to tell you he knows about the maid."

"What?" I regarded Mr. Grimes in pure dismay. "How could he possibly know?"

Mr. Grimes shrugged. "He's Danny."

"Drat him." I doubted Hannah had told him her true identity. She was very good at deception, but then, so was Daniel. "He didn't send her away, did he?"

"He didn't say. But I think he'd have told me if he had done."

I exhaled an exasperated breath. "Well, I hope he makes use of her instead of shutting her out. Blast the man."

Mr. Grimes clearly had no idea what maid I was talking about, but he nodded along thoughtfully. "Danny does what's best."

"Do you know anything about what he's facing?" I asked, my worries mounting. "Was the dead man the secretary he replaced?"

Mr. Grimes went somber. "Danny says so, though he don't know who killed him. Mr. Howard, secretary's name was. Gent from Northamptonshire, youngest son to a toff, come to London to make a living, poor chap."

Mr. Howard had accepted the wrong offer of employment, it seemed. Had it been chance that he'd found work with Viscount Peyton? Or had he been a supporter of the Fenians, an anarchist himself? Or, more troubling, had he been an envoy of this secret police the letters mentioned?

If Mr. Howard had been a police spy, he'd been readily dispatched. Which meant that if Daniel's true identity was revealed, they would not hesitate to dispatch him as well.

As much as I wished Monaghan and his cronies would act, I thought I understood why they hadn't simply carted everyone inside Lord Peyton's house to the nearest magistrate. Lord Peyton and his friends would have to stand trial, and if the police did not have enough of the right evidence, and Lord Peyton had a good barrister on his side, the judge might throw the case out or acquit him.

Lord Peyton also could be powerful enough to have judges dancing to his tune. Besides, he would face the House of Lords or a tribunal of some sort for treason—I wasn't certain about how such things worked—but he'd never kick his heels in Newgate and then be dragged through the tunnel to stand in the dock at the Old Bailey.

Monaghan and Daniel had to be careful to catch these people in the act of whatever they planned. To bring forth enough proof to outrage the Crown and end the danger of them once and for all.

Others would follow, a dim voice in the back of my mind told me. There had been bomb attacks before, and there would be again, until Ireland had its grievances addressed. Some of the stories I'd heard about the suffering in Irish villages were sad and horrible, and I sympathized with the people there. But again, it was *my* child in danger from their fellow countrymen's explosives.

Last October, bombs had gone off in Paddington Street Station, on the Underground, which had done nothing to endear me to that form of travel. I'd been careful to keep Grace from trains lately, especially after another incendiary device had detonated in Victoria Station only three months ago.

Daniel was trying to stop that. His ultimate task was to keep more violence from happening. Lord Peyton—or someone in his house—could point the way to the culprits.

I should leave Daniel to it, but as I'd reflected before, sacrificing Daniel for the greater good was not justifiable in my eyes.

"What can we do?" I asked in some desperation.

"We can watch." Mr. Grimes's usually sunny face held seriousness. "We can be ready to snatch our Danny to safety at a moment's notice. If you got one of the maids on your side, she can help, can't she?"

"She can." Hannah was nothing if not resourceful. She was also fast on her feet, slipping from danger like a clever fox from a snare.

Mr. Grimes pasted on his smile again. "Don't you worry, Mrs. H. Danny won't come to harm if *I* have anything to say about it."

I believed him, and I appreciated his adamance. "His brother is helping too. Mr. Fielding's got people watching." His lads lounged against railings in the shadows a little way along Mount Street even now, observing us.

"Wild Errol, the vicar?" Mr. Grimes's laugh rang out once more. "Well, he knows some who are plenty frightening. Dangerous even. They'll let no grief come to Danny."

"Thank you, Mr. Grimes," I said, straightening my basket. "You have made me feel much better."

Mr. Grimes touched his cap. "Happy to help. Danny's like a brother to me. One what kept me out of trouble—as long as I did whatever he said." He chuckled.

My tension eased enough to let me smile. "That sounds like

our Danny. Please visit again, Mr. Grimes. And tell me about *anything* that happens."

"That I will." He winked. "Any extra tarts wouldn't go amiss either."

I regretfully showed him my empty basket. "I'm afraid I've given away everything I brought out with me. If you stay a moment, I can fetch you something else."

"Naw." Mr. Grimes straightened to his full height. "I ate plenty of grub already today. Save it for another time. It will be my special treat."

"I will reward you well," I promised. Mr. Grimes would never have an empty belly again.

"I do look forward to that." Mr. Grimes rubbed his hands in tattered gloves together. "Good night, missus. And don't you worry. I'll look after him."

"Good night, Mr. Grimes." I knew he'd do his best to keep Daniel safe, and for that, I'd bake him a thousand tarts. "God bless you."

"And you, missus." Mr. Grimes tipped a grubby cap to me, sent me his brilliant grin, and ducked back into the shadows.

I waited until he'd disappeared before I gave Mr. Fielding's boys a nod and turned back to the kitchen stairs. I was still afraid for Daniel, but as I descended to the kitchen once more, I was bolstered by the knowledge that he had allies who'd fight for him.

The week's end passed without incident at Mount Street, with the exception of Mrs. Bywater scolding me for making so rich a dish as the apples à la frangipane. I'd give them all dyspepsia if I wasn't careful, she said.

Mr. Davis told me sourly that such concerns hadn't stopped Mrs. Bywater from eating an entire bowl of it.

In my annoyance, I decided it would serve her right to give her a tart that was as dry as toast, perhaps with a single smear of unsweetened jam as its filling.

I even began to rub a tiny amount of butter into a mound of flour I'd heaped upon my table. If I moistened it into a paste with water, the result would be crisp and dry, like the stalest bread.

"Are we out of butter?" Tess asked in passing as she glanced at my floury fingers. "I can run out and fetch some if you like."

"No, no." I snatched the cloth off the tub I had brought from the larder and cut more cubes. "If I want the dough to puff into leaves, I must add the butter a little at a time."

In the end, I could not bring myself to make a bad pastry. It would be like a famous soprano trying to sing out of tune, or a great ballerina faltering to the time of the music. If word got out that one of my tarts was inedible, my reputation would be in tatters.

I transformed the mound of flour and bowl of butter into a sheet of dough that I folded and rolled out, folded and rolled out, over and over. I layered the finished sheets into an oblong pan, alternating them with pears and cinnamon. No custard this time, but the pastry would not need it. I'd whip a cream to dollop onto the warm, finished pieces.

That sweet went up on Sunday night, and Mr. Davis proclaimed it a success. Tess and I, eating the remainder, agreed.

Monday after lunch, I donned my second-best frock and scurried away before Mrs. Bywater could come downstairs and demand I make six more of the pear tarts for tonight, as Mr. Davis had warned me she'd threatened to.

I'd nearly reached Oxford Street, when a hansom overtook me. I recognized the cabbie as one called Lewis, Daniel's friend, and paused my steps when Lewis halted next to me.

"Get in, Mrs. H.," Lady Cynthia drawled at me from the hansom's interior. The upright figure of Mr. Thanos sat next to her, with as much space between the two as the small cab could possibly allow. "Thanos and I would like to ask you a few questions."

Mr. Thanos, ever a stickler for courtesy, hauled himself from the hansom and steadied my ascent into it. Lewis, like most London cabbies, started the horse again in a hurry, and Mr. Thanos nearly got left behind.

Mr. Thanos landed breathlessly next to me, squashing me between the two.

"We are abducting you," Cynthia informed me. "Until you tell us all we wish to know."

"Not exactly," Mr. Thanos said quickly and apologetically. "Lewis has instruction to let you off in Cheapside."

"What am I to tell you?" I asked them both in curiosity.

"Why you didn't let on that McAdam wrote the direction on some of the letters Judith has collected for us," Cynthia stated. "Thanos recognized it straightaway, didn't you, Thanos? So tell us why you kept us in the dark, Mrs. H."

13

I haven't had the chance," I replied truthfully. Cynthia hadn't been down to the kitchen, and I'd been plenty busy with my day-to-day duties since Miss Townsend had showed me her letter. "You say there are more with Daniel's handwriting?"

"Indeed," Cynthia said. "Judes got her friends to cough them up. She has six of the awful things in hand now, all sent to women married to or related to people high up in government. Threatening them with dire fates if they don't do what they're told. Probably why I haven't been blessed with such missives. Papa barely knows where the House of Lords meets, let alone what they do there."

"So I had concluded myself," I said. "It is interesting that they have changed from demands for money to demands for influence."

"If McAdam is writing out these envelopes, he'll know who is sending them, won't he?" Cynthia asked.

"Not necessarily," Mr. Thanos broke in. "It could be part of one of these covert tasks McAdam has been thrown into for the police. He might be in on a plot to smoke out the blackmailer." Mr. Thanos peered at me hopefully from nearsighted eyes.

I hadn't let on to Cynthia or Miss Townsend about Daniel's current assignment, so I only nodded. "Something like that. I am sorry I cannot tell you more."

Mr. Thanos looked disappointed but understanding. "Please assure him that I will render any assistance I can."

"You've already rendered a great deal." Cynthia leaned around me to speak to Mr. Thanos. "Tell her about your chemical experiments."

Mr. Thanos beamed. "I happen to be friends with one of the foremost professors of chemistry at the Normal School of Science in South Kensington. Frederick Russell. As in Russell Square and Great Russell Street. Those Russells. He's an unassuming chap, in spite of his pedigree, and quite brilliant." He smiled broadly, wishing me to join with his pride in his friend.

"Go on," Cynthia prodded. "Tell her what he said."

"Oh, yes. Of course. Well, Russell tested the paper and envelope of the letters Miss Townsend received. He announced that they were very ordinary, full of wood pulp and not much linen. Cheaply obtained at any stationers on any street in London, sold for a ha'penny a packet."

"That does not help us much," I said, trying not to sound too despondent. "I had already concluded that the envelope was cheap, though I wasn't certain about the paper."

"Of a very similar nature. It is amazing how Russell can add droplets of colored chemicals to a scrap of paper and tell me exactly what it's made of by observing the colors or patterns that are formed. I am a theoretical scientist myself—all equations and diagrams—but I sometimes wish I could roll up my sleeves and swish chemicals about in beakers."

"It's rather a mercy you don't," Cynthia said in alarm. "You'd spill something incredibly dangerous and be an invalid the rest of your life."

"Exactly why I stick to books and papers." Mr. Thanos chuckled. "But it's fascinating to watch."

"You've left out the best part," Cynthia said.

"That is true. Forgive me, Mrs. Holloway. I'm apt to become interested in a thing, you know, and run off on a tangent. Russell said there was nothing remarkable about the paper. But the *ink*—now, that is a different story."

"Yes?" I asked, my hopes rising again. "What about the ink?"

"It turns out it is a combination of iron-gall inks mixed with indigo. This particular recipe, which Russell deduced from separating it into its parts, is manufactured in France, by a company that makes high-quality artist inks and also those for writing," Mr. Thanos finished, pleased.

"He means the ink can only be obtained either by a shop that imports it to London, or by traveling to Paris oneself and purchasing it," Cynthia elucidated. "In other words, expensive. Not something one would pop into the nearest stationers and buy for a few pennies."

"The bottles themselves are works of art," Mr. Thanos said admiringly. "Lovely glass stoppers. Russell showed me one—he of course can afford such things."

As could a man who lived in a luxurious house in Belgrave Square, who was visited by equally wealthy friends.

"We were thinking." Cynthia cut through my thoughts. "It wouldn't be difficult to find out who purchased the ink. Only a few shops in London carry it. Then we will know who wrote the letters."

Who had possibly written the letters, I amended to myself, but I nodded.

"If you do discover who bought this particular ink, please do nothing until we discuss it," I said. "Then we'll decide what to do."

"Go to the police and rout them," Cynthia avowed.

Mr. Thanos, who knew more about Daniel's past assignments than anyone, caught my concern. "Yes, we will proceed cautiously," he promised. "You are thinking this blackmailer might be more dangerous than a disgruntled acquaintance, Mrs. Holloway?"

I sent him a grateful look. "That is it exactly."

"Which is why I'd turn it all over to the police," Cynthia said. "But Judes also says no. Too many people could be hurt and embarrassed, she reminds me. They don't have the same stamina as Judith. Or me."

I slid my notebook from my coat pocket. "Can you tell me who else has had letters? If they would not be upset by me knowing."

"Don't worry," Cynthia said. "Judes has taken over all the letters received in her circle of friends, and they do nothing until she tells them to. In addition to Viola and Delia, there is Countess Buckenham, Lady John Langley, and Lady Edith St. Mary, whose father is a duke. She's a widow but hostesses all her father's dos, since her mum is gone."

I wrote down the names. "I will guess that their husbands, fathers, or brothers are important in government?"

"Cabinet ministers or leaders of the Tories or in some ministry or other, like Judith's father," Cynthia confirmed.

"And what does the letter writer want their male relatives to do?"

Cynthia drummed her fingers on her broadcloth-skirted

knee. "Harass the PM, remove restricting laws in Ireland and push for Home Rule, limit the powers of the police. The writer is a bit condescending to the ladies—they imply we women won't understand the policies the letter writer speaks of, but he assured them it is very important. So important that their nasty secrets will be exposed if they don't comply."

"Affairs and the like?" I asked gently.

"Affairs, ruinous gambling debts, children—heirs even—fathered by someone other than the lady's husband. One accused of causing the death of her maid, which we've always suspected is true, though accidentally, poor wretch."

I hid my distress at the last revelation by firmly jotting notes. "The writer knows quite specific things. I do not wish to be indelicate, but could your sister have had the liaisons her letter implied?"

"Yes," Cynthia said glumly. "Old Rankin was the very devil to live with. He's being generous to my family now, but I believe the shock of Em's death snapped something in him. Em never confided in me, but I am certain she had an affair with a French gent for a time. She'd have had to meet him in out-of-the-way places, because if Rankin had found out, he'd have never ceased punishing her about it."

"Then the writer must have been someone who knew her well," I said. "Or followed her about. What I am coming around to is: How does this writer know everything he or she claims? They make more than vague threats about exposing indiscretions. They are quite detailed."

"Someone who knows all of us well." Cynthia looked a bit sickly. "That could be any of us. Me. Bobby, even."

"Is Bobby interested in Irish Home Rule?" I asked with a touch of humor.

"I think Bobby might know where Ireland is," Cynthia

answered. "In a general sort of way. But no, she is not political, by any means. She says government is created by men for men, and until women lead the world, she wants nothing to do with such things. I can see her point."

Mr. Thanos broke in. "Jesting aside, I believe Cyn is right. There is a spy in your midst. Is anyone particularly adamant about the Irish question?"

"Yes, of course," Cynthia said. "Our bluestocking chats in Russell Square are about the state of the world and finding justice for everyone. Some ladies are a bit fanatic about reform—suffrage for women and rights of those crushed by the empire. At the same time, I can't imagine *them* writing scurrilous letters threatening to tell tales to get their way. They proclaim their views loudly and even walk about the streets with placards. Besides, it would be difficult for them to discover some of these things—who fathered whose child, and so forth. That points more to a society lady or gent who watches and collects the information."

"Someone with a relative in Ireland, perhaps?" Mr. Thanos suggested.

"Perhaps," I said hesitantly. "Or perhaps the collector of information does not write the letters. He or she passes on the bits, not knowing that they are being used in an attempt to manipulate powerful men."

"Why should they pass on the information?" Cynthia demanded. "For money? Perhaps *they* are up to their ears in debt."

"Or for someone they love?" I suggested. "Perhaps not wisely."

"Again, that could be anyone in Mayfair." Cynthia waved her hand at London in general. "And it might be a servant. A footman, a valet, a lady's maid. Someone intimate with a family. Speaks to other valets and manservants and gathers the particulars."

"I have thought of the possibility of a servant," I said. Mr. Davis, for one, knew much gossip about what went on in the homes of the titled, as did I. The cooks I was acquainted with liked to impart tittle-tattle, the juicier, the better. "Or a lady who wanders from home to home, insisting on hospitality."

Hannah had mentioned Lady Mortimer from the old days, who had been just such a person. Her husband's estate had gone to his nephew, and he'd refused to provide more than a meager allowance for her. Lady Mortimer's own parents had long since died, and so she'd prevailed upon the kindness of her friends for room and board. The fact that she stole small trinkets—and couldn't help herself—was a trial, but her friends had felt sorry enough for her to put up with her. Lady Mortimer had known a great many people in society and was in place to learn of any skeletons in their cupboards.

Hannah had also told me that Lord Peyton's sister, Lady Fontaine, was of similar character. I needed to know more about Lady Fontaine.

"I'm not acquainted with anyone of that nature," Cynthia said. "But Judith might be. She knows everyone in Britain, I believe."

Miss Townsend herself would be a perfect candidate. She mingled with all walks of society, in spite of her scandalous life, as no one wanted to offend the daughter of such a powerful family. Miss Townsend was also observant, intelligent, and determined, and she could dissemble well.

However, I viewed Miss Townsend as an honest woman who would directly ask for reforms instead of resorting to threats and underhanded means. But in my current state of mind, I was willing to believe anything of anyone.

"Do ask Miss Townsend," I said. We were approaching Cheapside, and I pocketed my notebook, ready to put this unpleasantness behind me for a while.

When Lewis halted the cab, Mr. Thanos scrambled out and held out a hand to assist me.

"Thank you very much for the transportation, Mr. Thanos," I said as I alighted. "It was generous of you."

"Not at all." Mr. Thanos gave me a gallant bow. "It is a long walk across London."

"I am robust," I assured him. "But it is a kind thought."

"Saves your feet for walking about with Grace," Cynthia called cheerily to me. "You never did tell us why Daniel was addressing the envelopes."

"Because I do not know," I said as Mr. Thanos climbed back into the cab. "If we find the letter writer, I believe all will become clear."

"As simple as that," Cynthia said wryly. "Good day, Mrs. H. Give my best to your girl."

I assured her I would. Lewis, in the impatient way of cabbies, started off, leaving me to wave after them. At least he'd let Mr. Thanos sit down first.

Once they were lost in the traffic determinedly making its way along Cheapside, I turned to Clover Lane, leaving off my troubles to immerse myself in the joy of my daughter.

O nce I'd had my walk with Grace and we'd returned to Joanna's house for a nice long tea, I turned my steps westward again, making for the Strand.

Joanna's afternoon tea had been in no way as fussy as the one I'd had to serve to Mrs. Bywater and her cronies. We had bread and butter, a few scones with jam Joanna had brought out as a treat, and that was all. But the conversation and merriment were far preferable to me to a tray of perfectly matched petits fours.

My belly and heart both full, I hurried along Fleet Street, passed Temple Bar, and turned south down Whitehall at Charing Cross.

Scotland Yard's entrance lay along the narrow lane called Great Scotland Yard, from which the Metropolitan Police had obtained its nickname. The police would soon move to new premises on the Victoria Embankment, but the construction on that building, on the site of what was supposed to have been an opera house, was slow.

The ground-floor hall was as busy as ever, with constables moving to and fro, members of the populace trying to get attention or to leave as quickly as they could, and general pandemonium. I walked purposefully to the desk near the stairs and spoke to the sergeant behind it.

"I would like to see Inspector McGregor, please."

The sergeant, whom I'd dealt with before, gave me a side-eyed glare. "He's busy."

"I imagine he is. Will you please send word that Mrs. Holloway has come to call on him?"

"That I won't, missus. Unless you have some information on whoever pushed that bloke's dead body into the Thames."

"I might, actually." I fixed him with a stern gaze. "I'd guess Inspector McGregor would be a bit put out if he does not hear it."

The sergeant wasn't going to give way. One of the constables though, a friend of Constable Greene, I recalled, came forward. "I'll take her," he offered.

"Then you get his wrath on your head," the sergeant muttered.

The constable ignored him. "Mrs. Holloway?" He gestured me to follow him.

I gave the sergeant a final disapproving look before I turned away.

The constable led me out to a smaller building in the court-yard, which now housed the Criminal Investigation Department as well as the Public Carriage Office, where cabs were licensed. Once inside, we went up a flight of stairs to a narrow corridor and so to the office to which Inspector McGregor had moved.

Inspector McGregor's outer office, in which his detective constables and sergeants worked, was indeed busy. The men scarcely raised their heads from desks filled with papers and books as the constable ushered me through.

Fortunately, the inspector was alone. He looked up when the constable tapped on the door and then opened it, his quick glance becoming an expression of dismay.

"You," Inspector McGregor growled at me. "What do you—? Thank you, Constable. Please go."

The constable sent me a surreptitious grin and disappeared, clicking the door closed behind him.

"I am busy, Mrs. Holloway. I have a murder to solve."

"Did Mr. Monaghan insist you look into that one?" I seated myself on a hard wooden chair without waiting to be invited. "He is one Milton Howard, former secretary to Lord Peyton of Belgrave Square. He was either dismissed or decided to flee. I would keep my eye on Lord Peyton's very large manservant, Inspector. However, that is not what I've come about."

"No?" Inspector McGregor regarded me with his usual irritation. His pale hair was slicked back from a forehead gleaming with sweat, and his equally pale mustache flickered as his lips twitched. "What is it? Tell me and depart."

"I have no other information, but I wish to ask you a question." I leaned forward, lowering my voice in case any of the constables had lingered to listen outside the door. "What can you tell me about Scotland Yard's branch of secret police? This is what Mr. Monaghan truly runs, is it not? And he has made Mr. McAdam be part of it, hasn't he?"

14

Inspector McGregor went so still for so long I wondered if he'd ceased breathing.

I'd expected him to launch himself to his feet snarling at me to leave off asking ridiculous questions and depart his presence, but instead he merely stared at me, color suffusing his face.

"So I am right," I said softly. "There *is* a department of secret police, and that makes you very unhappy."

Inspector McGregor's face reddened still more, revealing his distress well. "Did McAdam tell you that? Damn the man."

"Mr. McAdam never breathed a word," I said in truth. "He would not breach a trust, not even to his closest friends. I have simply drawn the conclusion."

From the relieved flicker in his eyes, Inspector McGregor believed me, but his ire remained high. "Never, ever speak of this, Mrs. Holloway. Not to me, not to McAdam, and not, for the love of God, to Monaghan."

"A man you dislike intensely," I said. "What has he done that is so unpardonable? Mr. McAdam implied that he was worse than the most dangerous criminal in London."

"He killed people," Inspector McGregor said bluntly. "Assassinated them, I mean. Instead of hanging for it, CID decided they needed his insight into criminal activity, and he walked free. That is not a secret. Everyone knows it."

I might have guessed something of the sort, with Monaghan's cold gaze and complete lack of compassion, but I shivered.

"That was long ago, was it not?" I asked in a faint voice.

"Does it matter?" Inspector McGregor snapped. "Yes, it was many years ago, and for a long time now, Monaghan has helped the police bring down dangerous men, so I suppose he has paid his dues. He hunts villains with the ruthlessness with which he must have hunted his targets."

"He puts Mr. McAdam in perilous situations because of it," I stated. Daniel had asked me not to discuss his current assignment with Inspector McGregor, but that was before a man had been murdered. I doubted Inspector McGregor would rush from this room to tell tales about me to Mr. Monaghan.

"I know," McGregor snapped. "I understand your concern, Mrs. Holloway, because I share it. But there is damn-all I can do." He cleared his throat. "Pardon my language."

"Think nothing of it, Inspector. Is there no one higher up than Mr. Monaghan? Surely he answers to someone. I am not averse to him stopping people who set off bombs in public places, but I wish he would not throw Daniel in front of them to do it. Daniel has proved to be a good detective, has he not? Surely he could be employed elsewhere."

McGregor listened to all of this with a scowl, and not because of anger at me. "I agree with you, but Monaghan has McAdam tethered. McAdam is not even a proper member of the police. He's considered more of an adjunct detective, meaning he answers to Monaghan alone. He can ask for assistance from any department, but those departments are not obligated to render it."

I recalled that when I'd gone with Daniel to the bridge on the Tamar between Devon and Cornwall, uniformed and plainclothes policemen had rallied around him, obeying his commands. I wondered now whether Monaghan had ordered them to be there or whether Daniel had compelled them himself.

I felt cold. "You mean, if he runs into trouble, he might be completely on his own."

"That is the truth of it, Mrs. Holloway. The reason McAdam has received help in the past is because the rest of Scotland Yard respects him as much as they fear Monaghan. However, if Monaghan instructs them not to assist McAdam, then they won't."

A wave of fury washed away my chill. "That is unfair."

McGregor's voice went hard. "It is how the ambitious, or those who simply want to keep their jobs—including me—remain employed."

"Daniel has been placed in great peril, but if Monaghan tells you not to help him, you will refuse?" I demanded.

"I did not say *I* wouldn't help," Inspector McGregor said. "If I could cause Monaghan's downfall, I would, though I doubt I can do anything about that. But I'll tell him to go to the devil if he endangers McAdam too much. I share your distaste for him sacrificing others for his cause."

McGregor's statement, delivered in his usual grumpy manner, made me feel marginally better. I realized I might have found an ally, but how much he could do remained to be seen.

"How will you determine when the danger is too great?" I asked him. "When Daniel is half dead or fighting for his life to escape? You might act too late."

Inspector McGregor planted his elbows on the desk, lacing his blunt fingers. "McAdam is a resourceful chap, remember. The chief supers wouldn't let an incompetent fool set Monaghan's snares for him. McAdam has probably already roped in assistance from among the many villains he knows from the streets. Also, he has you to come and bother the police."

"Which I will continue to do until Daniel is safe," I said with determination.

"Being a policeman is never safe, Mrs. Holloway. This is a building full of men who risk their lives to stop criminals robbing, beating, and murdering people. We investigate crimes committed by some powerful villains, and as long as McAdam does that, he will not be safe."

"I know that," I said in irritation. "I'm not a foolish woman wondering why my menfolk don't stay tamely at home. This is a different situation. Daniel is alone, in a nest of said criminals, and I have the feeling Monaghan will be happy if he perishes there. I'm certain your chief superintendents will praise Daniel's nobility for dying to protect the queen, but I'd rather he not need that honor."

McGregor thumped back in his seat in exasperation. "What would you have me do, Mrs. Holloway? March to my commanders and tell them to boot out Monaghan, disband the new branch, and set McAdam to investigating ordinary burglaries?"

I rose. "Yes, that would be a splendid idea."

McGregor also got to his feet, following gentlemanly rules in spite of his vexation with me. "I will assist McAdam in any way I can with his current investigation. If you have *any* information from whatever villains he's pulled in to assist, tell me right away. Monaghan doesn't necessarily need to learn about it."

Inspector McGregor's indignation and his dislike of Monaghan was heartening to observe. I decided to trust him with what I knew.

"Very well. In addition to the murdered secretary, there might be blackmailing letters coming out of the house in Belgrave Square, instructing ladies connected to prominent gentlemen to influence their husbands and brothers to grant Irish Home Rule and lift other restrictions. Otherwise, indiscretions will be revealed. I can't tell you which wives, because it's not fair to expose them. One of the letters mentioned the secret branch of police, which is how I came to hear about it."

Inspector McGregor grew red in the face again. "You are saying the Fenians know what we're up to?"

"I imagine they've guessed. There have been so many bombing incidents lately, they'd have to realize the police would respond in some coordinated way."

Inspector McGregor came around the desk to halt closer to me than he'd ever been comfortable with before.

"You must remain silent about this." His quiet voice held steel. "For your own good and for the safety of the men who are trying to thwart the bombings. The Fenians and those they fund believe that nothing but violence will do until Ireland is an independent state. The violence is what we are trying to stop."

I saw a mixture of fear, anger, and loathing in his hazel eyes. "I have said nothing to anyone but you, I promise. You agree with what this new branch is trying to do, but not with their methods. Am I correct?"

"They spy and pry," McGregor said in disgust. "Sometimes on people who turn out to be perfectly innocent. They do such things on the Continent, I know, but I thought we were above that here."

"Needs must, perhaps?" I suggested, though I shared his disquiet. "The Fenians are quite dangerous."

"Is it worth having a policeman at everyone's shoulder, including mine?" Inspector McGregor growled. "Go home, Mrs. Holloway. If you learn anything more, you tell *me* and no one else. Do you understand? Trust no one, not even Constable Greene."

I raised my brows. "Surely Caleb could help. He has proved resourceful in the past."

"No one." Inspector McGregor herded me to the door. "If I've found out you've peached to anyone, I will arrest you myself."

"No need for that," I said quickly. "I can keep mum."

"See that you do."

Inspector McGregor abruptly swung open his door. The constables in the outer office were all bent over their desks, making a show of working diligently.

Before the inspector could shove me bodily out, I hastened from him. I nodded at the constables and hurried into the outer hall, thanking the lad who'd leapt to open the door for me.

I did not breathe easily until I was out in the street and then joining the crowds in Trafalgar Square. A juggler entertained passersby in one corner, and a busker sang in another. A few beggars lined the sides of the square, cups out for stray coins.

Trafalgar Square was wonderfully normal, with Londoners hurrying on their business or loitering to watch the juggler or busker. Tourists from outside the city gawped at the classical edifice of the National Gallery, craned heads to peer up Nelson's Column, and took in the pretty church of St. Martin-in-the-Fields. I slid through the masses, cutting along Cockspur Street to Haymarket.

I felt eyes on me. I wasn't certain whether Monaghan's plainclothes constables dogged my steps, or Mr. Fielding's lads, or minions of the Fenians. I'd just left the headquarters of the Metropolitan Police, a suspicious thing to do.

I couldn't be certain of help if anyone cornered me. I was on my own, alone in a city of multitudes.

Luckily for me, I knew London better than most. As a girl, my entertainment with Joanna had been to explore, evading pickpockets, constables, and any who would've been delighted to snatch up two young lasses for whatever purpose they put us to. We'd been fast on our feet and cunning too.

I could not move as swiftly as I used to, having spent too many years eating well, but I knew these streets. An artery from Haymarket led to Whitcomb Street, and from there it was a step to Leicester Square. I popped in and out of a few shops there, buying nothing, then wound through more lanes, some clean and neat, others grimy, making my way northward.

Footsteps rang behind me in a quiet alley, and I scuttled away from them to emerge into busy Oxford Street.

As I crossed back and forth on this road, pretending to do more shopping, a wagon rumbled to a stop beside me, and a small boy leapt off its back.

"Get in, missus," he urged. "We'll take you off."

He might have been one of Mr. Fielding's boys, or even have been employed by Daniel or Mr. Grimes, but I did not recognize him.

"No, thank you," I sang, and dove into my favorite greengrocers.

The greengrocer was shutting up for the evening. "I've nothing left for you, Mrs. Holloway. You're quite late tonight."

"Never mind," I said sweetly. "May I exit through your back door?"

Without waiting for him to answer, I dodged through crates in a tiny storeroom and out into a yard. If I was right, the row behind this yard would lead me to Castle Street, which in turn spilled into Regent Street, not far from Cavendish Square.

Before the wagon or boy, or any of my other followers, could decide what I'd done, I sped across Regent Street, down another short lane, and emerged at the back of the Polytechnic, where Mr. Thanos lectured.

I'd met one of the charwomen here before, and sure enough, she was sweeping the back steps tonight.

"Good evening, missus," she greeted me cheerily. "Mr. Thanos has gone home, love, if that's who you're looking for. Between us, he's sweet on that young lady who assists him. Wedding bells ringing soon, I'm thinking. Course, they'll be poor as church mice."

"Ah, well," I said, offhand. "I thought I'd take the chance."

The charwoman leaned on her broom. "Have time for a cuppa, dear?"

"I'd love one." Without hesitation, I followed her down steps into the cellar, liking the sound of the heavy door swinging shut and the charwoman's key turning in the lock.

* * *

I spent a comfortable hour chatting with the cleaner, whose name was Mrs. Harmon. We speculated on the possibility of Mr. Thanos and Cynthia making a match—*He needs some-one to look after him*, was Mrs. Harmon's opinion. *The lady does her best, though she's not as practical as a tutor's wife ought to be. Still, they're in love. You can see it.*

I saw it too, but I agreed with Mrs. Harmon that they'd need money and an understanding of how to keep themselves clothed and fed. I'd be glad to help them, if my two dear friends could find happiness.

Mrs. Harmon also had gossip about other tutors and re-searchers, as very clever gentlemen tended to be a bit odd, in her opinion. One had a mistress nearly twice his age—*and he's not a young man himself, believe me.* Another had been caught using another professor's conclusions as his own—*You'd think he'd murdered someone, the way they carried on. Well, he's not here any longer, that's for certain.*

It seemed that places of higher learning were as scandalous as any circles in the *haut ton.*

I left Mrs. Harmon after we'd polished off some rather dry cakes and too-strong tea, thanking her for the respite and the chat.

The May twilight lingered, days growing longer as summer neared. Plenty of light for me to navigate south through Ha-nover Square, winding through back lanes and mews until I reached Mount Street.

I plunged down the stairs there after another quick glance about. I did see one of Mr. Fielding's lads but no one else.

Feeling better that he was there on lookout, I landed

breathlessly in the kitchen. Tess greeted me with her usual cheerfulness, and I began to relax in my haven.

Cooking was a worthwhile endeavor, I decided as I started helping Tess get on with supper, one I'd always taken pride in. For some, cooking was a necessary chore—one has to eat, after all—but it could also be a form of art, so to speak. The melding of scents, tastes, and even how the food looked could work together to please even the most unyielding curmudgeon.

Tess and I set about creating a roast with plenty of potatoes and carrots, plus fresh asparagus I'd found this morning, lightly steamed and then sauteed in butter, with a hint of garlic and lemon.

I tossed together another apple tart by folding slices in a crust that had already been spread with butter and dusted with cinnamon. Easy enough to bake, as Tess had cut up the apples into lemon water while I'd been away.

Cooking let my worries recede into the background, though they would never quite go away while Daniel was caught in a web of dangerous men that even the stalwart Inspector McGregor feared.

Inspector McGregor had said that Mr. Monaghan had been an assassin. An interesting choice of words. An assassin of whom? And why?

Sometimes men were employed in wars to kill important people on the enemy's side. Had that been what Inspector McGregor had meant? Or had Monaghan killed people in general, ones he thought needed to be taken down?

I shivered. If he thought Daniel needed taking down—or Inspector McGregor, or me—who would stop him?

I forced myself to push these disturbing thoughts aside

and bury myself in preparing the meal and then making a start on tomorrow's chores.

I was reminded of my dilemma not long after we'd sent up the supper when the young lad Hannah used to communicate with me appeared at the scullery door. He thrust a paper at me and held out his hand for payment.

"A moment," I told him. I opened the note which stated, in Hannah's plain writing: *Pub. Leicester Square.*

15

The paper contained no further information. I turned it over, but the back was blank.

"It is a place," I informed the boy. "But not a time."

He sent me an aggrieved look. "She said Thursday, soon as it opens."

I held out a bright copper coin but let it hover over his waiting palm. "What's your name, lad?"

He hesitated a beat too long. "Adam."

If he had to think about it, then he made up the name. "Would you like a cruller?" I asked him.

"No." Adam all but snatched the coin from me and disappeared up the stairs and into the darkness.

I shook my head as I closed the door. Hannah trusted the lad, which meant I should, but I worried about him.

"Wait, missus." A voice called to me from the outer stairs, a different one, belonging to another boy.

I swung the door open again to find Albie, his countenance far more cheerful than young Adam's.

"I come for another fivepence," he announced.

"Have you now?" I studied him sternly.

"I have. Been watching that bloke you told me to—Lord Pelsham—for a time." Lord Pelsham was the friend of Lord Peyton's that Hannah mentioned visited often. "His grooms are not so nice as the Lofthouses', and he's just returned from Ireland."

"Has he?" My severity lessened. "That is interesting."

"He didn't have the best time of it, from what I could tell," Albie went on. "Railing about how dreadful it all was. How his tenants there were sullen and nasty, and how he couldn't get shot of the place quick enough. Then Lord Pelsham climbs into his coach and rolls off to Belgrave Square, probably to complain about it more to his mate there."

Very observant of the lad. "You have done well, Albie. Your fivepence and, if you'll wait a moment, a cruller."

Albie took the coins I handed him, instantly dropped them into his pocket, and touched his hat. "Won't say no to that."

I went through the kitchen to the larder and the plate of fresh crullers I'd left for the staff. I wrapped one in an old but clean cloth and returned to Albie, who lounged against the doorframe. He grinned as he took the pastry, said good-bye around me to Elsie in the scullery, and dashed upstairs. The cloth fluttered back down to me as the cruller went straight into the lad's mouth.

As I retrieved the rag and carried it to the laundry, I mused over the difference between the two boys, who were of an age. Adam—or whatever his name might be—clearly hungry and dirty, who wouldn't take my food, and Albie, already an able earner of coins, happily devouring whatever I offered.

I'd have to tempt Adam next time I saw him. He didn't need to be so thin and bleak.

The next morning, Tuesday, Tess returned from her sojourn to the market, her face pinched. She said nothing as she sorted the produce, but she worked with bangs and slams.

"Please do not bruise that cabbage," I said sternly. "We'll have to throw half of it away."

"Sorry, Mrs. H." Tess dropped the dusty carrots from her hands and sat down hard on a chair. "I have much on me mind."

"Yes?" I took over the sorting, gently placing carrots, cabbage, brussels sprouts, and more spring asparagus into boxes I'd brought out for the purpose. "Tell me what it is, and we can work through it together. Is your brother all right?"

"Tommy's well, thank you. It's Caleb what's upsetting me."

I paused, asparagus stalks dangling from my hand. "Oh dear. He hasn't given you the push, has he? Or did you him?"

"No, nothing like that," Tess said quickly. "Only, Caleb has been promoted, you see. He's been made a detective."

I blinked at her. "Has he, the dear boy? That's good news, is it not?"

"So I thought." Tess looked mournful. "But he won't be walking his beat anymore, will he? I won't see him stroll by so I can go out and have a chat." Tears welled in her eyes, which she blinked resolutely away. "He's not sure what his day out will be, if he has one, so it might not be the same as mine. Add to that, he won't talk about what he's going to do. Might be writing reports on a typing machine, for all I know. I asked him, and he came over all quiet. Wouldn't say much of anything on the rest of our walk home."

I laid down the asparagus and patted her shoulder in sympathy. "I'm sorry, Tess. It's hard to be sweet on a policeman. Well I know this. It might be difficult for the moment, but when Caleb is in a routine, and you know when you'll see him, things will be easier. And he'll have better pay now, won't he?"

"Yeah, he's chuffed about a rise. But I feel like it's taking him away from me." Tess's face was so downcast my heart squeezed.

"It will feel like that sometimes, yes. The best thing we can do is be kind to our blokes while they're answering to their bosses, and be there for them when they need to take their minds off their troubles. Chasing criminals is a difficult business."

Tess sent me a grateful glance, but her eyes held a wry sparkle. "Is that why you scold Mr. McAdam about staying away long stretches and not sending word?"

I flushed. "Daniel expects me to scold him." I longed for him to be here so I could.

Tess's face fell again. "Mr. McAdam does come around almost every day when he can. Caleb won't be able to."

I had no answer for that, so I patted her shoulder once more. "If your day out needs to change, I'll make certain there is no objection."

"Even if it's Thursday?" Tess asked.

I hid a wince. "The time I spend with Grace is important, not which day it is. You'll go even on a Thursday. I'll change too if I have to."

Tess relaxed. "You're that good to me, Mrs. Holloway."

I knew when she used my full surname that she truly was grateful. I returned to the produce.

"At the moment, neither of us has a day out," I reminded her. "We must get on with the master's dinner."

"Right you are, Mrs. H."

As I resumed sorting and deciding how I'd use each vegetable, I pondered Caleb's news.

Would he work for someone sensible, like Inspector McGregor, or had Monaghan somehow seized hold of the lad? Caleb, a good-humored young man, never hesitated to talk about his work, within reason, of course. His sudden reticence plucked at my suspicions.

Likely Caleb simply didn't know what to tell Tess, because this was all new to him. Even so, I remained uneasy, and Tess was unnaturally quiet as we turned our hands to cooking.

Thursday morning, I left the house as soon as I could, determined not to let anyone—Mrs. Bywater with a last-minute request, Cynthia abducting me to pump me for information, or the multitude of spies following me—keep me from my time with Grace.

Hannah had requested a meeting in Leicester Square as soon as the pubs opened, which meant early afternoon. I could hardly take my daughter with me, so I explained to Grace and Joanna once I reached their house that I had to run an errand.

They both were surprised, as I never disappeared during my visits, but when I explained it had to do with Daniel, they rather shooed me on my way.

I took a circuitous route to keep off any pursuers, sticking to the areas of Fleet Street and the Strand. To come at Leicester Square from the north would mean cutting through the warrens of St. Giles and Seven Dials, which held far more potential danger than the most violent anarchists could imagine.

Hannah hadn't specified which pub in Leicester Square, but I chose the one that had opened earliest. If she wasn't there, I'd look in the others until I found her.

This public house lay on the north side of the square, its taproom already full of local men, who'd come in for luncheon and a pint. Ladies were allowed only in the snug, a small room down a corridor from the front door. This suited me for a clandestine meeting, and I made my way there.

The only person in the snug at the moment was an elderly woman swathed in a dark shawl, who stared in distaste at a cup of tea on the table before her. Her body odor was a bit unfortunate.

I moved to the other side of the room and sat at the table farthest from her, on a bench that ran the length of the back wall. A silent barmaid appeared, and I asked for a cup of tea. She gave me a sour look but nodded and turned to depart.

"'Ere," the old woman said as she passed. "Can't see your way to putting a drop of gin in this, can ye?"

"We don't have no gin, ma'am," the barmaid said impatiently. "I already told ya. It's ale or nothing in this place."

"I'll have a pint, then."

"I'll see your coin first."

The old woman snarled and waved the barmaid off with a stubby hand. The barmaid retreated so hastily that I hoped she'd remember to return with my tea.

"Ale's like piss," the woman informed me, hunching over her cup again. "Not worth it, mark my words."

"I am having tea," I assured her.

"Ain't much better."

She lifted her head, her gray hair scraggly about her face, and shot me a grin full of crooked teeth.

At this moment, the barmaid did return with a pot of tea and a cracked cup, which she more or less slammed onto my table. I slid a coin across the tabletop for her, which she instantly snatched up. She ran out, resolutely not looking at the old woman.

I carefully poured myself some tea. "Come over here, dear," I told the other woman. "It's warmer on this side."

She heaved herself up, lifted her cup and saucer, and hobbled across the room to my table, where she plunked herself down opposite me and helped herself to hot tea from my pot.

"I will have to meet your wigmaker," I said in a quiet voice. "She does wonderful work."

"She does," Hannah answered as softly. "But can't have the proper maid from my fine house be seen talking to you, can we? Or even sitting in a pub like this one."

"Are you well?" I asked anxiously. "I do not like the fact that someone in that house was murdered. It might have been a chance meeting with robbers on a street—"

"No." Hannah interrupted me. "They killed him. Depend upon it. Viscount Peyton ordered that murder, and it was done for him."

16

I had lifted my tea to sip, but I set it quickly back down. "Why are you so certain?"

Hannah's eyes glittered with adamance. "They're villains in that house, mark my words—his lordship, his manservant, and his pals what come to see him. They shut themselves into his study for hours. They pore over maps and papers and go instantly quiet when the helpful maid comes in to refresh the brandy or bring tea for the lady. They don't bother hiding the papers, because they think I can't read," she finished with some amusement.

"Are the maps and papers damning enough?" I asked in hope. "Can Daniel call in Scotland Yard to come in and seize them?"

Hannah's smile deserted her. "I don't know. When his lordship's mates leave, the papers are all gone, every bit of them. I've looked. If I could smuggle out one scrap, I'm certain the whole lot of them would be arrested, but they're too careful, and I haven't found nothing."

"Please *don't* snoop," I said quickly. "I don't want *your* body ending up in the Thames."

"Two people from the same house murdered would set the police's sights on them though, wouldn't it?" Hannah's eyes narrowed in thought, increasing my alarm.

"And please don't get yourself killed to bring the constables there," I begged her. "Such a sacrifice is not worth it."

Hannah went off in peals of merriment. The laugh became the cackles of an elderly woman just as the barmaid returned. Hannah began to cough, the reedy hack of someone in the first stages of consumption, and she rubbed her eyes with a rough-gloved hand.

The barmaid crossed the room to us, set a cloudy half-pint of ale in a glass next to Hannah's elbow, and waited. Hannah glared up at her with damp, bloodshot eyes.

"That's only a half."

"Half is what we give ladies," the barmaid said. "Landlord says drink it and clear off."

Hannah growled something inaudible, then fumbled in a pocket and counted out a few grimy pennies.

"It's a shilling," the barmaid informed her.

"What? Highway robbery, that is."

I'd already pulled out my small coin purse. "There you are. A bit extra for you too." I dropped a shilling and tuppence into the barmaid's palm.

"You shouldn't pay for the likes of her," the barmaid advised, though she slid the coins into her apron pocket readily enough. "If she's troubling you, I'll have her slung out."

"I'm simply practicing Christian charity," I said, a bit

primly. "When you are old and lonely, perhaps someone will stand *you* an ale and a chat."

The barmaid scoffed, rolled her eyes, and tramped away, her pockets clinking.

"Such lies you tell," Hannah said to me with glee. "Christian charity, indeed." I noted that her cough had magically vanished, and her eyes had dried.

"I do give to those who are less fortunate." I lifted my teacup again while Hannah sipped her ale. "I would like to think someone would do the same for me if I were on the streets with an empty belly."

"You always were unnaturally kind." Hannah took another sip of ale and made a face. "I'm not wrong about it tasting like piss."

"You were also right about the tea not being much better." I pushed aside my cup. "What does Daniel do during these meetings? Is he in the room with the conspirators?"

"Not always." Hannah shook her head. "He has his own chamber next to the master's study. It's not a very big room, only enough space for a desk and a bookcase. He's made to wait there when all the people come. Sometimes his lordship will send for him to bring in a book or another map or to take away some papers. Those papers must not reveal anything, or your man would hand 'em to Scotland Yard quick, wouldn't he?"

"They are careful." I traced the knob on the teapot's lid. The pot needed a good wash, but at least the water was scalding hot. "Do they suspect Daniel of being not what he purports?"

"Don't seem to. They ignore him, mostly. His lordship calls to him to write letters or take down dictation and send messages to his cronies, but those have nothing to do with villainy that I can tell. I hear sometimes what his lordship dictates, and it's dull tripe. Like wishing a man's corns heal up, or how many shirts to order from his tailor, or recommending a restaurant for a mate's wife's birthday."

"If any of that is code, Daniel will crack it," I said with conviction. "Is Daniel given envelopes to address? Even if he doesn't write the letter inside?"

"All the time. No one in that house can be bothered to write a direction themselves. His lordship's sister—Lady Fontaine, you remember I told you about her—always hands your man things to post and bids him write out all her envelopes. Also thrusts her shopping lists at him to give to the housekeeper, as though she can't do that herself. Lady Fontaine don't like anything that comes from a pen done by any but Daniel. Either she's a clever crook and wants nothing in her own handwriting, or she's sweet on him."

I shrugged. "Both could be true."

Hannah laughed again. "He has a way with him, don't he? Don't bother to hide it none either. He'll use it to charm his way safe, mark my words."

"As long as it keeps him well, I won't object." I could hardly be jealous of a sharp-tongued, penny-pinching ladyship if she wanted to make sheep's eyes at Daniel.

"Well, ain't you the one?" Hannah chuckled. "He never mentions you, of course, and he pretends no woman has ever entered his life—he being a skint gentleman what has to take small pay in a rich house. But I see the wistfulness in his eyes sometimes. He misses ya."

"You are kind to say so."

Daniel, that master of deception, would never let on, even with a flicker in his gaze, that he was anyone other than he appeared. Hannah was only trying to make me feel better. Daniel would never betray any sort of yearning—would he? I hoped not, for his sake.

"I ain't being kind," Hannah said. "The sooner he's out of that house and back courting you, the better."

"Do you know what sorts of letters Lady Fontaine writes?" I asked, pretending to ignore her last statement.

"I've had a good peek, so yes. More inane things, like ordering gloves or nattering on to a friend how annoying her brother is. Then she walks downstairs and fawns all over his lordship until he gives her more cash for what she's just sent me off to buy. She likes me to do her shopping for her, lazy old bat."

"Perhaps she fears to leave the house, in case her creditors are lurking," I suggested.

"Could very well be. Lady Fontaine got herself into some terrible debt. Part of it wasn't her fault—her husband left her destitute and owed many people on top of that. But she don't cease purchasing stockings, ribbons, hats—oh, so many hats—handmade shoes, shawls, and whatnot. I think Lady Fontaine sends me because she knows she'll be tempted to pinch a few odds and sods if she goes into a shop. She knows she can't help herself."

"Daniel addressed a batch of envelopes that turned out to contain blackmail letters," I said, as though this were nothing remarkable. "Could Lady Fontaine have written them?"

Hannah's eyes widened. "Blackmail letters?" She stared at me in astonishment. "Doesn't your Daniel know who wrote them?"

"Possibly not," I said. "If they were handed to him already sealed."

Hannah contemplated this a moment, then she shook her head. "I don't think Lady Fontaine would have anything to do with that. She's happy to criticize other ladies, great and small, and gossips like mad, but I can't picture her sitting down and organizing something as intricate as blackmail. Lady Fontaine's like an impatient teakettle, steam boiling from her at any provocation. Blackmailing takes a cool head and a calculating mind. Lady Fontaine has neither."

"Perhaps her tempers conceal her true character?" I asked, not very optimistically.

"Not her. I can spot a villain ten yards off, like I told you. Mostly because I am one." Hannah grinned. "She's desperate and angry—Lady Fontaine ought to be a great hostess, not a poor relation. But she can't curb herself. Do you know what I mean? She keeps herself out of the shops, but she can't stop herself nicking things from her own brother. Mrs. Proctor and I are forever finding trinkets that belong elsewhere in the house in her night table. We return them and say nothing. Lady Fontaine knows. She's ashamed and becomes wickedly rude to cover it."

"You go through her cupboards and drawers, then?"

"Mrs. Proctor and I do. Mrs. Proctor wouldn't let me at first, but she's come to trust me. If Lady Fontaine was secretly writing blackmail letters, I'd have found them by now. Besides, she has no money. Nothing tucked away, not a bob that don't come from her brother."

"Lord Peyton might be doing the blackmailing," I said. "Or one of his pals. Mrs. Lofthouse, perhaps. She'd know which ladies of the *haut ton* had secrets."

Hannah shook her head. "Not her. She's a bluestocking and loathes society. She's not invited to the outings even Lady Fontaine is. Pretends she don't care, but she seethes. She *might* blackmail to take out her hurt feelings, but she'd have to know who was doing what, and not many speak to her, from what I can tell."

"Hmm." I had an idea how the scheme was being worked,

but I'd need more details. "Since you were very surprised about the blackmailing, I will surmise that you haven't seen any letters of the sort while you've been prying."

"Not a sausage." Hannah wrinkled her nose. "Speaking of sausage, his lordship's cook's not good at those. Charred on the outside, almost raw in the middle. Nothing I'll be eating. I have to say, when I worked in the same house as you, I dined well. Until you interfered in my business, that is." Her eyes sparkled, our quarrel about that long since resolved.

"I too know a villain when I see one," I said, then I sobered. "Have a care, my friend. These people will kill to protect their secrets. I have to wonder if the first secretary—Mr. Howard—discovered what they were up to? Saw something he shouldn't?"

"I can try to find out. Discreetly—don't you worry none. If anyone offed someone, I'd say it was Fagan." Hannah shivered. "He don't say much, but he's a ruffian, good and proper. Mrs. Proctor says he almost went down once, a long time ago, for beating a man. But just before he went to trial, all the witnesses suddenly refused to swear what they'd seen. Mrs. Proctor and the master both claim he's reformed, but I make sure I'm never caught alone with him."

"Please continue to do so." I poured myself more tea. "Now, you shouldn't linger. Unless there's something else I need to know?"

"I wish I could tell ya." Hannah took a last sip of ale, made a face, and quietly dribbled the liquid into the corner next to the bench. From the stains there, others had rid themselves of the insalubrious drink in the same fashion. "Your man's growing impatient with them too, I can tell. He wants to nick the lot and be gone."

"I'd like him to be gone as well, but please don't let him walk into danger."

"I'll do me best." Hannah sighed. "You know, apart from me wondering if I'll be found out and killed any moment, it's not a bad place. Good wages, easy house to care for, and no one is demanding except for Lady Fontaine. Enough to almost make me want to turn my hand to honest toil."

"No, it doesn't," I said.

Hannah chuckled. "No, it don't."

"Daniel knows I know you," I said, recalling what Mr. Grimes had revealed to me. "I suppose it doesn't matter if you speak openly to him. As long as you're not caught, mind."

Hannah looked dismayed, then annoyed. "I didn't peach. Honest. Oh, I knew he were a clever lad as soon as I set eyes on him."

"I know you didn't say anything." I laid a hand on hers. "But if Daniel can discover you're there to spy, others can as well. Please take care, my old mate. If things become precarious, you go. Say nothing–just vanish."

"Aye, I'm good at that. For now, it's quiet. The blokes and lady who gather with his lordship, they don't even argue with each other much."

"Which makes me even more uneasy. Argumentative conspirators might never arrive at any course of action." I released her. "Well, nothing we can do about that at the moment. Send word when you can. The boy who brings your notes–you can trust him?"

Hannah's dimples pressed deeper into her cheeks. "Course I can. He's me son, inn't he?"

I blinked. "Is he?" I cast my mind back to my few encounters with the boy and realized that he did resemble Hannah. Same dark red hair–her natural color–same blue eyes. "You never said. How lovely for you."

Hannah appeared both proud and exasperated at the same

time. "He's a handful, he is. And least said about his dad, the
better. I shook his dust from me boots, like you did with your
bloke."

"I am so very happy for you," I said warmly.

Hannah flushed. "As I say, a handful." She climbed to her
feet, grimacing as an older lady might, as though unbending
her knees was painful. "But I loves 'im, I truly do. The wretch."

Hannah departed while I remained seated, so that we
would not leave together. We needed to be two strangers
who'd shared a drink and then went our separate ways, having
nothing more to do with each other.

I waited in the snug for another twenty or so minutes after
Hannah had gone, sipping bad tea and reflecting what she had
told me.

From her report, I was assured that Daniel had not yet been
found out, but realized he was becoming impatient to find
evidence to give Monaghan. That meant Daniel might do
something rash, and I prayed he'd refrain.

It might be worth it for Hannah to cultivate her acquaintance with Lady Fontaine, a mine of gossip, for information.
Whether Lady Fontaine knew what her brother was up to or
not, she might provide valuable insights on Lord Peyton and
his cronies. His next-door neighbor—Lord Downes, I recalled
his name was—might be useful as well. Mr. Fielding would
have to help me there, as his man was already in place as
groom to the neighbor's horses.

The sooner we could help Daniel find firm information, the
sooner he could come home and be out from under Mr.
Monaghan's thumb.

Not that I was convinced Mr. Monaghan would let Daniel

go that easily. But I would fight with every weapon in my arsenal to get him free, including using Miss Townsend's connection with the Home Office.

When I emerged from the pub into a rainy afternoon, I waved at Monaghan's young constables who had tailed me, much to their consternation. I ignored my other followers and made for shops in Oxford Street, as though I'd merely paused to refresh myself before running more errands.

I dove into a secondhand clothing store and browsed its wares, hoping to find an alternative to my worn-out best frock, but nothing there that might fit me was to my taste. I thought they were asking rather a lot of money for the frocks as well.

I decided to try to find fabric and a pattern to suit me, and ask Joanna to sew a new one for me. I'd offer to pay her, and though she'd refuse, I could bring her children little gifts or bake extra treats for her and Sam. I'd compensate her somehow, whether Joanna liked it or not.

I did purchase a pattern book from a secondhand bookshop along the road. It was two years old, but I liked the look of the frocks illustrated inside.

Fabric was expensive, of course, and I'd have to dig into my funds and search far and wide before I found the perfect material I could afford.

So ruminating, I wound my way along the backstreets, smiling as I imagined the frustration of my followers. Mr. Monaghan already knew about my daughter and where she lived, so I didn't bother trying to shake his constables, but I certainly didn't want any villains near her.

At one point, when I turned from a tiny lane into Farringdon Road and plunged beneath the Holborn Viaduct, I heard a scuffle behind me. I glanced back to see Mr. Fielding's lads engaging two others I didn't recognize. The villains would be dangerous, but Mr. Fielding would have chosen boys who knew how to fight.

I took advantage of the distraction to reverse my direction and hurry north to the next lane, which took me to Smithfield. I had no need of the meat market today, but I wandered through it as though deciding from which butcher to purchase my next week's provisions.

Mr. Fielding's recruits did their job well. No one dogged my steps as I passed the pile of St. Bartholomew's Hospital and emerged into Newgate Street. From there, I wasted no time hurrying along Cheapside to Clover Lane and shutting myself into Joanna's cozy house.

The afternoon flew by too quickly. Once Joanna's front door closed, I let myself become absorbed in Grace and her life. After assuring Grace and Joanna that my errand had gone as well as it could have, Grace clamored to see the pattern book I'd purchased.

I sat down in the parlor with a far better cup of tea than the pub had given me, and we pored over the book with Joanna and her two daughters. Between the five of us, we chose a frock that would flatter my rather plump frame. It had few frills but enough ruffles along the bodice and hem to please Grace.

To be honest, my heart sped with excitement at the thought of having a new and elegant frock that Joanna promised to sew to perfection. I wasn't certain when I'd become such a frivolous creature.

When it came time to depart, I hugged Grace hard before I made my way through the damp twilight to Mount Street. My followers found me when I reached the Strand, but as they must have already known where I lived, I didn't bother trying to shake them this time. I assured myself that Mr. Fielding's lads and whomever Mr. Grimes had conscripted would work to keep me safe.

How ridiculous, I mused, to have so many following one innocuous cook about the metropolis. It would be comical, if some of them didn't truly wish me harm.

Tess was in better spirits when I returned to the kitchen. She'd seen Caleb today, as he'd not yet taken up his duties in CID, or wherever he would be, and had a long chat with him. He'd assured her they'd be together as often as possible and that his elevated salary would let them do more, such as eat out on their days off.

"Fancy me in a Frenchy restaurant." Tess laughed as she sliced mushrooms. "I'll wager the food won't be up to much. I'll be sailing into the kitchen to tell the chef how much better you cook it."

"The restaurant would chuck you out." I began to peel and chop the onions I'd set out, knowing how much they made her teary. "Rather embarrassing for Constable Greene. I do not advise it."

"Nor would I, Mrs. H." A very familiar voice I hadn't heard in weeks sounded behind me. "Though I can picture you instructing the chef yourself. Now, I've brought the potatoes you ordered. All right?"

Daniel McAdam, in a scruffy wool coat, breeches, and boots, dumped a heavy sack onto the floor of my kitchen and stood there grinning at me.

17

I wasn't certain how long I remained frozen in place, knife in hand, a smattering of the onion's juices dripping to the floor.

This could not be Daniel, whole and well, in his work clothes, smiling at me as though this were an ordinary evening and he'd found an excuse to come and pass the time. He must still be in Belgrave Square, desperately searching for evidence to break an anarchist's ring. This was a ghost.

Except Tess saw him too. "Hiya," she sang. "Ain't you a sight for sore eyes."

Her greeting cut through my shock, spinning emotions through me so fast I felt sick.

I took a deep breath to shout at Daniel, remembered that I was below stairs with most of the house's staff within earshot, and rearranged what I'd been about to say.

"What are you thinking of?" I demanded, as though angry at an ignorant deliveryman's interruption. "That's a dirty sack on my nice clean kitchen floor, that is. You carry it into the larder, at once, as you know you're supposed to."

Daniel's smile widened. "Right you are, missus." He heaved the potatoes onto his shoulder and marched out of the kitchen and down the hall.

I dropped my knife with a clatter and sped after him, catching up to him as he entered the larder. "Just there," I pointed to a corner deep in the shadows, followed him into the cool room, and shut the door.

Daniel turned from dumping the sack onto the floor where I indicated. Before he could take a step, I flung my arms around the wretched man and held on tight.

"Damn you," I croaked. "Damn you."

"Kat." Daniel's voice held tenderness and wonderment. "Forgive me for springing myself on you like this. I didn't like to send a message."

I abandoned all pride and clung to him, sobbing into his shoulder. He held me, gently caressing my back.

"I was so worried," I choked out. "I thought they'd catch you and kill you, like they did Mr. Howard."

"No." Daniel's voice was warm in my ear. "They never tumbled. Thought I was a competent but dim impoverished gentleman from the moment I entered the house to the moment I left it late this afternoon."

I spent a while longer letting my pent-up emotion pour out of me, then I pried myself from Daniel's embrace. I kept hold of his shoulders, as though fearing that if I released him, he'd evaporate.

"Why did you leave them?" My face must be a mess, streaked with tears and flour. "Why did they let you go?"

"They rather insisted." Daniel's smile returned as he brushed a thumb across my cheek. "Lord Peyton sacked me.

Actually, he had his housekeeper do it. His lordship keeps himself distant from sordid domestic business."

"Sacked?" I wiped my eyes and stared at him. "What for, if they didn't suspect you?"

Daniel shrugged in his characteristic way. "Interfering with something not my affair. I was surprised his lordship took on so—I'd think he was grateful to me for not letting his manservant get into trouble, but he believed Fagan could do no wrong."

I barely stopped myself shaking him. "What are you talking about? Tell me what happened before I have apoplexy."

Daniel looked me up and down. "You appear in no danger of that. It was a trifle, which is why I say I'm surprised. Fagan, the manservant, got into a scuffle with a groom who works for the lordship next door to Lord Peyton. Came to blows, blood flying, stable boys cheering them on. I pulled them apart and gave them a lecture, as a stiff-necked, too-prim secretary would. The neighbor's groom seemed ashamed, but Fagan was furious with me. I thought he'd lift me and throw me across the mews. Lord Peyton dotes on him, so when he complained, Lord Peyton decided to give me the sack." Daniel grimaced. "Most unfortunately. I spent a few hours being dressed down by Monaghan for being so careless."

"Monaghan ought to be grateful you are in one piece, blast the man." I'd have much to say to Mr. Monaghan when I saw him again. "Was the man Fagan fought the groom Mr. Fielding sent in?"

Daniel's mouth popped open before he groaned and stepped back. "I ought to have known no one would be able to keep out of this. Do you know the name of everyone in the house, and all the staff next door?"

I planted my fists on my hips. "Did you think I'd stay in my kitchen baking bread while you were in such danger? If so, you do not know me as well as you thought."

"I certainly didn't want you found in the Thames like my predecessor," Daniel growled, then he went thoughtful. "The groom was Errol's man? I thought he was another copper Monaghan had put in to make certain I didn't make a muck of it. The groom did always manage to be in the mews whenever anyone emerged from the house."

"Did Fagan know? Is that why he attacked him?"

"Fagan was not at fault," Daniel said quickly. "Or at least, Fagan didn't throw the first blow. I heard words exchanged between him and the groom. Peeked out the window of my office above the mews to see them sizing each other up. I was worried about the groom, in case he was a copper about to be revealed, and I went down to persuade Fagan back inside. However, one doesn't order Fagan to do anything, not even Lord Peyton. I reached the mews in time to see the groom swing a punch at Fagan. After that, it became a brawl between the two. I inserted myself in it, pretending to be brave enough and foolish enough to try to separate them. No wonder the groom looked daggers at me instead of being grateful. Errol's friends are hard men."

"What was he thinking, fighting Fagan like that?" I demanded in exasperation.

"I didn't have the chance to find out. Either Fagan truly provoked him or the groom decided it would be odd for his character if he didn't strike out. A spy can be unmasked if they don't react the way an ordinary person would."

I regarded him sternly. "I suppose you pulling them apart was what an ordinary secretary would do?"

"The persona I'd been cultivating would. Thomas Delamarre—which is what I'd been calling myself—is a prig and a know-all. He'd certainly try to keep the peace and be quite self-righteous about it." Daniel sobered. "But also, I knew Fagan was a killer. I don't think he murdered the previous secretary himself, but in his past, he's done others. I didn't want him to forget himself and beat the groom to death. That would bring in the police, which might have exposed Lord Peyton and his friends, but I wasn't willing to sacrifice the groom so Monaghan could get a result." Daniel's last words held bitterness.

I knew then why I loved Daniel. He'd been willing to risk his job, his life, and his chance to be free of Monaghan to keep a man he didn't know from being hurt. He hadn't even had to think much about it before he acted.

Love.

I realized I'd just thought the word, and for a moment, I froze in stunned awareness.

Yes, I did love Daniel. The knowledge filled me like flame. I had done for some time, but I'd not let myself fully admit it.

"Are you all right, Kat?" Daniel studied me in concern. "As I say, I apologize for springing myself upon you—"

I silenced him by hugging him again, though less desperately than I had before. "I am simply happy you are out of it and safe."

"Not entirely out," Daniel said as his arms enfolded me, I resting again on his shoulder. "Monaghan is trying to find another way I can bring down the ring, which will probably involve something even more dangerous. I haven't fulfilled my mission yet."

I popped my head up. "Well, he can give you a few minutes to catch your breath, at least." I tapped his chest, happy he was here for me to touch. "By the way, how did you know about Hannah? I thought she'd be undetectable."

"Who is Hannah?" Daniel asked in perplexity. "Oh, you

mean the maid. She gave her name as Marjory Smith. No one, including me, suspected it wasn't."

"Then how *did* you know? I cannot believe she betrayed herself at any moment."

Daniel's amusement returned. "She never did—I'd never have had doubts about her at all, had I truly been Thomas Delamarre, that twit of a secretary. But there were a few things. She so conveniently turned up soon after I was instated, though I admit the other maid departing to marry couldn't have been foreseen. I was the one who checked Marjory's references—Mrs. Proctor, the housekeeper, said she was too busy to be bothered. They were excellent references, but I noticed that one house she claimed she'd worked in, you had also worked in. That might be a coincidence—there are only so many large houses in Mayfair where a person can be a servant. But then, she asked that her day out be Thursday."

"Ah." I'd told Hannah to use whatever day out she could get, but I suppose she'd wanted to make certain she could find me away from both our houses.

"No one else but me would have put those facts together." Daniel's eyes twinkled. "Conclusion—you sent her to watch over me."

"Mr. Grimes told me you knew, drat you."

"It was a clever ruse." Daniel regarded me admiringly. "If I'd not known as much about you as I do, I never would have guessed. Your Hannah is the perfect upstairs maid, but not so perfect as to draw unnecessary attention. She made certain she had flaws, such as scolding the downstairs maids if they weren't diligent and fawning to the upper staff."

"Hannah is still in the house," I said, stricken. "I didn't worry about her as much with you there to guard her, but now she is alone with them. They are Fenians, are they not?"

Daniel heaved a weary sigh. "If they are, I can't prove it. Lord Peyton's bookkeeping is excellent, and I couldn't find any evidence of him and his mates gathering money or purchasing weapons. The Fenians are definitely planning something, and they have agents all over the metropolis, but I couldn't find the connection to Lord Peyton." His shoulders sagged. "Needless to say, Monaghan is not happy with me."

"That is hardly your fault. How can Monaghan believe that you, by yourself, can expose the ring and thwart every plot the Fenians come up with?"

"Because he is unreasonable, and he is angry."

"Also a killer," I said, recalling what Inspector McGregor had told me. "I know that he—"

"Mrs. Holloway." The shocked tones of Mr. Davis rang behind me, accompanied by a draft that told me he'd opened the door. "Have a care for your reputation," he went on, aghast, then his voice hardened. *"You.* Out." He pointed a thin finger at Daniel and made a sweeping gesture into the hall.

"Don't you worry none, Mr. Davis," Daniel said merrily. "I'd never let harm come to our Mrs. Holloway. All right, all right, I'm going. The rest of your order is arriving tomorrow, Mrs. H." This last Daniel said to me as he eased past Mr. Davis. "I'll send me lad around instead so our Mr. Davis ain't scandalized."

I strove to recover my aplomb. "See that you do." It was a weak statement, but the only one that sprang to mind.

Daniel threw a last wink at me, and then he was gone. I heard Tess's joyful greeting to him as he went through the kitchen, with a few of the footmen calling out to him as well. Everyone liked Daniel, with the current exception of Mr. Davis.

"Do not lecture me," I told Mr. Davis as he drew breath to

speak. "I've not seen Mr. McAdam in some days, and we were catching up. I can't help it if the door blew shut."

Mr. Davis's expression told me he didn't believe me for a minute. "I care not what you get up to with McAdam on your days out. You might have a second home and ten children with him for all I know, though I presume you have more sense. But if the mistress catches you canoodling with such a man, you'll be out before you can speak."

"I was hardly canoodling," I said indignantly. "What an appalling expression. I'd never do such a thing in the larder, of all places. In any case, it really isn't your business, Mr. Davis."

"I recall a day when you meddled in *my* business." He referred to the afternoon he'd caught me coming out of his bedchamber when I'd gone in to snoop. I'd been worried about Mr. Davis's absence and was trying to discover what had happened to him, but he'd been right to be angry. "It *is* my concern, Mrs. Holloway. I am fond of you, and I do not want to see you dismissed. Or throwing your life away on a waster."

A felt a trickle of warmth that Mr. Davis professed such friendship for me but was still affronted on Daniel's behalf. "Mr. McAdam is not a waster. He has employment and looks after his son just fine."

Mr. Davis remained unconvinced. "That is all very well, but if you wish to marry, you should take up with someone who can provide for you, like an innkeeper or a gent who owns a shop. You've drudged all your life—you ought to be able to put your feet up afterward."

"No thank you," I said decidedly. "An innkeeper or shopkeeper would be pleased to have me cook for them or assist in the shop without wages. At least my drudging brings in a salary. I am saving for my future, as you advised me, and am not thinking of marriage to anyone."

Not quite the truth. I'd pictured myself and Daniel snug in a house together with Grace and James often enough. But that vision was hazily in the distance, not an immediate reality.

Mr. Davis continued to frown. "Thought I'd give you a friendly warning."

"I appreciate your concern." I moved pointedly toward the doorway Mr. Davis blocked, and he stiffly stepped out of my way. "I know it was kindly meant, but please do not make me jump out of my skin again."

"Do not let any doors blow closed, and all will be well."

We shared a cool stare, then I ducked around him and strode back to the kitchen. There, emotions and sensations chased each other through me so fast that I had to sit down for some time before I could carry on.

I slept very little that night. Daniel did not return before I retired, though I lingered well into the darkness, sharpening knives, making notes, and straightening the kitchen. I imagined Mr. Monaghan was keeping him on a short tether.

Once abed, I lay awake worrying not only about Daniel but about Hannah. I'd need to find out if she was still all right, alone in that house of villains. I'd ask Mr. Fielding to tell his groom—if he too hadn't been sacked—that she was there and to look after her.

I longed to speak to Daniel again, to ask him about the things I'd not had time to: the blackmail letters, the envelopes he'd addressed, the secret police Inspector McGregor had more or less confirmed Daniel worked for, and many other things.

Most of all, I longed to snatch up Grace, take Daniel by the hand, and run with him far, far from Monaghan, the Fenians, the police, and anarchist plots. I'd seen photographs and paintings of the Lake District, in the north of England, which appeared quite beautiful and also remote. I could open a tea shop there as easily as anywhere, couldn't I?

I knew from experience that such things would not be as simple. But it was nice to daydream, which had a calming effect. I dropped off in the early hours of the morning, waking when the high window in my bedchamber lightened.

The sun rose early in May so I was downstairs before anyone else, despite my interrupted sleep.

My restlessness allowed me to make a start on the meals for the day, including another couple of the star breads, one savory with roasted onions and herbs and the other sweet, with the last of the apples. I'd make an apple butter to spread on the second bread, flavored with cinnamon and sugar.

My head was still reeling with Daniel's return and fear that Monaghan would send him somewhere worse—might have already done so—and working was the only way I could keep myself calm.

I had the doughs mixed and resting and the breakfast mostly done before Tess came downstairs.

"Sara says Lady Cynthia wants to speak to ya," Tess informed me after she'd exclaimed over how much of the tasks I'd already finished. "She's still in her chamber, but I'd guess you could go up to see her, since we're so far ahead."

"It isn't fitting for the cook to rush up to a lady's bedchamber," I said as I turned to stack toast onto platters. "Cynthia knows that."

"You could take her a tea tray," Tess suggested. "Would save Sara some work. The mistress has Sara running off her feet, she says."

I knew that Lady Cynthia liked to lie abed late after one of her nights out with her friends, demanding very strong tea and toast when she woke.

Tess's idea was a good one, and truth to tell, I was curious about what Cynthia had to say. I prepared a pot of tea, adding a silver container of sugar and a ceramic pitcher of cream to the tray. Several pieces of the hot toast, dripping with sweet butter, went alongside the tea things.

I reflected as I carried the heavy tray up the stairs that I was lucky I was rarely required to tote things I made from the kitchen. I'd collapse if I had to carry the supper dishes upstairs every night instead of putting them in the dumbwaiter that went to the dining room. I gained new respect for Sara and the other maids for running up and down with loads like these.

Sara sent me a grateful glance when I emerged into the second-floor hallway. She had her hands full of towels and dashed from the hall cupboard toward the mistress's bedchamber, from which Mrs. Bywater's voice rose.

"No, this water is too cold. Take it away. Where *is* Sara?"

Mrs. Bywater's bedchamber door banged open, and a footman scuttled out with a large basin of water. Sara whirled past him and inside, slamming the door behind him.

The footman started when he saw me, slopping some of the water onto the floor. He glowered at me and disappeared into the discreet opening in the paneling that led to the backstairs.

I tapped on Cynthia's door and received a groan in reply. Taking that for permission to enter, I fumbled with the door handle and carried the tray into the room.

Cynthia's chamber was dim, the curtains drawn against the morning light. She let out another groan as she cracked open her eyes.

"Mrs. H.," she wheezed in surprise. "How splendid. I hope

that tea is strong. My head aches something fierce." She put a weary hand to that appendage.

"As dark as I could brew it," I assured her. "You need to drink the whole pot. I've also brought some toast, fresh and hot."

"Put it over there." Languid fingers emerged from the bed-covers and fluttered at the nearby table. "I'll see what I can manage."

I set down the tray where indicated, but I did not depart and leave her to it. I poured out tea, dolloped some cream into it along with a lump of sugar, laid a thick piece of toast onto a plate, and carried both to her.

"Get that down you," I instructed. "Then you can tell me what you wanted to say."

Cynthia sent me a faint smile. Even in the half light, I could see dark smudges beneath her bloodshot eyes.

"Yes, Mum." She obediently took the tea. "You know, you're better at mothering me than my own mama."

"You and I are the same age," I pointed out rather coldly. "Or near as. Drink."

Cynthia sipped the tea, raising her brows as the smooth liquid entered her mouth. She drank several noisy slurps before lowering the cup again.

"Sister, then," she said. "My own never had much use for me."

"I would be honored to be considered your sister," I said. "Now eat some toast."

"Quite the dragon, you are." Cynthia nibbled a slice, then her face changed and she devoured the entire piece. "This toast is lovely." Her voice gained strength. "I must have you bring up my tea every morning."

"I hardly have the time." I poured more tea into her cup.

"Now, Sara told Tess that you wanted to speak to me. Please do before your aunt finds me here and scolds the life out of both of us."

"No fear." Cynthia took another noisy sip of tea. "She's dressing for one of her charity dos and will be some time perfecting her ensemble. I wanted to inform you that Thanos and I have been sleuthing. We've been up and down the Strand and Bond Street looking at shops that sell high-priced ink. We found it." Cynthia beamed at me, color entering her pallid face. "In the Burlington Arcade. Beautiful bottles of artist's ink from France. I have a list of who purchased them. I went all wide-eyed and innocent and asked for the shop's clients, saying I might want to purchase some of the same ink as gifts for my friends, but of course, I didn't know which friends actually used it. Hold on a tick."

Cynthia rummaged in the drawer of her bedside table and produced a sheet of paper. The handwriting on it was neat and firm, which told me neither she nor Mr. Thanos had made the list.

Squarely in the middle of it was the name of Viscount Peyton, resident of Belgrave Square.

18

"Excellent," I cried, forgetting to worry about who would hear me.

Cynthia shook her head, her triumph fading. "Not so quickly. There are quite a number of names on that list. It is a popular brand of ink with aristocrats."

Indeed, I recognized the name of Lord Downes, Lord Peyton's neighbor, and more ladies and gentlemen in Belgrave Square and Mayfair.

"Even so, it was well done, my friend." I sent her a broad smile. "Please give Mr. Thanos my thanks as well."

"Thanos." Cynthia's face fell, her weariness returning. "He is put out with me. I believe my adventure in assisting him is finished."

"What are you talking about?" I quickly fetched another piece of toast from the tray and dropped it onto her empty plate. "Mr. Thanos is never put out with anyone. He is the most genial of gentlemen. You must have misunderstood him."

Cynthia shot me a dark look. "I did not misunderstand him taking me to task last night for overindulging and getting thrown out of a gentleman's club with Bobby. No one tumbled to Bobby's being a woman, but they guessed at me. The door-man threatened to summon the police, and only Bobby and Thanos, who said he happened to be passing, prevented him. They told the doorman they'd take their foolish woman home and she'd never bother them again. Which means that the club is forever closed to me. Bobby left me in Thanos's care, and he lectured me something fierce all the way home. I don't remember much about the ride, but I recall that."

Tears welled in her light blue eyes and trickled down her cheeks.

"Oh dear." I took the cup from Cynthia's hand, set it on the night table, and dared seat myself on the edge of her bed. "Mr. Thanos is only worried about you. *I* worry about you. You can be reckless sometimes, and he, like me, doesn't want you to come to harm."

"He was following me about." Cynthia's gaze was defiant through her tears. "Happened to be passing. Ha. He knew I'd gone to that club. He was hanging about, waiting for me to be thrown out so he could scold me."

"Nonsense. Mr. Thanos might have been keeping an eye on you, but not because he was waiting to lecture you. He was con-cerned, as I say, and trying to help. He cares for you, Cynthia."

"I doubt that very much. If so, he has a damned funny way of showing it. I find his books and sort his papers, write out his long equations that I don't understand one whit of, make cer-tain his shoes match, and that he doesn't lose his spectacles. Thanos thanks me profusely, but does he give me one look of tenderness? Try to press my hand or steal a kiss? Not a bit of it.

If I try to sit too close to him, he draws away in a hurry. It is humiliating."

"Mr. Thanos is painfully shy." I picked up her teacup. "And very much a gentleman. If foolish gestures of passion are what you want, then break the poor man's heart and find another gent to give them to you. You are a lovely young woman—I'm certain you will find many a gentleman willing to kiss you. But they will not be as kindhearted as Mr. Thanos."

Cynthia regarded me with a stunned stare as I made this speech. "I, break *his* heart? I doubt I can. I disgust him. You did not hear what he said to me last night."

"Which was?"

Cynthia blew out a breath. "That I was wild and silly and too anxious to impress my unconventional friends. So much so I'd come to grief." She broke off sullenly. "Much of what *you* say to me, in fact."

"You know I never scold you out of disgust," I said. "It is because I do not want to see you paraded through Bow Street nick where unsavory sorts will taunt you. I quite understand your fondness for Bobby and Miss Townsend, because I have grown fond of them too, but you have no need to go to jail for them. Nor would they wish you to."

"Bobby and Judes come from powerful families," Cynthia conceded. "They can get away with much more than I can. I might be an earl's daughter, but my pa would never bestir himself from Hertfordshire to throw his weight about." She reached for the teacup. "My way of saying you and Thanos are right, and I am an idiot."

"Your father would certainly bestir himself." I thought of Lord Clifford, the feckless gentleman who loved his family more than he'd admit. "He'd race to London and land himself in great trouble, as usual, and we'd have to pry him out of it, as we have before."

Cynthia softened enough to laugh. "Again, you are right, Mrs. H. Shall I go to Thanos on bended knee and beg his forgiveness?"

"You should go to him, in any case. After you drink all this tea and finish your breakfast." I rose from the bed. "At this point, Mr. Thanos is probably in great anguish, certain he'll never see you again."

A gentle light entered Cynthia's eyes, one that showed me more than she realized. "The poor chap. He'll never tie his cravat right if he's upset, or find his lecture notes. He does need me, doesn't he?"

"Indeed." *And you need him,* I added silently. *Someone who sees your worth and loves you for who you are.*

"I know I've torn it." Cynthia took a gulp of tea. "But fear not. I will put on my prettiest frock, fly to the Polytechnic, and grovel. Will that satisfy you?"

"It is not me who needs to be satisfied," I said. "Now drink up. And thank you very much for the information about the ink bottles. It is helpful."

"Is it?" Cynthia peered at me doubtfully. "Seems we proved nothing but that those in Belgrave Square are willing to spend much on their ink."

"I will pass your findings to Daniel. He might be able to make something of them."

Cynthia's brows rose. "I thought he was gone to the ends of the earth on some covert assignment for the police?"

"He was." I still could not be effusive about what he'd been doing until I asked him whether Cynthia and Mr. Thanos could be brought in on his secrets. "He has returned, at least for now."

"Well, give him my best." Cynthia downed her tea in several swallows and reached for the toast. "And thank you for the repast, Mrs. H. Exactly what I needed."

My little rebuke about Mr. Thanos hadn't hurt either, I saw. "I am pleased I could help."

I left Cynthia munching happily, her good spirits restored. I reflected as I slipped into the backstairs—I could still hear Mrs. Bywater ordering the staff about in her chamber—that I was glad Mr. Thanos had made known his feelings for Cynthia, if in an awkward way.

I hoped their reconciliation brought about the touching of hands or stealing of kisses that Cynthia longed for. Though I had the feeling Cynthia would have to instigate any kissing with Mr. Thanos. But all would be well between them.

If not, I'd sit them down and explain how lucky they were to have each other. Not everyone was so fortunate, a lesson I was learning myself.

D aniel did not return that day, or Saturday either. I would have worried, but James visited, telling me his father was well. Daniel was spending much time at Scotland Yard, James relayed, explaining to his guvnor everything that had happened in the Belgrave Square house.

I imagined that would take some time, even if Daniel had learned little. Mr. Monaghan was thorough, so Daniel had told me.

I went over the list Cynthia had given me many times in my idle moments, of which I hadn't many. With Lord Peyton's name on the list, I felt I could ignore the others, but I decided to be cautious. The likelihood of Daniel writing envelopes for anyone but Lord Peyton was small, but still, I put a tick mark next to several of the wealthy people who lived nearby and had purchased ink.

I hoped Daniel would be able to get away from Monaghan on Monday, so Grace and I could spend time with him. Grace had not seen Daniel in weeks, and I knew she missed him.

Cynthia did seek Mr. Thanos at the Polytechnic, and they made things up. She did not tell me this, but I saw her leave on Friday morning, after our chat, and when she returned, she was in fine spirits. She did not come down to the kitchen, as her aunt had her busy with helping with her charity gatherings, but Cynthia beamed a large smile at me in passing when our paths happened to cross.

I finished my work on Sunday evening and lingered well into the night, hoping for but not truly expecting Daniel to visit. I was buoyed by anticipation of spending the next afternoon with Grace, so I waited less anxiously than I might.

When the knock came on the back door, however, I was across the dark and quiet room in an instant, ready to pull Daniel into my embrace.

I wrenched open the back door . . . and saw no one. That is, until my gaze moved downward to find a much smaller personage than Daniel had come to call.

It was Adam, Hannah's son and messenger. My heart beat hollowly in concern—had Hannah met with some danger?

Adam, with his characteristic silence, handed me a folded paper.

I opened it, my blood chilling as I read Hannah's words. They proclaimed:

Peyton died tonight.

19

Having delivered his message, Adam started to turn to rush back up the stairs.

"Wait!" I all but shouted at him. "What does she mean? How? What happened?"

Adam regarded me with the arrogant impatience of ten-year-old boys. "I dunno, do I?"

"I need to speak to your mum. Can she meet me tomorrow?"

Adam's eyes flickered at my knowledge that he was Hannah's son, but he shook his head. "She's got to stay in. No leave. Says her ladyship's upset, and Mum's not allowed a day out."

From which I gathered that Lady Fontaine was distraught—and well, she must be—and refused to let any of the servants out of her sight.

"Will you tell Hannah to send word as soon as she can get away? We must confer."

"All right." He turned to go again.

I guessed that Adam could not read what his mother had written, or he'd not be so ready to dismiss it. He'd either be upset that his mother was in a house where a man had recently died, or he'd revel in the excitement of it.

"Adam," I called.

He didn't turn right away, reinforcing my idea that Adam was not his true name. I'd have to ask Hannah what it was.

"What?" he asked from three steps up.

I fumbled in my pocket. "Don't you want your coin?"

"A bleedin' ha'penny?" He regarded me with scorn. "No thanks, missus."

"Very well, a penny this time. It's more than I pay most of the messenger boys."

"You gave Albie fivepence," Adam said indignantly. He'd seen that, had he? And knew Albie, presumably.

"He was running errands for me, not simply bringing me a scrap of paper," I said. "But wait there, and I'll fetch you a bun."

"Just the penny." Adam held out his hand. He wore gloves, which were worn and stretched.

I held the coin between my fingers. "Well, if you'd rather go hungry than have a nice, fat, currant bun still warm from the oven . . ."

Adam hesitated, his appetite winning. "All right, then. Only if you're quick about it."

I returned the coin to my pocket. "Simple gratitude would not go amiss, young man. Stand there."

I strode back into the kitchen and took up the currant bun I'd set aside in case Daniel came, wrapping it in a cloth. I returned to the outside stairs with both bun and penny but kept hold of them, knowing Adam would disappear the moment he had them in hand.

"Tell your mum that if she wants to go home, I'll understand." If Lord Peyton's death had been murder, the police would swarm the house, and Hannah would do better to avoid them.

"She likes the wages," Adam said. I at last handed him the coin and bread, which he snatched away. "Thank you, missus," he muttered as an afterthought.

"Mrs. Holloway," I informed him. "Look after your mum, Adam. She'll need you."

Another glower. "I always do." He turned from me and stomped up the stairs, and this time, I let him go.

I closed the door on the cool night air and again studied the note Hannah had scribbled.

Lord Peyton was dead. Just like that.

Killed? Topped himself? Died a natural death? I'd never learned why he had to use a wheeled chair, except that it was some ailment that prevented him from walking. It might have been a wasting disease that had finally finished him off.

I could know nothing standing in the kitchen in the dark, but I wasn't certain when I'd be able to discover anything further. Daniel was being sequestered by Mr. Monaghan, and Hannah was restricted to the Belgrave Square house.

Caleb might have been recruited by Monaghan, putting him beyond my reach. Caleb was a bright young man, who I knew could go far, but I wondered if one of Monaghan's motives in taking him from his beat was so I could not use him as a resource.

"Drat," I said with feeling.

In the morning, I'd send Albie, if I could put my hands on him, to spy on the Belgrave Square house and tell me all that happened. I'd instruct him to seek out the groom Mr. Fielding had put in place next door. Together the two *must* be able to give me some information.

I crumpled the note into my pocket, put away my things, and ate the second currant bun I'd left out—no sense letting it go to waste—before I took myself to bed.

I lay awake ruminating on the problems much of the night. Had Lord Peyton been murdered, and if so, why? Had he truly been the ringleader of an anarchist group funded by the Fenians? Or had someone in his circle been the anarchist, and Lord Peyton had found him out?

Lord Peyton had purchased the very ink used in the blackmail letters, and Daniel had addressed the envelopes, which meant the letters *must* have come from within Lord Peyton's house.

Written by Lord Peyton? Or his sister, Lady Fontaine? Or one of his frequent visitors? Or one of the staff? Mrs. Proctor, the housekeeper?

I tossed and turned, beating my pillow in frustration. I hated having to wait to ask questions, but I could not rush about in the middle of the night, pounding on doors and demanding information.

As I'd worked hard all the day long, my body at last demanded rest. In the wee hours of the morning, I fell into a deep sleep, swimming awake in an awkwardly twisted position as sunshine touched my window.

I heaved myself from bed, wincing as my muscles unbent, and hurried through my ablutions. Today was Monday, my afternoon out, and I chafed to leave the house.

Downstairs, I raced through breakfast preparations, once again having most of it done before Tess entered the kitchen. I broke off my tasks a half dozen times to hurry up the outside stairs and down again, to Tess's consternation.

"Everything all right?" Tess asked me when I returned from one trip.

I'd been searching for Albie, so I could set him to watch over Hannah. Tess eyed me fearfully, so I shook my head.

"I'm sorry, Tess. A man Daniel had been sent to observe has died, and I am at my wits' end."

Tess would learn of the death soon enough if the journalists were as quick on the scene as usual, so I saw no reason to keep it from her.

"Were he a crook?" Tess asked as she slathered butter onto the piles of toast. "Would be if they sent Mr. McAdam to watch over him. If he's dead, it's a good thing, inn't?"

"A sudden death is never a good thing, Tess. But this is nothing for you to worry over."

"I'll ask Caleb," Tess offered, then became mournful. "If I ever see him again."

"He might not be able to help us anymore, that is true. But don't fret so much. Everything will be well."

I was placating her, and Tess knew it. Caleb's new job could very well hinder their courtship, but I would have to tackle that problem later. Tess returned to buttering toast, downcast.

"Caleb adores you," I told her, wishing I could comfort her. "He said he'd find a way for the two of you to be happy, did he not?"

I believed he'd let little stand in his way of seeing Tess, and she must also know this, because she gave me a wavering smile. I left her to it, and I charged upstairs to the street again.

To my relief, I saw Albie trotting my way. I waylaid him and told him what I wanted him to do.

"I was just coming to tell you the gentry-cove died," Albie said. "His friends are cut up something awful over it. The Lofthouse people are packing for the Continent."

"Are they, indeed?" Not suspicious at all, was it? I handed Albie his fivepence. "Here's your payment, Albie. More when you tell me about what is happening in the Belgrave Square house today. Don't forget to find the groom." I'd described the man, though I had yet to discover his name.

"I know what to do." Albie grabbed the coin but regarded me in a more good-natured way than Adam had. "I won't let you down." He shot me a grin and raced away, his legs in knickers moving in a flash.

I closed the door on him, wishing I could run off with him.

I had no more word from or about Belgrave Square as I worked to fix a light repast for Mrs. Bywater and Cynthia's midday meal. Mr. Davis was busy this morning and didn't leave a convenient newspaper lying about, and I had no time to find one or ask him about articles in them regarding Lord Peyton. The mystery of the viscount's death remained just that, a mystery to me.

When at last I could depart for the afternoon, I changed my frock and bade Tess farewell.

"Save the hardest work for me, Tess," I told her as I pulled on gloves and snatched up my basket. "I'll be back as soon as I can."

Tess nodded at me, no doubt ready to be rid of me and my impatience. "Give my love to Grace and Mrs. Millburn," she said, with a hint of her usual cheeriness.

I promised I would and hurried away, heading for Piccadilly and making my way east along it. I turned south at Haymarket and dodged crowds through Charing Cross until I reached Great Scotland Yard.

I didn't bother with the sergeant at the desk this time but went straight to the edifice of the Public Carriage Office, intending to take myself to Inspector McGregor directly.

A constable in the courtyard moved to intercept me. Before I could begin to argue with him, a heavy hand fell on my arm.

I recognized the touch, so I did not struggle away. "I am here to speak to Inspector McGregor," I informed him. "The Lofthouses are leaving for the Continent."

"So it seems," Daniel said.

"Of course you'd know what I rushed here to impart," I said in annoyance. Truth to tell, I was quite happy to see Daniel, and anything he said would not dim my immediate joy. "Shall we speak to Inspector McGregor together?"

"No." Daniel moved his grip to my elbow and steered me back through the courtyard toward the street. "I want you nowhere near Scotland Yard, in case Monaghan decides to detain you."

I shot him a startled glance. "He would not dare."

"In his current mood, he might. Now, it is your afternoon out—let us get you to Clover Lane."

"Do not placate me, Daniel McAdam. I still have a friend in the Belgrave Square house, and it is my fault she is there. I must—"

"You must go to the Millburns'," Daniel said firmly.

We'd emerged to Charing Cross by that time, Daniel guiding me unyieldingly. Once in the Strand, Daniel let out a piercing whistle, similar to the one James had used only a few weeks ago. A hansom immediately pivoted in a sharp turn and pulled in next to us.

I clung to Daniel's hand as he assisted me in, fearing that if I let go, he'd send the hansom on and fade into the crowd. I relaxed when he climbed in beside me and the cab jerked forward, taking us in the direction of Cheapside.

"You must tell me what the devil happened," I said once we

were rumbling along the cobblestoned street. "Was Lord Peyton murdered?"

"I don't know." The furrow in Daniel's forehead told me his frustration matched mine. "No one is certain whether it was an accident, a natural death, was self-inflicted, or a murder. The viscount was found at the foot of the staircase, his wheeled chair at the top of it. No one, not even Fagan, knows why he was in the upstairs hall or how he came to fall."

"Someone must have killed him, then," I said with conviction. "If he was an invalid, how could he throw *himself* down the stairs?"

"He could stand," Daniel said. "Shakily, and only if he held on to something, usually Fagan. He would last for about thirty seconds before he had to sit down again. Lord Peyton had some sort of palsy, and even his doctor wasn't certain exactly what his ailment was. He might have heaved himself out of his chair for some reason, lost his footing, and fallen. According to everyone in the household—Inspector McGregor and his men questioned them all—they heard him cry out, and then the crash of him on the stairs."

I winced, not liking to picture the poor man, whether he was a villain or no, desperately trying to stop himself as he tumbled to his death.

"He might have been asleep or under the effects of laudanum," I suggested. "To prevent him struggling or calling for help when the murderer pushed him to the top of the stairs. Not waking until he knew he was falling."

"As I have not been able to see the scene of the crime, I am guessing as much as you are," Daniel said. "The back wheels of the chair are large enough that Lord Peyton could propel himself about, though he didn't like to. It was difficult for his weak hands, but he *could* have taken himself into the hall. From what Fagan told Inspector McGregor, the chair wasn't at the edge of the stairs, but a few feet back. Lord Peyton could have tottered the short distance himself for whatever reason he thought he should. Or he might have had a seizure of some kind. He pulled himself to his feet to shout for help but wasn't able to summon anyone before he fell."

"The police surgeon will be able to determine whether Lord Peyton had apoplexy or his heart had given out, won't he?"

"Possibly." Daniel scanned the traffic around us, as though watching for followers. "The actual cause of death was a broken neck, so the examiner might not bother to search for other ailments. Even Monaghan does not seem that interested. The subject of Monaghan's investigation is dead, and he's satisfied the man can cause no more trouble."

I heard the skeptical note in his voice. "But you are not?"

"I'm not convinced Lord Peyton was a criminal mastermind who was planning and funding bomb attacks around London. He is for Irish Home Rule, but so are others in the Lords and Commons, without resorting to violence. Viscount Peyton had sympathy for those who need to better their lives, but I believe there his complicity ended. I went over all of his correspondence and his accounts multiple times, and a less guilty-looking man, I have never met."

"Mr. Monaghan was adamant though."

"He was," Daniel said. "I thought Monaghan would be all over that house this morning, digging into every corner, but he's lost interest, it seems."

"Rather an odd reaction."

"Monaghan is a rather odd man. He turned me away when I asked him why he wasn't following the investigation on

Peyton's death. Which means either there is something he doesn't want me to know, or he was wrong about Peyton and refuses to admit it."

"Well, you did your best," I said emphatically. "Monaghan cannot go back on his bargain that he'd let you go because he was wrong about the culprit."

"He can, and he will," Daniel said, a bleakness in his eyes. "I haven't put myself into sufficient danger to satisfy him yet."

My ire rose. "If Mr. Monaghan does not release you, I shall have something to say about it. Inspector McGregor is not happy with him either, and Miss Townsend's father works for the Home Office. She likes you, and she'd be pleased to help."

"Miss Townsend's father is right-hand man to the home secretary," Daniel said. "But the home secretary might be on Monaghan's side, in this case." His voice softened. "It is kind of you to worry about me, Kat."

"It isn't kindness," I said in vexation. "You know it isn't."

Daniel stilled for a long moment. "Do I?"

"Of course you do. I am quite fond of you." I drew a long breath, remembering what I'd admitted to myself when he'd held me in the larder. "More than fond." I had difficulty saying the words with him gazing at me with his blue, blue eyes. "Grace loves you too," I finished in a faint voice.

"Don't, Kat," Daniel said fiercely. "Don't give me hope."

I stared straight ahead at the gleaming brown back of the horse pulling us through London. "I know I've pushed you away," I said, choosing my words carefully. "I did because I've been frightened. I thought myself in love once before, but it made me miserable and wretched. Not until I held my daughter did I understand what loving truly was." My heart had swelled with immeasurable joy that day, but I'd also felt great terror. "Even when I understood that you were nothing like Joe, I was still afraid, because of Grace. I didn't want your ties to Scotland Yard to hurt her. So I kept putting you off."

When I faced Daniel again, I found him watching me with a stunned expression. I continued: "When you went into that house in Belgrave Square, and I thought you might die there, every harsh word I've ever said to you came back to me." I rested a hand lightly on his knee. "I am so sorry, my friend. You have been good to me, and I repaid you poorly. I ought to have learned how to manage my fears, or told you to go, instead of trifling with your feelings."

Daniel's shock turned to amazement. "You have been thinking all this?"

"Yes, and I know that rattling through London in a hansom is not the place for such a discussion—"

Daniel put gloved fingers to my lips. "I am the selfish wretch who should have told *you* to go. You are right that what I do is dangerous—very dangerous—and I have pulled you into that danger from the beginning. But looking forward to being with you keeps me from despair every day. Makes me want to be good at what I do, and moral, and even admirable. So you will look at me and tell me it has all been worthwhile."

I reached up and gently grasped his hand. We both wore gloves but the warmth of his fingers flowed into my every limb. "Seeing you is all I need. *That* is worthwhile."

"Damn Monaghan," Daniel growled. "I need to be free of him. Soon. So I can come to you as I truly wish to."

"With a sack of potatoes?" I asked coyly.

"Oh, Kat." Daniel silenced anything else teasing I might say with a strong kiss on my mouth.

I returned the kiss, clinging to him, but the bumping hansom had us soon drawing apart, laughing.

We spent the rest of the journey without speaking, but something between us had profoundly changed.

E ven the passionate kiss and our near-declarations of devotion to each other did not erase the need to solve the dilemma of Lord Peyton's death, the former secretary's murder, the blackmail letters, and whether Lord Peyton, his manservant, or his friends had anything to do with Fenian bombs.

However, we could not discuss the problems when we reached the house in Clover Lane, with Joanna beaming at Daniel, and Grace so excited to see him.

I half expected Monaghan to turn up and drag Daniel away by his ear, but Daniel seemed in no way worried about this. He announced he'd accompany Grace and me on our walk.

I did not want to go far, to Grace's disappointment, because we still had watchers. I sensed them, as did Daniel. I saw him surreptitiously signal to someone unseen as we strolled along Cheapside, possibly one of Mr. Grimes's men ready to intercept whoever stalked us.

We paused to observe Mr. Bennett's complex clock strike the hour and then meandered to our tea shop. The waitress there, who was usually sour to me, always had a smile for Daniel and Grace. She was almost pleasant today, serving our tea and cakes quickly and not glaring when we lingered to talk.

"James should come to tea with us sometimes," Grace suggested as we finished our repast. "Though he would likely devour the entire tray of sweets."

"James is working now," I reminded her. "Delivering goods while his father lazes about eating scones."

Daniel licked a bit of lemon curd from his thumb and grinned at us.

"Still, he might enjoy it," Grace said.

She proposed this in all innocence. I wondered anew if she regarded James as a potential beau rather than a friend, and which opinion James held of her. A mother's worry never ceased, I supposed. I was happy my own mother never knew of the mess I'd made of my earlier life.

James was a good lad and would never hurt Grace as my husband had me, but it was still too soon for this direction of things, I decided.

I hugged Grace tightly when we said good-bye and swallowed a lump in my throat as Daniel led me away from her.

I laced my arm firmly through his. "Now, Mr. McAdam, we will find somewhere to talk about Lord Peyton and all the things you learned in that house, and decide who murdered him."

Daniel opened his mouth, likely to make some quip about my eagerness, but we were interrupted by the form of Inspector McGregor, who stepped out of the crowd at the turning of Cheapside to Clover Lane.

"McAdam," he said.

"Inspector." Daniel touched his cap. "I thought I saw some of your lads watching us. Seeing us observe a masterfully engineered timepiece and then take tea must have been entertaining."

Inspector McGregor's mustache twitched with his annoyance. "They were ready to arrest you, but I held them back until you took the little girl home. Viscount Peyton's sister and the manservant have insisted that *you* killed Lord Peyton, McAdam, and that we should detain you immediately."

20

He never did," I stated at once, earning Inspector McGregor's glare. "I know full well that Mr. McAdam is not capable of throwing a weak and impaired gentleman down a flight of stairs."

Inspector McGregor did not appear to be as convinced. "I'll need a statement from you as to your whereabouts at ten o'clock last evening," he said to Daniel.

That must have been the time the examining surgeon had decided the man had died. If his neck had been broken it would have been very quick, which was a mercy.

"I can answer that easily," Daniel said, the least tense of the three of us. "I was with Monaghan. He was explaining to me, as he has been for the past few days, what a poor excuse for an investigating officer I am and how the little evidence I've gathered wouldn't convict a beggar of loitering. I was in his office, which is above yours, by the way, while he harangued me. He let me go about midnight, but only because he wanted a meal before crawling back to the hole he lives in."

"And you went home?" McGregor demanded.

Daniel nodded. "I slunk to Southampton Street and my rooms there and slept heavily. Plenty of constables saw me leave the Yard—and plenty heard Monaghan going on at me before that, I'm certain. My landlady greeted me when I went in, with disapproval of the late hour. She prepared me a fine breakfast this morning, however, so all must be forgiven."

Inspector McGregor listened with his usual surliness. "Monaghan will have to confirm your story."

Daniel shrugged. "He will. I suppose he might try to deny I was with him for the amusement of watching me be dragged to Newgate, but as I said, there were witnesses, and not all of them fear Monaghan. Sergeant Scott, for example. He was there."

"Scott is an upstanding fellow," Inspector McGregor conceded. "I'll ask him, if Monaghan tries to play a game." He turned his scowl on me. "My advice to the pair of you is to go home and stay there. Avoid Monaghan as much as you can until this blows over."

Daniel sent him a wry smile. "Monaghan will blame me for everything, even though I can prove I was far from Belgrave Square when the man died. My fault he was killed, or fell, or whatever happened, in his view."

"No sign Lord Peyton was pushed," McGregor said. "No bruising on his back, chest, or arms, except what he got from the stairs. No convenient handprint the exact size of his killer's."

"Then how did he fall?" I could not stop myself from asking. "Where was his manservant?"

"Fagan was in his bed, sleeping the sleep of the just, according to everyone in the household," McGregor surprised me by answering. "He seems broken up about Lord Peyton's death, though the sister is furious at him for not being by his master's side all hours."

"He usually was," Daniel said. "Odd that he went to bed last night."

"I asked him why," Inspector McGregor said. "Fagan claimed he was exhausted, but now is saying someone put something in his tea to make him sleep. There was no sign of that though, or remains of any substance in his teacup. He still had it on his bedside table."

"Convenient for any killer," Daniel said. "But it might not have been in the tea. Fagan was known to have a nip of gin when he thought no one was looking. But if you say there's no sign of anyone pushing the man, we might have to conclude it was an accident. Lord Peyton wheeled himself to the top of the stairs for whatever reason, stood up, and fell."

"Both the manservant and that Lady Fontaine are insisting it was murder," Inspector McGregor said. "Lady Fontaine is already starting to be like a burr under my skin."

From the way Hannah described her, I believed him.

"Did you find any evidence of the blackmailing letters I told you of, Inspector?" I asked.

This was news to Daniel, who blinked, but Inspector McGregor shook his head.

"Lady Fontaine has a diary of tittle-tattle gossip, according to the housekeeper, which her ladyship refused to let us see, though I can insist if necessary. But no letters of the sort you mean. The only correspondence we found was the usual—notes to a man of business, orders to buy or sell shares of stock, instructions to the viscount's land steward about the estate's farm. Most written by McAdam here, who logged them neatly into a ledger."

"As a good secretary would," Daniel said with a modest nod. "I saw nothing of the kind you are talking about while I was there either." He regarded me in bewilderment.

"Lord Peyton bought the ink they were written with," I continued, making both men stare at me. "A tutor at the Polytechnic did experiments on the paper and ink, and the ink proved to be rare and expensive. Lord Peyton bought bottles of it from a shop in the Burlington Arcade."

Inspector McGregor's breath gurgled in his throat. "Mrs. Holloway—"

"I have given you a place to start, Inspector," I continued. "Someone is sending letters all over Mayfair, intimidating highborn ladies into influencing their gentlemen to act in the letter writer's favor. The letters ask only to use their powers of persuasion now, but what if the victims are soon requested to do other things, such as deliver packages to government leaders or perhaps leave an innocuous parcel at a railway station?"

"Ones that might detonate," Daniel said grimly. "She has a point, McGregor."

"I am looking into it," McGregor said in exasperation. "Heed what I've told you, Mrs. Holloway. Go home. Stay there. Forget about Lord Peyton, blackmailers, and Fenians, and bake pies, or whatever it is you do."

I fixed him with an admonishing gaze. "You need a wife, Inspector, one who will chide you when you say silly things about cooks. And to make certain you are properly dressed each day. Your collar is half twisted inside out, you know."

Inspector McGregor put a self-conscious hand to the offending collar, while Daniel chuckled.

"You'd probably eat better as well," he said.

"Enough." Inspector McGregor cut us off. "McAdam, I will quiz Monaghan about your alibi. But I suggest you lie low for a few days, or an enterprising constable will try to haul you in. Good evening to you both."

He tipped his hat with a stiff hand, turned on his heel, and marched away to Cheapside, snarling at small boys who dared dart across his path.

"I agree with the inspector," I said before Daniel could speak. "I'd feel better knowing you were home, with Mrs. Williams to look after you."

"Not until I see *you* safely to Mount Street." Daniel did his sharp whistle again, and a hansom turned to halt for us. This time, the cabbie at the reins was Lewis, Daniel's friend, as though he'd been dogging our steps.

I let Daniel assist me into the cab. "I am glad you are seeing me home, because we have much more to discuss. Much, much more."

Daniel scrambled in beside me and closed the doors on us. "I am happy to continue talking about what we did on our ride here."

His smile sent a frisson of pleasure through me, but I felt a bit fragile after confessing such feelings.

"I am afraid it is something more serious." I turned in my seat to face Daniel squarely, so I could watch his expression when I asked my question. "Does a secret branch of the police exist, and are you and Monaghan a part of it?"

Daniel was very good at masking his true reactions, but I'd caught him off guard. His surprise and dismay told me I'd guessed correctly.

"I see," I said.

"*Secret* means just that," Daniel said in a quiet voice.

I did not relent. "Inspector McGregor more or less admitted

that such a thing was true. It was mentioned in the blackmail letters Miss Townsend received. I asked her about it, and she pretended to not know what the writer meant. But I could see that it rattled her."

Daniel let out a breath and briefly covered his eyes with his gloved hand. When he looked up at me again, it was with unhappiness and resignation.

"I never meant to lie to you, Kat. I was compelled to say nothing to anyone, on threat of being tried for treason. Though as time passes, many more know, or suspect, the truth."

My throat was tight. "I did not want to be correct."

"It hardly matters now. You understood right away that Monaghan was a hard man who didn't seem to be under anyone's control. Now blackmailers are writing about us in letters. The home secretary instigated this project a few years ago, and as I said, Miss Townsend's father is his right-hand man. As the cabinet comes and goes, so does the home secretary, but Mr. Townsend stays. We more or less answer to Townsend and him alone. Miss Townsend is a clever young woman. She either inferred this new branch's existence or her father trusted her enough to tell her."

"The goal is to chase Fenians?"

My chest felt tight, my fears rising. A branch of the police ruled only by the Home Office would be powerful but also vulnerable. Inspector McGregor had said that Daniel could command any constables he wished, but that those men didn't necessarily have to help him when he called.

Who knew when the secretary would decide to shut the project down, and what if he did it at the very moment Daniel had infiltrated a group of dangerous bombers? Leaving him without recourse?

"More or less," Daniel answered me. "The branch was formed in response to the assassination attempts on the queen and for the incendiary devices left hither and yon, injuring and killing people. The Metropolitan Police alone don't have the resources to fight both the bombers and the more usual criminals, so the Special Irish Branch was formed. There is talk of removing 'Irish' from the name, as more people than Irishmen are disgruntled at the British Crown and seek vengeance."

"So you will chase men of all nationalities who wield dynamite," I said faintly. "That does not make me feel better."

"I was pleased when they chose me to join," Daniel confessed. "At first, anyway. When I realized that Monaghan used it as an excuse to thrust me in front of every hazard he could, I was less happy, but I'm good at this, Kat. I've found villains and saved people from harm."

He had indeed, well I knew.

"So Monaghan will release you only when you've endangered yourself to his satisfaction?" I demanded. "He promised to when you were finished with Lord Peyton, and now you are finished."

"He promised, if I got a result," Daniel corrected me. "Which I did not. Something is brewing, Kat. All the signs are there. Peyton, I am willing to believe, had nothing to do with it. His friends might have, but so far, they all seem to be exactly what they appear to be. And now Peyton is dead. Very suspiciously."

"Inspector McGregor said he wasn't pushed."

"True, but there are ways to kill a man without touching him. I will have to look at the postmortem results."

"Inspector McGregor also told you to stay out of it," I reminded him.

Daniel sent me a grim smile. "I don't answer to McGregor, remember? Or his superiors. I advised Monaghan, when he stopped raging long enough to listen to me, not to pull all his watchers from that house. There is something . . ."

I knew there was something amiss as well, of which Lord Peyton's death was part, though I had no details as to what. "Hannah is still there. She can have a nose about."

Daniel shook his head. "Send word to her to go. Two people have been killed. If anyone tumbles to the fact that your Hannah is not actually a maid, she will be in grave danger, and I'm no longer there to protect her."

"She actually is a maid," I said. "At least, she was, years ago. She is also the best confidence trickster I have ever met, even beyond you and Mr. Fielding. I will warn her, of course, but if she chooses to stay, she would be of invaluable help."

Daniel blew out a breath of exasperation. "I can't stop her doing anything she likes, I suppose. Or you, apparently."

"My dear Daniel." I slid my arm through his and rested my head on his shoulder. "You never could."

D aniel did not accompany me inside when we reached Mount Street. We shared another kiss in the hansom, which I insisted let me off around the corner, and once I'd descended, Lewis took Daniel on.

I hoped Daniel would heed Inspector McGregor's advice and stay home for a bit while Monaghan cooled his temper, but I knew Daniel well. He might rest for a few hours but be out again trying to find answers.

For my part, I had my own resources and fully intended to use them. Monaghan held enmity for Daniel, and I wagered he'd not be satisfied until Daniel died to assuage Monaghan's grief and anger. There was no way I'd sit back and let Monaghan take his vengeance. If my efforts could help release Daniel from his bargain, then I would act.

Once I'd resumed my work dress, I took up a basket of scraps from the day's cooking and went back out into the now dark evening.

I found Mr. Fielding's lads straightaway. They approached when I beckoned, and I handed them a tea cake each—Tess had baked a nice batch this afternoon.

"Do you know the boy who sometimes seeks me?" I asked them. "Scruffy clothes, dark red hair, blue eyes. Goes by the name of Adam, though I do not believe that is his true name."

"Yeah, we knows 'im," the black-haired boy said. "Slippery little eel, but we'll catch 'im."

"Politely," I said. "He is the son of a friend of mine. Please bring him to me—I need him to deliver a message."

"Right you are." The second boy touched his cap and sped into the darkness. The first paused long enough to shove an entire tea cake into his mouth, then he sprang after his friend.

I shook my head, handed out the rest of the scraps to the men and women who gathered, and returned to the kitchen.

"I might have to change me day out to Wednesday," Tess told me unhappily when I joined her at the work table. "Caleb thinks that will be his day off, but he's not certain. He might not be able to take any time at all, at first."

"Who will he be working under?" I asked, as though off-handedly. "Inspector McGregor?"

"He won't tell me." Tess scowled at the bread dough she kneaded. "He's gone all secretive."

"It could be he doesn't know. Those higher up in the police don't impart information to one and all."

I meant to comfort Tess, but I wondered anew if Monaghan

hadn't clamped hold of Caleb. I hoped Inspector McGregor or perhaps someone like Sergeant Scott could make certain Caleb didn't work in this special Irish branch Daniel had told me about.

The work they'd been set up to do was important, I recognized. I was all for stopping explosions in railway stations and on streets—but I did not want Caleb to forfeit his life for it. Tess hadn't had much happiness in her years on this earth, and losing Caleb would crush her.

Tess continued to be sullen, and I left her alone. I couldn't tell her all would be well when I had no idea if it would be.

I sent Tess to bed early, as I usually did when I took my days out, and finished up sitting alone in the kitchen, making notes in my book.

Culinary problems did not occupy me tonight. Instead, I jotted more thoughts about the deaths of Lord Peyton and his secretary, the blackmail letters, and the list of those who'd purchased the ink bottles. I also spent time wondering how on earth Daniel would go about finding out what the anarchists were up to.

If they were up to anything at all. Daniel had found no evidence of Fenian plots in Viscount Peyton's house—had Monaghan truly got his information wrong? Or was he setting up Daniel in some sort of scheme to make him fail?

If Daniel watched people who had nothing to do with the bombings, and terrible things happened elsewhere, Daniel might be blamed.

Would Monaghan risk people's lives to ruin Daniel? Thinking of the hard-eyed man, I believed he could.

But was he? Or was I simply reaching for explanations?

Just before midnight, I heard a tap on the back door. I opened it cautiously to find Adam on the doorstep.

"What yer want?" he asked ungraciously.

I forbore from scolding that a young lad should be in bed, not running about in the dark, and handed him a folded piece of paper.

"Can you get that to your mum without anyone seeing?"

The scorn Adam did so well flowed from him. "Course I can."

No doubt Hannah, the expert, had taught him well.

"I would be grateful," I said. "Here's tuppence for your trouble, and a tea cake as well. Has plenty of currants."

Adam pocketed the note and the pennies, snatched up the tea cake, and took a large bite. "'S'good, missus," he said grudgingly.

That would be all the thanks I'd receive, I imagined. "Tess baked them. She will be pleased to hear it."

Adam eyed me skeptically, then shrugged and trudged up the stairs without looking back.

Poor lad. With Hannah moving from house to pub to living with a man who might or might not have been Adam's father, he probably didn't know whom to trust. I believed Hannah loved him, but life with her would be unconventional.

I sighed as I shut and bolted the door. As I'd had to leave my own baby on my friends' doorstep, I had no call to express superiority over another's mothering skills.

I made certain the kitchen was ready for the next day, blew out the candle, and went upstairs to bed.

In the morning, as Tess and I sent up breakfast and took a few minutes to munch our own, Adam returned.

He handed me a paper—my note reused—and held his hand out for his expected payment. I gave him another tuppence and a buttery muffin wrapped in a cloth. He looked less ungracious but again ran away without thanks.

I went down the hall into the empty larder to read Hannah's reply in privacy.

I can get you into the house, the note promised. *Greengrocer's, Oxford Street, today.*

21

As always, Hannah's directions to a meeting were cryptic. *Today* was a vague stretch of time, and there were several greengrocers on Oxford Street.

Nevertheless, I brought out onions and mushrooms to make into a thick soup for luncheon, instructed Tess how to start, and took up my basket.

"I can go to the shops for you," Tess said hopefully. She likely wanted a chance to encounter Caleb, who she'd told me would continue his beat until officially moving into his new position.

"Next time," I said, not liking how quickly her eagerness faded. "Or perhaps you can take a short walk this afternoon to get some air."

Tess brightened and returned to her chopping. I dashed up the stairs and out into the street.

The morning was warmer, June quickly approaching. I walked purposefully north through Grosvenor Square to Oxford Street and headed for my usual shop. Hannah would likely know which one. She probably had instructed Adam to report to her all my haunts.

An elderly beggar woman lingered by the greengrocers, hunched over a bundle she held close to her chest. I had become used to Hannah's disguises and pretended to ignore her as I approached the open-front shop.

The beggar started to rise, tripped, and fell into me. Her bundle crashed to the ground, and half-squashed fruits and vegetables tumbled and began to roll into the street.

"Let me help you, love," I said quickly. I bent to retrieve her things as she sniffled, noting that she was quite odiferous.

"You dropped another," Hannah's voice came from behind me. I looked up to see her, dressed as herself, holding out an apple to the elderly woman.

"You've ruined all me things," the beggar snarled at me. "Watch what you're about."

"Nonsense," I said, trying to recover my surprise. "Most of these are fine, and I'll buy you a few new cucumbers."

She sniffled again. "All right."

I ducked into the grocers to procure the fresh vegetables while Hannah remained to put the woman to rights. I handed the beggar the replacements when I came out, and she shuffled off without much gratitude.

"That's an old trick," Hannah said as we watched the woman hobble along the street. "She'll do it again at the next shop—crash into someone and spill her wares so they'll buy her better ones. You're too good to the likes of her."

"I thought she was you," I said. "And yes, I do feel sorry for her, ruse or no."

Hannah laughed at me. "Like I say, you're a bright-winged angel. I didn't have time to do much more than change me dress and squash on a hat." The hat was large, covering all of Hannah's hair, and her gown was the one I'd seen her wearing at her Portobello Road stall. "Her ladyship and the house-keeper think I'm at the shops. Marjory the maid went into Fortnum's on an errand, and is still there waiting for an order to be bundled up, for all anyone knows."

Meaning she'd walked into Fortnum's dressed as an up-stairs maid, changed her appearance somewhere in its re-cesses, and walked out the back door as herself. She'd reverse the procedure when she went back. Hannah's ruses could be simple, but effective.

"Let us step somewhere we can speak, then," I suggested.

"Don't you need to buy your veg?" she reminded me. "So those in the kitchen think you're shopping like I'm meant to be?"

"I will purchase the things when we are finished. Every-thing needs to be fresh as can be, and they won't improve be-ing tucked into my basket for an additional half hour."

Hannah shook her head good-naturedly. "You really enjoy being a cook, don't you?"

"There's nothing wrong with being a cook," I said, a bit stiffly. "Preparing good food is a skill I'm not ashamed to have cultivated. There's a tea shop a few doors along. Let us pause for a cup."

Hannah remained amused but followed as I went into the shop in which I sometimes took refreshment. I chose a table in the far corner, away from the few ladies who'd also decided to spend a moment off their feet.

The waitress brought us a pot with cups and two dispirited biscuits, announced she had nothing else to give us this early in the day, and left us alone.

"*How* do you propose to let me enter the house?" I asked as

I poured out the steeped tea. "I've been itching with curiosity. Is the cook leaving now that the master is gone?"

"Not a bit of it." Hannah accepted the cup I handed her. "Lady Fontaine wants the household to stay together as long as she can. The next viscount is a distant cousin, and she can't be certain he won't sling her out when he finally reaches London. Lady Fontaine's trying to decide what to do. Poor lamb. I feel sorry for her, even if she's a right old bitch. But her surliness comes from never knowing where she'll be welcome."

"If not as cook, then what?" I asked. "A relation of Marjory? Come to make sure her sister's all right?"

Hannah shook her head and took a noisy slurp of tea. "I have to say, this shop does a much better tea than that awful pub in Leicester Square."

I agreed. "They buy it from Twinings, even if it is the lowest quality they sell. Now please cease teasing me and tell me what you have in mind."

Hannah's grin showed me she was enjoying herself. "Lady Fontaine is agog to know what happened to her brother. She at first insisted the secretary—your man—did it, but the police told her this morning that he has an unbreakable alibi for the time in question." She paused to sip more tea. "Isn't this exciting? Like a detective story in the magazines."

"Not really," I said severely. "Daniel barely avoided being blamed. Who does Lady Fontaine think did it now?"

"She don't know, but she wants to find out. Seems she loved the old geezer. He was one of the few who didn't run her off after a few weeks."

"If you think to bring me in as a detective, I will refuse," I said. "The police truly are investigating, even if they seem slow about it."

"Nah, her ladyship don't have any faith in policemen or

detectives. She wants to consult the spirits." Hannah's dimples showed. "She does this for many a problem."

"The spirits." I regarded her with misgivings. "How will she do that?"

"A séance, of course. Spirituality is all the rage among the quality, if you didn't know. I can't tell you how many crystal balls and fake Romani table draperies I sell from my stall. People will believe anything."

My alarm grew. "What has this to do with me?"

"Can't you guess? I told Lady Fontaine I knew a medium who'd done wonders for my last lady. Can speak to the dead and everything. That medium will be you." Hannah finished this astonishing statement and plopped her biscuit into her mouth.

"No," I said immediately. "As much as I wish to look about that house, I refuse to do anything so silly. If Lady Fontaine is an avid spiritualist, she will know immediately that I am a fraud. I'm not even certain what mediums do."

Hannah noisily swallowed the biscuit. "They pretend to go into a trance and let the dead talk through them, so you only need to roll your eyes a bit and speak in a mysterious way. Mediums are the best confidence people I know—they take money for telling their dim clients something vague that their late relatives want to impart. Though, most people try to ask the dear departed things like who they really wanted the silver tea service to go to, or where is that extra hundred pounds they'd hidden a few years back."

"My dear friend," I said when Hannah paused for breath. "I could not possibly. Why don't you do it? I'm sure you'd fool them beautifully."

"Would if they didn't already know me. But I'm a respectable maid trying to help her ladyship find a bit of peace. I made out that I don't really believe in spiritualism, but my former employer seemed to draw comfort from it. If I suddenly declared I could sense Lord Peyton's ghost and he had a message for Lady Fontaine, she'd smell a rat. Much more believable if I bring in a stranger I pretend to barely know. They've never seen you or know anything about you."

I regarded her in consternation. "Good heavens, you mean for me to do this."

"Why not? You'll get into the house and have a look around when you say you need to take in the atmosphere. Walk where the dead man walked, sit where he sat. I can't think of a better opportunity. Besides, she'll pay you ten guineas."

"Ten guineas?" My voice rose enough to attract the attention of the other tea drinkers and the waitress. I cleared my throat and sipped tea until they looked away.

"That's what I told her your fee was," Hannah said. "She said she could scrounge it up from the money her brother left lying about. If nothing else, you'll have a bit of extra cash for all this worrying you've been doing."

Ten guineas was a lot of money. With it, I could purchase the fine fabric for the new gown I needed, plus something nice for Grace and have plenty left over to tuck into my building-society fund.

"Charlatans truly charge that much?" I asked in astonishment. "Perhaps I ought to reconsider how I make my living."

Hannah's dimples showed again. "Now you're seeing wisdom. Don't sound so daft now, does it?"

I tamped down my eagerness. "I could not in good conscience take money for fooling people. Although . . ."

"Although what? You're liking the idea. I see it in your eyes."

"If I do discover what happened to Lord Peyton—through

means that involve *this* plane of existence—then I won't really be fooling her. Will I?"

Hannah's laughter filled our corner. "This is why I love ya, Katie, me darling. You come over all scrupulous, but you're willing to overlook a little deception in the name of practicality. Like not peaching on a maid filching money from a mistress's desk to feed her poor little boy."

My eyes narrowed. "Your son isn't old enough for you to have been stealing for him the night I caught you."

Hannah shrugged. "I had other reasons, I'm sure."

"What is his name?" I asked in curiosity. "He told me it was Adam."

"It never is, the little imp. It's Sean. That's Scottish. Or Irish. I don't know. I just liked the name."

Was it perhaps his father's name? I wondered, but decided not to ask. "Where does Sean live, with you gone from home now? If I'd known you had a lad, I wouldn't have asked you to be a live-in maid."

"He stays at my place," Hannah said over the rim of her teacup. "Where'd ye think?"

"He was wandering about very late last night."

Hannah's amusement faded into annoyance. "He's a sturdy tyke and can take care of himself."

"I apologize," I said. "I wasn't implying you were lacking as a mum. I'm merely worried for the boy. I can find someone to look in on him if you wish."

"No." The word was sharp. "I let him run about and do as he likes, because if I'm too strict with him, he'll leg it, and I know it. He's already gone off a few times when I tried to put me foot down. I don't mind giving him his freedom, Kat. He's all I've got."

The fact that she addressed me by my correct name while

her eyes moistened told me she was sincere. I made a soothing gesture.

"I would never interfere," I told her. "But if you ever need help, you come to me. All right?"

"Cease being so bleedin' kind. You'll turn on the waterworks." Hannah wiped her eyes. "Can I tell her ladyship you'll be there to ask the spirits what became of her brother?"

I debated another moment then heaved a sigh. "Yes, I will do it. I can come on Thursday afternoon, no sooner."

"Night's better. The sitters will already be spooked by the darkness and more inclined to believe you."

I shook my head. "It's much more difficult for me to slip away at night. If I'm caught, I'll get the sack. Nothing is worth that."

Hannah regarded me impatiently. "I've never understood why you willingly slave for a living. You're better than that."

I answered with equal heat. "Because I need the money to keep my daughter fed and clothed. Besides, there's nothing wrong with honest work."

"So you've told me. I'll wager if you set up with a stall like mine and sell them cakes and tarts you do, you'd make a fortune."

My retort died on my tongue as she put forth this tempting idea. My dream was my own tea shop, of course—one much nicer than the one in which we sat—but a stall in a market could be a start.

However, I made myself be practical. "Such an endeavor would mean purchasing my own supplies. I cook fine cakes now because the kitchen I work for pays for the ingredients. If I had to compromise on quality to save money, I'd sell nothing for long."

"We'd find some way around that," Hannah assured me.

"Very well. Thursday afternoon it will be. Don't drape yourself in scarves and whatnot. Mediums only do that on the stage. A plain and sensible frock will be fine."

"As I only have the one, it will have to do." I drained my cup and set it down. "Now I must go, or I will be out a place sooner than I think."

"Give it up," Hannah advised me. "Have your little girl help you with your stall and sleep under it if you have to. Worth it."

I wanted more for my girl than hawking wares in a cold and windy market, but I didn't want to hurt Hannah's feelings by explaining that to her. She understood, I believed, because she only raised her brows and went back to her tea.

We parted cordially, and I skimmed to the greengrocers to pick out the best of what he had before hurrying back home, my thoughts troubled.

I continued to argue with myself for the next few days about turning up in Belgrave Square, pretending to be a medium.

On the one hand, it might be my only opportunity to enter the house and have a good look around. Daniel wouldn't have missed much when he'd been employed there, but as someone trying to get in touch with Lord Peyton's spirit, I could wander into rooms he'd been shut out of.

It was important to find out how and why Lord Peyton had died, which might provide a valuable clue about whatever the anarchists were planning. If I could offer any information to the police, I would.

Then I'd tell myself I was mad to even consider Hannah's scheme. Lady Fontaine, if she was as interested in spiritualism as Hannah claimed, would immediately spot me as a fake.

This worried me so much I came up with several plans for how to escape from her house if I were caught out.

Daniel, of course, would forbid me to go if I told him. I never had the chance to speak to him about it, in any case, because he didn't turn up all the rest of Tuesday and not on Wednesday either. I hoped he was lying low, as Inspector McGregor had instructed, but it was more likely he was running errands for Monaghan, dangerous ones.

I found my thoughts turning too many times to the discussion of my true feelings with Daniel in the hansom cab, and the warm kiss that had followed. I'd told him more plainly than I ever had what he meant to me, even though I don't think he'd quite believed me.

I'd not have blamed Daniel for running out of patience with me long ago, but he hadn't. That told me clearer than words how much he cared for me. For *me*, as I was, not someone to mold into the woman he wanted me to be.

That was worth more than riches, any day.

Thursday morning, I donned my brown frock and hat and left the house. I'd see Grace first, as she was the most important person in my world, and then I'd go to Belgrave Square.

I confess it was the ten-guinea fee that clinched the matter.

T he front door was opened at the Belgrave Square house that afternoon by a very tall man in a black suit. I gazed up past wide shoulders to a craggy face and found red-rimmed eyes peering down at me.

Fagan, I decided. The manservant.

"I am Mrs. Crowe," I told him. Hannah and I had decided on that name before we'd departed the tea shop. It was brief, easy to remember, and held a hint of the macabre. "Her lady-ship is expecting me."

Fagan made a polite bow and gestured me inside and to a reception room. I strolled into this chamber, pretending dignity, and tried not to flinch when Fagan closed the door behind me with a loud click.

Reception rooms were meant to awe the visitor with the house's grandeur and yet not let them become too comfortable. Guests reposed here on hard but elegant chairs until the master or mistress of the house resolved whether or not to welcome them.

This room had furniture with modern, clean lines, eschewing the carved mahogany and overly cluttered decor of past decades. The walls were painted a light green, which went well with the dark walnut chairs and tables. Landscapes of a beautiful countryside hung on the walls, the skies in them an arching blue.

How lovely it would be to live in a village with flower-studded meadows and woods all around one. I told myself that in reality there would be plenty of insects and other small creatures to contend with as well as mud and damp, but the paintings made it appear so tranquil.

The door opened behind me as I contemplated one of these pictures, a heavy silence telling me Fagan had returned.

"You're to come upstairs," he rumbled.

His accent put him from the north, possibly Birmingham or thereabouts. No matter where he hailed from, he was clearly morose, as though Lord Peyton's death was a blow from which he was still reeling.

Fagan was the first person who'd jumped to mind as soon as I'd heard Lord Peyton had died. He'd accompanied Lord Peyton everywhere, at all hours, and was strong enough to heave the man out of his chair and drop him down the stairs. Inspector McGregor had said there were no signs of anyone having pushed Lord Peyton, but as Daniel had hinted, there were other ways to make certain a man fell.

Fagan now climbed lugubriously up a polished staircase, presumably the one Lord Peyton had tumbled down. Ivory-colored paneling made the hall light, as did a large window on the landing.

This tall window reached all the way up to the next floor and looked out onto the mews, its draperies open. I'd noted the window from the other side, when I'd spied on the house several weeks ago. The curtains had been drawn then, muffled like all the windows in the back of the house.

I wondered if Lord Peyton had insisted the drapes be kept closed and now that he was gone, that rule had been relaxed. Or else the household was distracted, and the opening and closing of the curtains was the least of their worries.

Fagan hesitated at the top of the stairs, and his shoulders quivered. I caught up to him, astonished to find the man weeping.

"Now then," I said gently. "I know it must have been a shock."

Fagan wiped his eyes, but more tears rolled past his large nose. "It were here, missus." He pointed at the floor beneath his feet. "The master fell right here. He died, and I wasn't there to prevent it." He put his hands over his face and sobbed.

22

The sound of Fagan's weeping filled the silence of the upper hall. His entire body shook, and I reached out a tenuous hand to touch his great arm.

"I am so sorry," I said, scarcely knowing what to tell him. "It was an accident, the police said. Nothing you could have done."

Fagan jerked from my touch. "I should have been with him. I left him alone because he sent me to bed. If I'd been here, he'd still be alive."

He broke down, his chest heaving, his choked sobs pathetic to witness.

"You can't blame yourself," I tried. "You had to have slept sometime. His lordship would know that, else he'd not have sent you to bed."

"I don't know why he did. It was late, but I could have stayed with him all night. He needed me." Fagan's breath wheezed, tears streaming down his large face.

"You have no idea why he was at the top of the staircase?" I asked.

"None at all."

I gazed past the weeping Fagan down the steep flight we'd just ascended. The window gave an excellent view along the mews, all the way to the corner I'd peeked around when I'd walked the road with Grace.

We were directly over the back door, I realized, the one that had the entrance between the walls. James had been correct that no one in the house could actually see that door. Once a visitor passed between the walls below, they'd vanish from sight.

I studied the scene for a time, while Fagan's sobs slowly faded to a soft gasping.

A door opened somewhere behind me. "Where are they?" a woman's stentorian voice demanded. "Go and find them. I want to make a start."

I turned as a maid in a black frock with a white pinafore glided from a room at the far end of the hall. She had dark hair in a smooth bun and a neatly starched cap pinned securely atop her head.

I'd never have recognized Hannah if I hadn't known it was she. Her face was impassive, and her eyes took in her surroundings and revealed nothing.

"This way, madam," she said to me. "That will be all, Fagan."

Hannah gave the last command in perfect imitation of a maid at the end of her patience with a manservant who at present was, in her opinion, shirking his duties.

Fagan turned and lumbered down the stairs, wiping his eyes with the heel of his hand. Hannah stood unmoving by the door she'd opened, waiting for me to enter.

I moved quietly toward her, reminding myself I was here as

a guest, not a domestic. I had no need to scuttle inside in obedience, no need to curtsy to the reedy woman—Lady Fontaine, I assumed—who waited for me there.

The chamber I entered was a drawing room filled with furniture in the same style as that of the reception room. This room was still formal but more comfortable, with pillows strewn about, books waiting on low shelves, gas lamps lending a glow even on this sunny afternoon. Apparently Lady Fontaine did not share Mrs. Bywater's alarm at the expense of lighting.

Hannah followed me in and gave Lady Fontaine a precise maid's curtsy that would do whoever had trained her proud. "Mrs. Crowe, your ladyship."

The thin woman in black looked me up and down. Her gown was simple in style, no bustle or stiff skirts, with a ruffle-trimmed bodice the only extravagance. Her iron-gray hair was likewise dressed in an uncomplicated braided coil. Lady Fontaine's face was sharp, her nose beaked, her eyes brown and watchful.

At the moment, that assessing gaze ran over me, not liking what it saw.

"She doesn't look like much," Lady Fontaine said to Hannah.

Hannah bobbed another curtsy. "Lady Mortimer swore by her, your ladyship. Said she did wonders to ease her mind about her late husband."

I hoped Hannah had not laid on her praise too thick. As Lady Mortimer had passed on, Lady Fontaine would not be able to check Hannah's claim, but Lady Fontaine could presumably quiz Lady Mortimer's acquaintances about the fictitious Mrs. Crowe.

"Lady Rankin as well," Hannah went on.

I hid my unease, as a reference to Lady Rankin was literally closer to home. But then, of those who'd worked for Cynthia's sister, besides myself, only Mr. Davis, Sara, and Elsie remained. Mrs. Bywater would have no idea if Lady Rankin had employed "Mrs. Crowe," and Cynthia would go along with the ruse once she learned of it.

Lady Fontaine sniffed. "Lady Rankin was a tart. Behaved as though she couldn't lift a finger but kept as many trysts as she pleased. Does her sister still run about in trousers?"

"I believe so, your ladyship," I said with feigned sorrow.

"That whole family is scandalous," Lady Fontaine answered decidedly. "I have nothing to do with them. But I suppose if Lady Mortimer approved of you, you'll have to do."

I contrived to look modest. "Thank you, your ladyship."

Hannah must have won Lady Fontaine's complete trust, because despite her apparent misgivings, the woman gave me a nod.

"Why were you lingering in the hall?" Lady Fontaine asked abruptly. "Fagan has become a useless lout. He'll have to go, if indeed he didn't murder my brother. That is what you are here to tell us, Mrs. Crowe."

"It wasn't Fagan's fault I remained in the hall." I felt sorry for the man now that I'd seen his true grief, and it was easy to come to his defense. "I wished to stand in the precise spot your brother met his unkind fate. To absorb the vibrations, you see."

"Ah, yes." Lady Fontaine's eyes softened the slightest bit. "I shiver mightily whenever I have to pass the staircase. I've barely been able to go downstairs since it happened."

"I'll fetch tea." Hannah snapped off another perfect curtsy and glided from the room.

Lady Fontaine continued to study me. "I suppose you will need candles and other accoutrements. We'll have to draw the draperies for the candles to even be noticed."

"Not at all," I said with feigned confidence. "The spirits are here, whether it is midnight or broad daylight." I gestured at the windows, through which May sunlight poured. As the days had warmed, the coal-smoke pall which usually coated the city had lessened.

Lady Fontaine gave me a minute smile of satisfaction. "Exactly what I always say. You don't need a crystal ball and black cloths to impress the departed. They float freely in the ether and are beyond caring about such things."

"Indeed," I managed.

"Well, make yourself comfortable, Mrs. Crowe. Marjory will return with tea, and we can make a start."

I gave her a nod and wandered about the drawing room, as though looking it over for the best place to contact the departed Lord Peyton.

I had to wonder again about the curtains, which were as wide open as the ones on the landing. Had Lord Peyton been the one who liked the drapes closed, and now that he was gone, Lady Fontaine preferred to see out?

This chamber was in the front of the house, and a glance from its two tall windows showed me the road that encircled Belgrave Square and the iron railings enclosing the park across that street. Trees and shrubbery promised tranquil walks in the green space, an oasis in busy London.

I turned from the windows and examined the rest of the room. It was fashionable these days to load mantelpieces and tables with photographs of family, but there weren't many photographs in here.

One of the few I saw was of Lord Peyton, standing stiffly

upright. It must have been taken in his younger days, the picture now faded as many from the early era of photography
did. A photograph of a slender young woman stood next to it,
and I realized with a start that she was Lady Fontaine.

The younger woman had been pretty, if not lavishly beautiful. I wondered if Lady Fontaine's marriage and her ailment
of stealing everything in sight had etched the lines of bitterness now on her face.

I noted that as she watched me, she remained in the center
of the room, far from the few knickknacks on the tables near
the walls. I wondered if Lady Fontaine had learned to do so to
keep her compulsion under some control.

Hannah skimmed back inside, balancing a full tea tray in
her hands. I curbed my instinct to help her, as an invited guest
would expect the servants to do any heavy work.

Hannah carried the loaded silver tray as though it weighed
nothing and placed it in the middle of the table. She began to
set out cups, three of them.

"Lord Downes will not be joining us," Lady Fontaine said to
her. "I invited him, as I told you, but he declined. Womanly
nonsense, he said." Her voice took on a tender note. "Lord
Downes has been like a rock. He lives next door, you see. Has
been holding my hand through it all. Well, not literally." Lady
Fontaine barely stopped herself from giggling.

If Lord Downes, the gruff and blustering neighbor Mr.
Fielding had sent his man to work for as groom, had lived in
Belgrave Square long, he'd have come to know Lady Fontaine
through her visits to her brother. Perhaps he'd grown fond of
her and she of him. Marrying him might solve her financial
dilemma for now, though I wondered if Lord Downes would
carry his fondness that far.

Hannah showed no annoyance that she'd brought an extra

cup and tea cakes for nothing. "Will that be all, your lady-ship?" she asked with faultless courtesy.

"*You* will stay with us, Marjory," Lady Fontaine announced. "I wanted Lord Downes to make a third party—the spirits pre-fer more of the living to interact with. Mrs. Proctor—she's our housekeeper—said she'd not have any truck with ghosts, and Fagan would be useless. So you will stay. You are not afraid, are you?" Lady Fontaine sent Hannah a piercing gaze, as though ready to mock her if she betrayed any fear.

"Not at all, your ladyship," Hannah answered without changing expression.

"Good girl. Now pour out the tea. Mrs. Crowe and I will drink, and then she will read my leaves."

I started. "No, your ladyship. I cannot."

Hannah flicked a glare at me, which Lady Fontaine did not notice. "Why ever not?" Lady Fontaine demanded.

"I am not a clairvoyant," I said quickly. "I can sense the de-parted and let them communicate through me, but I can't foretell the future. They are two different things."

"Oh," Lady Fontaine said in disappointment. "I didn't know that."

I would not have known it either, but I'd once worked with a housekeeper who was very certain she had second sight. She'd told me many things about spiritualism, whether I'd wanted to hear of them or not. I shared Hannah's opinion, that mediums and fortune tellers were charlatans, but that house-keeper had been very certain she gleaned things that others did not.

Perhaps she did. I hadn't the heart to take away the one dream she had of becoming a celebrated clairvoyant, so I'd kept my skepticism to myself.

"The tea looks splendid, in any case," I said. "While we partake, perhaps you can tell me more about your brother." When Lady Fontaine regarded this remark in surprise, I hurried on. "It will help me recognize him when I seek him out. I've never met him, and he might be more comfortable if I know things about him."

Whether Hannah approved or disapproved of my ruse, she made no sign. She poured tea and laid out cakes without a word.

"Of course." Lady Fontaine gestured me to the table, where Hannah continued to work. "Sit down, Mrs. Crowe, and I will tell you all I can."

I deferentially stood by and let Lady Fontaine be seated first—though I was not a servant in this scenario, I was not in her class—then I took the chair opposite her.

Hannah could not sit if Lady Fontaine did not invite her, so she finished serving and retreated to the window. She stood like a statue, the attentive maid who would keep a discreet distance until called for, while not so far as to inconvenience the lady who needed her.

"My brother was not the paragon others thought him, I will tell you plainly, Mrs. Crowe," Lady Fontaine began. "But I loved him dearly." She brushed an invisible tear from the corner of her eye.

I sipped the tea, pleased to find it of fine quality. If I did nothing else useful in this house, at least I would partake of a decent cup of tea.

"I am certain you did," I said in a soothing tone. "I can sense it."

"Edwin was a handsome youth, so athletic when we were growing up." Lady Fontaine's gaze went remote, the rigidity in her face easing as she warmed to her topic. "He won all the races with his friends as a child, and when he went to school, he did races and things there as well. Won many awards. Lord Downes was also quite an athlete in his day—though you'd never know to look at him now. Of course, he is a bit older than Edwin." Lady Fontaine sighed. "Then Edwin somehow got a wasting disease. No doctor could decide what was happening to him. He simply walked more and more slowly, or one leg or the other would seize up for no reason. When Edwin started to fall more than walk, he resigned himself to the wheeled chair. He was never ill a day in his life, and he was quite hearty, even with the weakening of his limbs."

Lady Fontaine brought out a lace handkerchief and dabbed her eyes, this time wiping away true tears.

"He had many friends," I said gently. "I can sense that as well. This house was lively, was it not?"

Lady Fontaine brightened. "Oh, yes. Edwin always had people coming and going. He was personable, brilliant at conversation. I looked forward to my visits."

"No quarrels of any kind?" I asked as I nibbled a tea cake. The cake was far too dry, and any currants in it were miniscule. Daniel had told me the cook doted on Lord Peyton, but she obviously skimped for Lady Fontaine.

"Perhaps there were disagreements on politics and such," Lady Fontaine said. "But argued with only the greatest respect. Not that I understood much of those conversations. Ladies don't need to, do they?" Her gaze encouraged me to agree that women should be political dunces.

"He did sometimes have a lady here besides yourself." I closed my eyes briefly as though searching the ether for visions of Lord Peyton's past. "One who spoke about politics with him."

"Well, there is Mrs. Lofthouse." Lady Fontaine waved a dismissive hand. "Such a bluestocking. She and her husband stated adamantly that the Irish should break from us. What nonsense. Ireland has always been a part of Britain."

Even I knew that was not true, but I did not correct her. "Your brother agreed?" I asked.

"Edwin? Not a bit of it. He vehemently opposed her. Vehemently. He believed that Ireland should have *some* independence—Home Rule, I think it is called—but should always remain connected to England. Whatever would they do on their own?" Lady Fontaine scoffed. "The whole place would fall into the sea, I should think, without us to anchor them."

Certainly Lady Fontaine would never be recruited by the Fenians for the Irish cause. Lord Peyton, however, was more difficult to pin down. Daniel had said he argued for Home Rule, but he'd found no evidence of any more radical beliefs or funding for those beliefs.

Perhaps it was the Lofthouses, after all, that Monaghan had in his sights. They were blatantly for Irish independence, they went to meetings in or near the British Museum with those of like mind, and they'd absconded to the Continent as soon as Lord Peyton had died.

I hoped with all my heart that Monaghan was after them, would capture them, and make them confess an association with the Fenians. If Monaghan discovered the "something brewing" Daniel had told me of, then Daniel would be released from his obligation to Monaghan, and we could all breathe again.

"Did your brother have any enemies?" I asked. "Someone who would be happy if he was out of the way?"

Lady Fontaine regarded me with indignation. "Good heavens, no. I told you, everyone adored Edwin. When he argued his point, it was in debate, not with anger. He rarely saw eye to eye with Lord Downes, even when they were at school together, but they are still—were still—great friends." Her breath caught on her accidental use of the present tense.

I understood why Hannah pitied her, and I now felt sorry for her as well. "Let me see what I can do."

Lady Fontaine drew a shaky breath. "How can I help?"

I'd drawn on my experience with the fortune-telling house-keeper while I'd prepared for this meeting.

"Do you have anything of his I can hold?" I asked. "A hand-kerchief, a letter, a watch chain? Something he'd have carried with him?"

"I had anticipated that." Lady Fontaine rose and went to a box on a table near the fireplace. She withdrew a polished pipe and brought it to me. "My brother did like his tobacco, though I always thought it a nasty habit. He did not smoke as much in these later years, as his doctor advised against it, but he liked to hold this even if he no longer used it."

She laid a small, polished pipe made of briarwood on the table in front of me. Lady Fontaine let her fingertips rest on it a moment before she returned to her seat.

"What now?" she asked.

"We should all sit," I said. "Including you, my dear," I added to Hannah.

Hannah, as an obedient servant should, looked to her mistress for confirmation. Lady Fontaine nodded, and Hannah moved noiselessly to the table and sat on my left side.

I touched the pipe, finding the wood soft and pleasant to my fingertips. Many gentlemen these days still smoked meer-schaums, which could be carved into fantastical patterns, but some now liked the briarwood, which remained cooler to the touch. Mr. Bywater, on the rare occasions he enjoyed a pipe, out of his wife's sight, he used a briarwood.

The pipe told me only that Lord Peyton had expensive

taste, as it had been finely made. The remnants of tobacco inside had also been costly, I could tell from its odor. I'd worked in houses where gentlemen had spent much on their tobacco and in some where they'd used dreadful-smelling cheap and damp leaves.

I admit I was on the lookout for poison as I delicately sniffed the end of the pipe. Someone might have introduced a noxious substance into it, which Lord Peyton could have inhaled when he sucked on the unlit pipe to comfort himself. Certain substances, like arsenic or strychnine, could make a man rise from his chair, clawing his throat or chest, and topple down a flight of stairs.

However, I smelled nothing but tobacco. Not that I had firsthand knowledge of the odor of all poisons, but as a cook who used scent to tell me whether vegetables and fish were fresh, or cooked food was done, my nose was rather practiced.

I laid the pipe gently onto the table and placed my fingertips on it.

"Do we need to hold hands?" Lady Fontaine asked. I heard the hesitation in her voice.

"That will not be necessary," I answered. "I only need to concentrate."

Lady Fontaine looked relieved, Hannah impassive.

I closed my eyes. I had no idea if I should make any sort of noises, like the groans Hannah had suggested, but I decided to simply sit still.

I pictured Lord Peyton in his wheeled chair. Daniel had told me he could trundle himself about in it when Fagan was abed or engaged in other duties. Had he taken himself into the hall and to the head of the stairs? For what reason?

I recalled the spot in which I'd stood with Fagan, the staircase opening before me. The wide window filled the landing, rendering the entire mews visible to anyone sitting at the top of the stairs.

Lord Peyton had been there at ten o'clock at night, but that did not mean the mews would have been fully dark. This part of London had plenty of lighting. If the mews didn't have its own lamps, the carriage houses likely did, or the grooms and coachmen would tote lanterns about as they carried on. A servant's work did not always cease with the setting sun.

I might be wrong about this vision, if it had been Lord Peyton who liked the drapes to remained closed. But perhaps he'd ordered them opened, or Lady Fontaine had wished it, or a servant had forgotten and either opened them or left them that way.

I imagined Lord Peyton gazing out of this window and seeing something that made him stagger to his feet. Whatever it was had amazed or frightened him enough that he had fallen forward, tumbling down, down, down the highly polished stairs, to end up in a broken huddle at the bottom.

I gasped and opened my eyes. The vision had been so vivid I wondered a moment if I didn't actually have second sight.

"Lord Peyton," I whispered. "What did you see out of the window?"

23

My question was hoarse enough and dramatic enough that even Hannah flicked a startled gaze to me.

Lady Fontaine leaned forward. "Have you contacted him?" she asked eagerly.

I couldn't bring myself to lie to the poor woman, so I didn't answer the question directly. I continued to skim my fingers along the pipe.

"He came into the hall," I said. "Did he hear a noise? See a flash of light? Why was he on this floor at all?" I asked Lady Fontaine in a more normal voice. "Did he use this drawing room?"

"His bedroom and study are the other chambers on this floor," Lady Fontaine answered impatiently. "It was easiest that way, so he didn't have to move up and down more than necessary. There's a cubby behind his study, which the secretary used as his office." Her lips pinched. "I still think the secretary was to blame. He was very charming, but I always thought there was something furtive about him."

I was certain Daniel would find that interesting.

I resumed my observations. "His attention was caught somehow, and he entered the hallway. Or he simply wanted to look out of a window. He could take himself about if he wished?"

"Oh, yes," Lady Fontaine answered. "His chair is wicker, with cushions, so he could be comfortable. Edwin could move the wheels easily by himself, though Fagan usually insisted he do the pushing." Her eyes filled again. "I can't bear to look at the thing, waiting in the corner of his study. I will have to burn it, to purge myself of the memories."

I did not tell her that she could donate it to a hospital or other home for invalids instead, so another could get some use out of it. I reminded myself that if she wanted to make a pyre to her brother, it was her business, no matter how much I disapproved.

"He moved to the top of the stairs," I said. "Something he saw out of that window frightened him, or angered him. He stood up . . . and fell."

I closed my mouth, and Lady Fontaine regarded me limply, the tears trickling to her cheeks.

"Poor Edwin."

"Can you think of anything that would upset him so?" I asked.

Lady Fontaine shook her head. "I can't imagine what. Perhaps a burglar, coming for the house. But there are usually grooms or stable lads in the back, at all hours. They'd stop a burglar, surely."

Or Lord Peyton saw someone else. Someone he didn't expect, or maybe someone he *did* expect, and feared. Perhaps he'd ordered the curtains to remain open so he could watch for that person.

Why then, would he have sent Fagan to bed, instead of having him stand guard? Unless he hadn't wanted Fagan to know whom he looked out for.

I released a breath and removed my hands from the pipe. "That is all, I am afraid. But your brother loved you very much, and misses you," I added quickly as Lady Fontaine eyed me morosely. "He said to tell you that." That sort of small falsehood I could bear, because it was probably true. Lord Peyton would have found ways to keep Lady Fontaine from his house if he hadn't cared for her.

Lady Fontaine relaxed. "Dear Edwin. He always looked after me."

Hannah, who'd barely moved for the entire conversation, rose to her feet. "Her ladyship should rest now. Thank you for coming, Mrs. Crowe."

Lady Fontaine put a fluttering hand to her chest. "Yes, yes, I need to lie down. See our guest out, Marjory, and then help me to my chamber."

Hannah gestured me coolly to the door. I sent Lady Fontaine an encouraging smile as I rose and compliantly exited the room.

I glanced at the closed doors which I guessed hid Lord Peyton's study and bedroom, but Hannah guided me inexorably down the stairs, a maid who wanted an unnerving guest to cease upsetting her mistress.

When we reached the ground floor, which was deserted, Hannah abruptly seized my elbow and steered me into the reception room.

"Stay here until I tuck the old dear into her bed," she whispered to me. "Her chamber's up on the fourth floor, so she'll be well out of the way. I'll fetch you, and you can have a rummage round."

"What about the housekeeper and other maids?" I asked with uneasiness. "And Fagan?"

"I'll keep 'em out of the way." Hannah gave me her impish smile. "Here's your ten guineas." She handed me a thick envelope that a peek showed me contained a wad of one-pound notes. "I collected the fee for you beforehand, so she couldn't change her mind." She winked. "A good day's graft, innit?"

I spent the time waiting for Hannah's return studying the landscape paintings I'd noted before. One portrayed a lavish country house built in a square, classical style with many columns and porticoes. Meadows dotted with flowers surrounded it, and wooded hills became misty blue in the background.

A closer look showed me tiny figures in the meadow, possibly a young Edwin and his sister, though I couldn't be certain when this picture had been painted. A man with a shotgun blasted away in the distance, which was ridiculous. The scene was of spring or early summer, and one didn't shoot grouse and other birds until autumn. I suppose the painter was trying for an ideal picture of the house, presumably Viscount Peyton's country estate.

Hannah returned before I'd had the chance to examine more than the one painting. She put her finger to her lips and guided me out.

We went quietly back up the stairs to the floor where we'd met with Lady Fontaine. I feared we'd encounter the housekeeper or Fagan shuffling about, but we saw no one. I was prepared to make an excuse that I'd left my handbag behind or perhaps had another message from Lord Fontaine, but it proved to be unnecessary.

Hannah deftly unlocked the first door from the staircase and opened it noiselessly. I couldn't see if she had keys or had picked the lock.

Once we were inside, Hannah closed the door behind us.

"What are we looking for?" she asked.

"I wish I knew." I stood in the middle of the neat room, surveying its entirety. "Anything that tells us who killed Lord Peyton, or anything tying him or anyone in the house with either the blackmail letters or Fenians."

Hannah's eyes widened. "Fenians?" her whisper held alarm. "You threw me among *them*, did you?"

"I'm sorry I couldn't tell you before. I was sworn to secrecy."

Hannah regarded me in disquiet, then she blew out a breath. "Don't matter. If I see a man who might be laying a bomb, I'll hit him with a brick and drag him off to the police. Don't like that it's not safe to walk in the streets without worrying about being blown to bits." She shivered. "D'ye think Fagan is one of 'em? I can see him blowing things up and feeling justified."

"I once thought so, but I'm not certain now that I've met him," I confessed. "He is very upset about Lord Peyton's death."

"That don't mean he ain't a mad anarchist. He'd a done anything for Lord Peyton, including plant dynamite in train stations."

"In any case, we'd need to find proof that Lord Peyton asked him to do it." I paused as we surveyed the large and rather cluttered chamber. "Why were the draperies open?" I asked.

Hannah blinked. "Eh? What draperies?"

"The window curtains on the landing. Whenever I've seen

this house, the drapes have always been drawn in the back. Now they're wide open." I gestured to the drapes in this room that had been pulled back from the window, which also looked out into the mews. "Why were they open that night?"

Hannah regarded the curtains in bewilderment. "I don't know, but now that I'm thinking it through, you're right. Lord Peyton liked everything closed up tight. After he died, Mrs. Proctor had me open all the drapes in the upstairs rooms, saying they needed light and air." She thought a moment. "The ones on the landing was the only ones open when Fagan found the viscount, and we all came rushing downstairs. I don't know why. I'll ask Mrs. Proctor if she knows."

"Thank you. That will be a help."

We fell silent and searched. Lord Peyton's wheeled chair stood in the corner, as Lady Fontaine had indicated. Made of wicker, it had a deep cushion on the seat and a smaller one for Lord Peyton's back. Blankets that must have warmed his legs had been neatly folded on the seat.

Hannah and I thoroughly looked through the desk, shelves, and tables, finding nothing but innocuous books and letters. Hannah knew how to locate secret drawers or nooks in the furniture, including chairs and the sofa, that might contain valuables and other things worth stealing. Between us, we had every possible hiding place opened and explored.

We moved to Lord Fontaine's bedchamber, reached by a connecting door. It had fewer furnishings, but we searched those too, and Hannah slid under the bed to look for things tucked beneath the mattress.

After a half hour of this, we'd turned up no stacks of blackmail letters or envelopes addressed to the victims, nor any damning plans of how anarchists or the Fenians would terrorize London until their demands were met.

Nothing in the study or bedchamber hinted that Lord Peyton was anything other than a formerly fit man who did little more now than read books, debate current politics with his friends, tolerate his sister for their childhood's sake, and once in a while suck on a pipe he could no longer smoke.

"Well, I don't know what they were talking about in here so furtively," Hannah said when we returned, disgruntled, to the study. "I could swear they were planning something sinister, and your man, Daniel, was certain of it too."

Daniel could not have been wrong. Likewise Hannah had much experience with crime and would have recognized the signs of a conspiracy.

Lord Peyton had been in on a plot, I was certain, but what plot, we couldn't say. I was equally certain that both Lord Peyton and his former secretary had been killed for it.

We could remain no longer. Hannah had warned the other servants to stay below stairs and make no noise to disturb Lady Fontaine, but at some point, they'd have to continue their duties on the main floors. The more I lingered, the less plausible my explanation would be for doing so.

As I began to follow Hannah out of the study, my eye fell once more on the wheeled chair.

Hannah turned back when I paused, giving me an anxious gesture to come away. I ignored her and approached the chair, fixing it with my gaze as though commanding it not to move.

I lifted the folded blankets that reposed on the chair and handed them to Hannah, who'd joined me. She took them, mystified, while I pried the cushion from the seat.

There was nothing beneath it. I probed the wicker, thrusting my hands down the sides of the chair to seek anything tucked there, but I found nothing but bits of broken-off wicker.

As I turned the cushion over, my fingers brushed something

beneath the velvet that rustled. Quickly I examined the cushion's edges and found tiny hooks that secured the fabric together.

With Hannah's breath on my neck, I undid the hooks and pulled out what had caught my attention.

It was a paper, thick and worn, that had been much folded into a two-by-two-foot square. I handed Hannah the cushion and carried the paper to the desk and spread it open.

It was a map, or rather, several maps drawn on one page. The most prominent and largest was of London, from Kensington in the west to Stepney in the east, from Hampstead Heath north to Lambeth south.

Small X's lay here and there, some larger than others. A few were underlined, and two had question marks next to them.

An X at what I knew to be Victoria Station, a few streets south of Buckingham Palace, had *Feb* written beside it. Marks next to the Westminster Bridge Underground station and also Paddington station were labeled *Oct*. Other X's were designated *Mar* and *May*.

The May X's had the number *30* next to them as well. Those lay in Pall Mall and Trafalgar Square, and also in Whitehall, right next to the buildings of Scotland Yard.

Last October, the Westminster and Paddington Underground stations had been rocked by explosions. This past February, one had gone off inside Victoria Station.

I did not recall any incendiaries detonated last May. My breath came faster.

If the May dates were in the future, then Scotland Yard and a building in Pall Mall were due to see explosions on the 30th of this month.

Tomorrow, in fact.

24

We stared at the map with its damning markings in shock.

Small wonder that neither Daniel nor Hannah had been able to find it. Lord Peyton had been literally sitting on the evidence of the Fenian connection. When he retired for the night, the chair would have been right next to his bed. I wagered even Lord Peyton's coconspirators hadn't known where he kept the map.

But Fagan would have.

"I must go," I said hastily. "So should you. Give your notice, or simply disappear, but please go home and take care of Adam—I mean, Sean."

Hannah shook her head. "I don't like to, not yet. Lady Fontaine's a daft old bag, but she don't need everyone deserting her now."

"Now who is being astonishingly kind?" I demanded. "It won't be safe for you here—or for her either."

Hannah regarded me stubbornly. "But his lordship's gone now, ain't he? His friends haven't darkened the door since he pegged it. Even his doctor looked his lordship over, pronounced him dead, and couldn't run off fast enough. I reckon the Fenians are done with this place."

"There's Fagan," I pointed out. "He won't be happy when he finds this map gone."

"You're taking it, then?" Hannah asked. "Why not call the police back in to discover it for themselves?"

"They didn't find it the first time they searched the house, did they? Besides, Fagan could move it by then. He had to know where his master hid it."

"You have a point," she conceded.

"If you wish to look after Lady Fontaine, then take her to a hotel or a lodging house," I urged her. "They can be paid from Lord Peyton's estate."

"I can't take her to no hotel, Katie. She'll get us slung out for stealing all the candlesticks and whatnot. At least here, whatever she takes stays inside the house. Don't worry about Fagan. I can handle him."

I wasn't certain she could, but I admitted that Hannah was smart and resourceful. Hopefully she wouldn't have to worry about him at all, once Scotland Yard had this map.

"If anything untoward happens," I said emphatically, "anything at all, even if you're not frightened, you send for me."

"I will," Hannah said. She was the sort who'd try to face down any peril on her own, and I prayed she'd heed me.

I gave her an impulsive hug. "Thank you," I said. "For everything."

"You knew I couldn't resist an adventure." Hannah squeezed me back, then helped me stuff the map into my small handbag. "Off you go then, Katie, love."

We'd put the rooms to rights when we'd finished searching, and it appeared as though no one had disturbed them. I left Hannah fastening the cushion together again and restoring the blankets to the wheeled chair.

I pattered down the staircase as quietly as I could, my heart pounding, the map feeling like a stone in my bag. At any moment, I expected Fagan to jump out at me, seize me, and find the purloined map. What he'd do then, I shuddered to think.

The staircase and ground floor hall remained empty, however, the servants seemingly obeying Hannah's stricture to not awaken Lady Fontaine. They were no doubt happy to leave the fussy woman in Hannah's capable hands.

I didn't breathe easily until I sped out the front door and carefully closed it behind me.

Belgrave Square appeared refreshingly normal, with a pair of ladies strolling arm in arm toward the park in its middle, maids hastening after them with blankets and baskets. Carts and delivery wagons rolled along the main streets, the business of London continuing.

A carriage pulled up in front of the house next door, disgorging a small man with a bushy beard and sharp face beneath a tall hat. He didn't glance at me as I lingered by the railings to stare, but an unremarkable working-class woman in an unremarkable gown was unlikely to draw his attention.

He growled something at the footman who'd opened the carriage door for him, then clumped past him and into the house.

I recognized the groom who'd appeared to take hold of the horses while the man descended. The coachman drove the carriage on and around the corner toward the mews, with the groom ambling behind it.

I fell into step with the groom. "Is that Lord Downes?" I asked him.

The groom blinked at me in recognition, then back at the house as we rounded the corner. "Aye, that's 'im."

I said nothing more until the carriage was rattling into the mews. I stopped the groom following it with the touch of my hand.

"The night Lord Peyton died," I asked him. "Did anything happen outside in the mews that Lord Peyton might have seen? That might have frightened him?"

The groom looked surprised. "Can't think of anything. It were an ordinary night—we were looking after the horses and cleaning harness. Lord Downes likes every buckle to shine. At least, head groom says that. I think Lord Downes just likes to squeeze as much work out of us as he can." He grimaced.

"Shouldn't be much longer," I told him. Once the police were finished and Lady Fontaine moved on to whatever house she'd stay in next, the groom could go home.

He shrugged. "I don't mind. I like the beasts."

"Lady Fontaine seems a bit smitten with Lord Downes," I remarked.

The groom's lips twitched. "She is that. Buttonholes him anytime she sees him coming out of his house. Morning, evening, and night."

"Is he as taken with her?" If Lord Downes felt enough for Lady Fontaine to marry her, she'd not have to worry about whether her brother's heir would support her.

"Not certain he is, no. But he's kind, I suppose, to listen to her natter on. She can certainly talk, can Lady Fontaine. Delays him for long stretches, but he don't run her off."

"Very gentlemanly of him," I said.

"Aye, Downes ain't a bad sort. Apart from being a stickler about his harness." The groom went thoughtful. "Lord Downes *was* marching about with his shotgun the night Lord Peyton died. Might have put the wind up Lord Peyton, though I don't know why it would."

"Shotgun?" I repeated in alarm.

"Aye, the old duffer likes to walk about with it draped over his arm. Lord Downes is a great one for shooting in the country, or so he tells us. Over and over again, about how much game he's shot. Never goes to the country—stays in London most of the time. He don't load the gun neither. Just wanders about with it. Reliving the old days, most like."

I recalled the painting of the country house in the reception room, with the man firing off his shotgun in the background, the two children in the meadow in front. Lady Fontaine had said admiringly how fit Lord Downes had been in his youth, implying they'd all been acquaintances then, as well.

I wondered if the painting had depicted Lord Downes, though the figure could simply have been the Peyton family's steward, not an old friend. I had no way of knowing which without quizzing Lady Fontaine again.

"Does Lord Downes wander about with the shotgun most nights?" I asked.

The groom nodded. "Lord Peyton would have seen him many a time. So I can't think why that frightened him."

I agreed. But *something* had . . .

I might suspect the affable groom himself if Mr. Fielding hadn't vouched for him. Mr. Fielding was careful, more than most people would be, so he likely was trustworthy.

I thanked him and took my leave. The groom touched his cap, and I sped on down the road, keeping a lookout behind me all the way.

At the next hansom stand I encountered, I climbed into a cab and instructed the driver to take me to Scotland Yard.

* * *

I kept my hands over my bag as the hansom bumped across the metropolis, certain every villain knew what I had. I half expected one to grab the horse and stop the cab, dragging me out and tearing my bag from me.

Nothing so dramatic happened. When I reached Scotland Yard, I handed the cabbie coins for the fare, clutched my handbag to my chest, and hurried into the building that housed the CID.

Inspector McGregor was busy. At least, I heard him rumbling at somebody behind his closed door. That opened as I approached it, and the detective called Sergeant Scott emerged.

Sergeant Scott was a slender man in his thirties, with pale hair pomaded flat and light blue eyes. I'd first encountered him late last year, when he'd been investigating a fraud, and I'd learned he had sharp intelligence and dogged resolve.

Sergeant Scott did not greet me, only skewered me with a cool gaze.

"Who is it?" Inspector McGregor called irritably.

I ducked past Sergeant Scott and into the office. Though I'd come to trust Scott, I didn't know him well, and I wanted to hand the map only to Inspector McGregor.

Inspector McGregor regarded me with his usual impatience. "I thought I told you to stay home."

"You did. But I could not remain idle when I found evidence of a plot to set off bombs all over London tomorrow."

I set the map on McGregor's desk with a flourish.

I admit I enjoyed the drama of my move, but Inspector McGregor remained unimpressed. "How could you have possibly found . . . ?"

He trailed off as he unfolded the map and gazed at it, becoming still. Sergeant Scott pushed his way around me and peered at it over the inspector's shoulder.

"The X's are places where explosions have occurred or will occur." I poked a gloved finger at Victoria Station, then moved to the Underground stations and Whitehall. "These have already been done, as you know. But *these*." I pointed to the square that represented Scotland Yard. "I believe this hasn't happened yet."

Inspector McGregor gaped at the map and then at me. "Where the devil did you come by this?"

"The home of Lord Peyton," I answered serenely. "It was hidden inside the cushion of his wheeled chair."

Inspector McGregor's face went nearly purple. Sergeant Scott remained impassive but watched me closely.

"Parker!" Inspector McGregor bellowed past me into the outer office. "Take some constables and get around to Lord Peyton's in Belgrave Square. Find that manservant, Fagan, and bring him in. Take firearms—he's got form."

"Yes, sir," Sergeant Parker said smartly, and gave orders to others in the office.

McGregor snapped his attention to Sergeant Scott. "Those Lofthouse people, were they detained in Dover?"

"They were, sir," Sergeant Scott answered. "But as they'd committed no obvious crime, they have consulted solicitors and are talking about bringing suit against the police."

McGregor sprang to his feet. "Wire the Dover constabulary and have the Lofthouses arrested for conspiracy to commit a felony and transferred here to me. And bring in any of the others Lord Peyton met with." As Inspector McGregor started around the desk, his gaze fell on me, as though he'd forgotten my presence. "Where's McAdam?" he demanded of me.

"I haven't seen him since Monday evening," I said truthfully.

"Get him in here," he told Sergeant Scott. "And *you.*" Inspector McGregor pointed a thick finger at me. "Take yourself home, *stay there,* and cease interfering in police business."

I regarded him without alarm. "You're welcome, Inspector."

Inspector McGregor growled something ungentlemanly at me, and I decided the best thing to do was to scuttle past him and out of his office.

Once outside in the courtyard, I drew a breath, and then coughed. Someone was burning paper or some such nearby, and smoke coated the air.

I went around the corner of the brick building and nearly ran straight into Daniel.

He steadied me as I rocked on my feet, hands planted on my shoulders. "Sergeant Parker tells me you solved the case." Daniel gazed at me with a mixture of exasperation and admiration. "That Lord Peyton's cronies are being rounded up as we speak."

Daniel's touch helped my usual composure return. "I would not say I solved anything. The situation is much more complicated, I am certain. I simply found something in Lord Peyton's house that was overlooked. Even by you," I could not resist adding.

Daniel's eyes narrowed. "Found it *where?*"

"In the cushion of his wheeled chair. You'd never have got past Fagan to search it, so do not blame yourself."

"No, I mean . . ." Daniel took a deep breath. "What were you doing in Peyton's house at all?"

"I was holding a séance to speak to the spirit of the departed Lord Peyton," I said. "Though it wasn't much of a séance—no candles or knocking or anything of that nature."

"You were holding a séance." The words were quiet and careful.

"Yes, at Lady Fontaine's invitation. Hannah recommended me."

Daniel released me to put both hands to his forehead and draw them down his face.

"You were—" He broke off. "Kat Holloway, you'll be the death of me."

"It was a good job I did go, or we'd not have warning of explosions planned for tomorrow. When Inspector McGregor questions Fagan, have him ask what Lord Peyton could have seen out his window on Sunday night that frightened him so much. I doubt that his neighbor with an unloaded shotgun could burn fear through him, so there must have been something else."

Daniel regarded me, dumbfounded. "What am I to do with you, Kat?"

"Never mind about me. Make certain Inspector McGregor asks the question."

Daniel pulled off his cap, crumpled it in his hand, then smoothed it out and returned it to his head. I could not express how much happiness filled me watching him do such ordinary things.

"Monaghan might intercept the lot of them and lock them in a deep cellar," Daniel warned. "Preventing McGregor questioning them at all. I'll do my best to prevent that."

"I don't believe Fagan is guilty of anything but devotion to his master," I said. "Even if he was a villain in the past."

"You might be right, but Fagan's head could hold all sorts of useful things." Daniel peered at me. "Why are you so taken with him, if you only met him today? I assume you only met him today," he finished darkly.

"Because he wept with genuine sorrow." I recalled how the big man had shuddered with sobs. "Not remorse or guilt, but true grief. I think he loved Lord Peyton, or at least felt immense gratitude toward him. Yes, I met Fagan for the first time today, but one can tell much by how another reacts to a loss."

"I suppose," Daniel said dubiously. "Very well, I'll be gentle with him, if he lets us."

"Lady Fontaine cried as well," I continued, "but more for nostalgia of the old days, I think, plus worry for what's to become of her. In my opinion, someone should be sent to talk to her and let her natter, as Mr. Fielding's man said she likes to do. Lady Fontaine could be a mine of information, even if she is not aware of the fact."

Daniel's eyes began to twinkle. "Can you wait while I fetch a large sheet of paper and write all this down?"

"Don't be daft. Now, please tell Inspector McGregor I will toddle home as he bade, after I finish my day out with Grace. I'll not keep myself from her any longer. Now that the police are forewarned, they can keep a lookout."

I half expected Daniel to continue expressing his exasperation with me, but instead he seized me and crushed me into an embrace.

The scents of warm wool and Daniel filled me, making me want to be nowhere but here, even if the yard was smoky and constables milled around us.

"It was well done," he whispered into my ear. "You will confound the lot of them."

I wasn't certain whether he meant the Fenians or the police, but I returned his hug with a tight one of my own.

"Take care, my dearest friend," I said. "I couldn't bear it if you came to harm."

We held each other for another moment, then Daniel released me with every show of reluctance. He brushed gloved fingers along my cheek.

"Go on to Grace," he said. "I'll come to you when I can."

"And you will tell me *everything*," I said emphatically. "Leaving out no detail."

"As though you'd let me." Daniel bathed me in his warm smile. "A candlelit evening with Kat Holloway. My greatest pleasure."

My face warmed. "With the best of my scones, you mean. Or cakes, or tarts. You will have to wait and see which one it is."

"I look forward to it, my dear Mrs. Holloway."

"It will be my pleasure, Mr. McAdam."

I started off to Cheapside to finish what was left of the afternoon with Grace. There was not a hansom to be had at this busy time of day, so I strode along the Strand, anticipation propelling my steps.

Not until I crossed Farringdon Street and entered Ludgate Hill did I realize my danger. As I passed a narrow lane, hands seized me and two men half dragged, half shoved me from the main street into a tiny passageway filled with shadow.

They tore my handbag from my arm and thrust me face-first into a brick wall.

25

I struggled mightily, but to no avail. My captors were large men in homespun breeches and woolen jackets such as Daniel wore. The faces I'd glimpsed were clean-shaven, and their lack of odor told me they regularly saw a bath, but I knew at once these were hard men who would have little mercy with me.

The feeble contents of my handbag clattered to the worn cobblestones. One lout pawed through them while the other held me in an iron grip. I could not move even to strike out or attempt a kick.

The man going through my things abruptly swept them aside in disgust. The one who held me dug my face harder into the wall.

"Where is it?" he barked.

I gulped for air. "What?"

"Whatever you took from that scum Peyton's." His accent

was nondescript, as though he'd practiced to sound neutral, as I had when I'd gone into service.

"The police have anything important." There was no use in lying. They'd beat the truth out of me if I tried to put them off.

"The police and their rotten spies are done for," the man who'd rifled through my bag vowed. He gave my things another kick, sending my pencil and notebook slamming into the wall beside me.

I prayed he did not take the notebook, where I'd listed so many details about this case. Either he wasn't able to read what I'd written when he'd opened it or else he thought a cook's scribblings were unimportant.

They could have released me and run off once they knew I had nothing they needed, but the first man kept a clamped hold of my neck.

"We'll show 'em what we think of spies." He shook me, and I cried out in pain.

He and his friend were prepared to kill me, and I knew it. Whether they'd leave my body here or throw it into the Thames, I couldn't guess, but there was no doubt they had murder on their minds.

The Thames was the most likely, I reasoned. Surely these were the men who'd disposed of poor Mr. Howard, leaving the post open for Daniel at Lord Peyton's.

"Why did you kill the secretary?" I asked them. If they were going to murder me, I might as well find out what I could. "Did you think he was a spy?"

"Orders, weren't it?" the man who held me said chillingly. "He were even easier to catch than you."

"Stop talking to her," the second man said. "Get on with it."

Pleading for my life would not work, I knew. I could weep

that I had a child I would leave alone and destitute, but to my last breath I would not give these men Grace's name.

If they'd been following me, they'd already know about her, but somehow, I thought these were not the same watchers I'd been evading in the past weeks. I'd not sensed them, meaning they were professionals, plus they hadn't hesitated to grab me off a crowded street.

I love you, Grace, was all I could think. *And you Daniel, my heart-mate.*

I continued to struggle, because I would not tamely let them cut me down, but both men had immense strength.

Pounding footsteps sounded behind us, and I heard a grunt as the man who'd gone through my things suddenly folded over onto himself. I felt a hot pain as a knife scored my neck, and then my captor was ripped from me, a massive fist crashing into his face.

"Knife," I called in warning, but Mr. Grimes already had it twisted out of his opponent's hand.

Three more ruffians about Mr. Grimes's size had sailed in with fists and clubs, and they began to beat my captors remorselessly.

The men who'd nabbed me cursed and groaned as they fought, but they were outnumbered and couldn't withstand the assault. I might feel sorry for them if they hadn't been about to cut my throat.

A small hand gripped mine, and I looked down to see Albie, my loyal lad. "This way, missus."

"Help me with my things." I bent down and started to scrabble for my coins, notebook, and pencil.

Albie studied me in disbelief, then he got down on his small knees and grabbed my belongings, stuffing them back into the bag.

I didn't have so much in my life that I could afford to lose the bits and pieces I carried with me. Besides, Joanna had given me that notebook.

Once I had everything, I let Albie tow me back to Ludgate Hill.

Mr. Grimes joined us after a moment. From the sound of it, his friends were giving the assassins a thorough going-over. Two more men jogged past us, Mr. Grimes nodding at them to join the fray.

Mr. Grimes looked none the worse for wear, with only a small bruise on his cheekbone to show for the battle.

"Let's get you indoors, Mrs. H.," he said. "Home is best, I think."

I nodded shakily. As much as I wanted to rush to Grace and hold her tightly, I did not want to risk leading any other toughs waiting for me directly to her. I would forego my need to be with her to keep her safe.

"Please keep watch on Joanna's house," I begged him. "In case they send others to Grace."

"My men are already there," Mr. Grimes assured me. "No one's going near that house or your daughter."

"These men deal in explosives." Panic was overtaking me. "They can set up their dynamite and flee."

Mr. Grimes shook his head. "They won't get close to the road, even. We don't feel sorry for those who hurt and murder others only to gain attention. Cowards."

I'd glimpsed his colleagues beating the lives out of the men who'd assailed me. While I did not condone such savagery, at the moment, I could only be grateful to them.

Mr. Grimes hailed a hansom, which came to us without hesitation. Daniel and Lewis must have recruited every cabbie in London to speed to my aid.

Mr. Grimes not only handed me in, my legs still wobbling, but he climbed in beside me. Albie touched his hat and ran off before I could ask him why he'd left Belgrave Square, and the cab lurched forward.

"Thank you for your timely rescue." I tried to sound normal, but my words wheezed, and I had difficulty catching my breath.

"The boy Albie followed you from Belgravia," Mr. Grimes said. "He saw those villains tailing you and had one of my lads alert me. Albie thought you'd be all right once you were at Scotland Yard, but he said they were still lurking. I'm sorry I didn't get to you sooner," he finished morosely, his gaze despondent.

"You were soon enough." I'd known in those seconds before he reached me that I was going to die.

It had been unreal, as though another woman had been standing in my place, waiting for the end. I couldn't quite grasp that they'd been about to kill me without contrition, but at the same time, I'd known it with all my heart.

Sitting in a hansom now instead of being dead in the lane was almost as unreal.

"You're all right, Mrs. H." Mr. Grimes clasped my shaking hands, his voice kindly. "Remind yourself of that. You're breathing air, with your feet on the ground. Or at least in a hansom."

The cab jolted over a hole, jarring us and reminding me that I could still feel.

I took a long breath, then another one. Mr. Grimes held my hands the entire time, watching me encouragingly. In his violent life, he must have made this speech many times, comforting those in his gang who'd escaped a dire fate.

When I could breathe somewhat normally again, I squeezed his large fingers. "Thank you. You are a good friend."

"As you are to me." Mr. Grimes smiled at me, his words ringing with sincerity. "Better now?"

"I think so."

"Don't worry if you ain't happy for a while. It was a close-run thing. Just keep on with what you do, and don't let what they almost did stop you from living."

I suddenly wished I'd had this giant of a man to pat my hand when my husband had disappeared, leaving me with a baby on the way and nowhere to turn. Of course, I'd likely have been terrified of Mr. Grimes—I'd been much unnerved the first time I'd seen him, before I'd known his true character.

The baby I'd feared for all those years ago was alive and well and being looked after by the best friends on earth.

I huddled in the cab all the way back to Mount Street, feeling rather sick. Mr. Grimes noticed and passed me a flask, wiping the mouth of it with a handkerchief first.

I was not one for spirits, but I readily downed a few swallows of the fiery liquid inside. Not gin—Mr. Grimes didn't have the half-drunken, red-eyed look of one taken with gin. Whiskey, and not a bad one. I used whiskey in some of my apple dishes and had to have a nip of it now and again to make certain it had the flavor I needed.

I thanked Mr. Grimes and handed him back the flask. He wiped it again and took a long drink himself.

I insisted the cab let me off in South Audley Street. I did not need to be lectured by Mrs. Bywater about getting above myself swanning about in cabs. Not today.

Mr. Grimes helped me down. He forestalled me rummaging in my handbag for shillings by telling me he'd already paid the fare.

I clung to him a moment, trying to get my feet back underneath me. He was a rock, this man, kind to me and to Daniel.

Others would consider him a villain, and I'm certain the police would be happy to question him about his past, but I knew few kinder men in the world than he.

"Good night, Mr. Grimes," I said. "And thank you. Turn up any evening, and I'll save the best of what I bake for you."

His grin split his face. "No need, missus. Though them crullers were a treat."

"I'll make a special batch for you. Now, please make certain Daniel doesn't fall prey to these people. I'm certain they know he was in Lord Peyton's house to discover their plans."

"You leave it with me." Mr. Grimes pressed my hands again, then released me. "You've no cause to worry with me and me mates looking after you."

I thanked him one more time—the words would not cease coming out of my mouth—and made myself stride purposefully toward Mount Street, wiping blood and dirt from my face with my handkerchief. Mr. Grimes rather ruined my quiet exit by waving and bellowing a good-bye to me.

The ordinariness of my kitchen closed around me like a warm blanket as soon as I entered it.

Elsie sang as she scrubbed pots, the sleeves of her work dress rolled to her elbows. Tess was lecturing a footman who presumably had come in to pinch a tidbit from the work table. Tess waved her chopping knife in emphasis, to the footman's alarm.

Mr. Davis and Mrs. Redfern were having a loud discussion about linens in the passageway between kitchen and butler's pantry. Pots burbled on the stove, and the scents of broth, roasting meat, and baking rolls wafted to me.

I let out a long breath of relief as I hung up my jacket and hat.

Tess caught sight of me and beamed me her usual grin. The footman, startled by my sudden presence, scuttled away.

"Cheeky lad," Tess said to the footman's retreating back. "Had a nice day out, Mrs. H.? How's that sweet Grace?"

I sank down into a chair, uncertain that this afternoon I'd actually performed a false séance, searched Lord Peyton's house, taken the map I'd found to Scotland Yard, and then been attacked and nearly killed in a street I'd walked along for most of my life.

"It was fine," I forced myself to say. "But I wouldn't mind a cup of tea. A strong one, if you'd be so kind."

I f I'd been the lady of the house, I'd have gone straight to bed with plenty of scalding tea laced with brandy and a hot brick to warm my feet. I'd have remained there as long as I liked, being waited on by anxious servants, not rising until my trembling ceased.

As it was, I had to get on with finishing supper for the By-waters. A domestic in a large house was not allowed to let anything, even nearly being murdered in a back lane, prevent her from finishing her duties.

I did not fancy going to bed anyway. I'd only lie awake, hearing the man's snarling voice and feeling his hot breath on my neck, followed by the cold touch of a knife.

The blade hadn't drawn blood, I saw when I changed my frock. Mr. Grimes had reached me quickly enough. I had a faint mark on the side of my throat, along with bruises on my neck from where the wretch had held me against the wall. My left cheek was scratched, but when I washed what little brick dust I hadn't wiped away already, the scratches scarcely showed.

I'd come out of the affair with few injuries, thanks to great good luck and Mr. Grimes's rescue.

I returned to the kitchen. Tess barely glanced up at me, so hard-pressed was she to have the vegetable dishes finished in time.

I took up a knife and helped her, noting that my hands stopped shaking once they were busy doing what they knew best. I let myself work, the routine consoling me, as did the satisfaction of turning out a dish well done.

We cleaned up after supper was finished and had gone upstairs, Tess and I partaking of a bit of the roast and fresh string beans she'd prepared.

She'd braised the beans then dressed them with a bit of butter and parsley, with a snipping of chives to finish off. All her own idea, Tess said with a mixture of pride and apprehension. I praised her for keeping the dish simple yet delicious, and she flushed with pleasure.

I sent Tess to bed soon after that, as usual on my days out, as she'd carried the burden of the workday by herself.

Once the rest of the staff retired, I turned down the gas and lit my candle, opening my notebook to add to my lists.

My pencil stilled where it touched the page, however, refusing to write. The sound of the villain's voice in my ear came to me as clearly as if he stood over me now, and I gasped, my stomach roiling.

I closed my eyes and drew a long breath, reminding myself what Mr. Grimes had said in the hansom.

You're all right, Mrs. H. Remind yourself of that. You're breathing air, with your feet on the ground.

I inhaled another long breath, trying to quell my rising hysteria. I'm certain I'd have given way to quivering sobs, had not a knock on the back door made my eyes pop open.

Did I freeze in terror, believing more villains had come to

find me? No, I knew exactly who'd come, and I flew across the kitchen and through to the scullery to open the door without hesitation.

Daniel pulled off his cap as he stepped inside, and I plunged straight into his arms.

26

"K at." Daniel's whisper caressed my ear. He held me close, a pillar of warmth in the cool May night. "Kat, my love."

I did not have to explain to him what had happened. He knew. Mr. Grimes or one of his men would have told him.

I didn't realize I was crying until Daniel cupped my face and brushed away my tears with his gloved thumbs.

"I am so sorry." His words were hoarse. "I sent you off because I knew Grimes's and Errol's lads were following you. I never thought they'd grab you like that, in the middle of a crowd."

"They didn't care. These people have no interest in what happens to those who get in their way. I suppose that's why they call them anarchists." I tried to laugh at my little quip and ended up sobbing instead.

Daniel closed the door against the breeze and held me for a while, hands strong on my back.

"I told Monaghan tonight that I was finished with him."

Daniel's abrupt statement made my head pop up, my weeping fade. "What? You can't, love. Not until this case is over. If you try to quit now, he'll stop you and accuse you of all sorts."

"He endangered you." A grim light I'd never seen before entered Daniel's eyes. "I don't mind the assignments he sends me into, but he put *you* in danger, and I can't permit that. Not you, not James, not anyone you or I love."

"Is James all right?" I asked in concern.

"He's in Kensington, sleeping hard." Daniel moved his touch to my shoulders, resting his hands lightly there.

"Thank heavens for that," I said in relief. "I thought he'd try to be in the thick of things."

"Why do you suppose I sent him to do all my deliveries?" A note of amusement entered Daniel's voice. "I told him I couldn't afford to give them up, because I'll need that work afterward. I'm not sure he quite believed me, but at least he's keeping safe."

"Mr. Monaghan didn't actually endanger me, you know," I pointed out. "I did."

Daniel bolted the door before he led me to the kitchen and my table. He fetched the kettle from the stove before I could protest and refilled the teapot I'd prepared, then unhooked a cup from the dresser for himself. I could only sit like a lump and watch him.

Daniel seated himself in his usual place across the corner of the table from me. I was so glad to see him there.

"You would not have inserted yourself into that house if Monaghan hadn't sent me to it," Daniel said. "He could have assigned me to the wilds of Scotland or the far reaches of Prussia, instead of a quarter hour's stroll from where you live. Of course you would go in—and you were very clever to find that map. Inspector McGregor is most impressed with you."

"Kind of him," I said distractedly. "But listen to me, Daniel. You can't walk away from Monaghan. He will not let you."

"I'll continue helping my colleagues prevent the bombings and catch the culprits behind them. I've made it clear I'm not doing it for Monaghan. He has shattered his last tie to me."

"He'll arrest you." My own distress was ebbing to be replaced by worry for Daniel. "Did you not hear me?"

"He won't." Daniel's mouth was a hard line. "McGregor is on my side, as are the few superintendents Monaghan will heed."

While I prayed this was the case, I wasn't as confident as Daniel appeared to be. "All will soon be resolved though, won't it? You have a map of the bombings, past and future, and Scotland Yard has arrested Lord Peyton's colleagues."

"Yes," Daniel said hesitantly.

"They were arrested, were they not?" I asked in surprise. "Inspector McGregor was most adamant they should be."

"They were, indeed. Fagan came in more quietly than anyone imagined. The Lofthouses, especially Mrs. Lofthouse, were far more unruly. McGregor's constables also found the doctor and the Earl of Pelsham, who were both part of the group. The trouble is, none of them seem to be the villains we are looking for. I suspected that already, but it was made clear today."

I sat back in confusion. "None are the villains? Then why did Monaghan have you sitting in Lord Peyton's house all these weeks?"

"Because his information was wrong. Even he admits that, though grudgingly."

"Then what on earth were they doing?" I demanded. "What about the map with the incendiary devices marked on it?"

Daniel lifted the teapot and calmly poured out tea for both of us. "According to the Lofthouses, Lord Peyton was adamantly working to *prevent* the Fenians and other anarchists from wreaking more havoc. He was gathering as much information as he could to rally his friends around London and in the government to act. He had no faith in the police, the Home Office, or the new Special Irish Branch, which he opposed being created."

"What did he suppose his friends could do that the police could not?" I asked in bewilderment.

"Peyton had connections in the highest of places, including Gladstone and ministers close to the queen. I'm not sure what he'd have them do, but I suppose they could even summon the army if they had to."

"Well, he died for trying to take matters into his own hands, didn't he?" I said in both pity and disapprobation. "As did his secretary, Mr. Howard. Did Lord Peyton know *you* were with the police? Is that why he kept you out of the meetings?"

"Kat." Daniel caught my hands to still my flow of questions. "Let us enjoy our tea, and I will tell you everything." He sent me a smile. "A bite of something wouldn't go amiss."

I huffed in feigned exasperation as I threw off his touch. "I ought to have known you came here tonight to satisfy your stomach." I rose as I spoke and hurried down the hall to the larder to fetch what I'd put aside for him. "Tess made an apricot tart," I announced when I returned. "Her baking is coming along well."

I laid the piece of tart, with apricot preserves in a buttery crust and a dollop of cream, in front of Daniel and resumed my seat.

Daniel dug in with pleasure. "Tell her it's the finest apricot tart I've ever eaten," he said after the first bite.

"I will. Now tell me."

Daniel took another bite and sip of tea—to plague me, I suppose—before he spoke.

"Fagan gave us the most information, in the end, though he was the least willing to speak at first. He was devoted to Lord Peyton, grateful to the man for giving him a chance to earn an honest crust when so many wouldn't. Fagan was arrested in the past for brawling, given hard labor for a few years for mangling another fellow, and he had difficulty finding work after that. Lord Peyton needed him, and Fagan appreciated that. Fagan was a go-between among the group, and also a guard, making certain they were undisturbed."

"I don't quite understand all this," I said when Daniel paused to enjoy finishing off the tart. "I thought Lord Peyton was *for* Irish Home Rule."

Daniel nodded as he scraped the plate. "He was. This is quite well done, you know," he said as he set the plate aside. "You are right that Tess is becoming accomplished. Viscount Peyton supporting Irish Home Rule made him unpopular, but rather than being a radical, he was a man of moderation. He did not believe in having Home Rule at any price. He thought there ought to be a separate parliament in Ireland, but one still subject to the British Crown. He was fervently opposed to Fenians, as were all in their group."

"Mrs. Lofthouse is a staunch supporter of the Irish, according to Lady Fontaine," I broke in.

"Mrs. Lofthouse is indeed an agitator. She told us as much. She marches about for the causes dear to her heart, including Irish Home Rule and women's suffrage. But she is quite opposed to the use of violence against innocents to achieve an end. She agreed wholeheartedly with Lord Peyton about that and gave him what support she could. Lord Peyton used her as a source of information on the reformist groups that Fenians try to infiltrate, because she is a member of them all."

"And the others? The doctor and Lord Pelsham?"

"The doctor claimed he was there to make certain Peyton didn't overexcite himself and become ill. Lord Pelsham, of like mind to Viscount Peyton, used his various contacts, including ones in Boston, to gather information on Fenian activities. He provided the intelligence about the bombs scheduled for the thirtieth, and Mrs. Lofthouse confirmed it." Daniel huffed a laugh. "They were all more interested in chastising Inspector McGregor for not preventing the previous bombings than in talking about their meetings. None of them have any trust in the police."

"If Monaghan is an example of who they'd need to trust, I don't blame them," I said. I'd downed my slice of Tess's tart while Daniel spoke and now studied my empty plate, sorry I'd not paid sufficient attention to what I was eating.

"Lord Peyton never allowed me into the meetings, because he couldn't be certain I wasn't a Fenian myself," Daniel said with a wry smile. "I turned up very conveniently after Mr. Howard departed, didn't I? My references were good but from gentlemen out of the country for one reason or another."

"The men who attacked me more or less admitted they killed Mr. Howard." I shuddered, pitying the poor man and knowing that they'd have dispatched me as heartlessly. "Was Mr. Howard in on the group's plots?"

Daniel shook his head. "Fagan was unshakable in his opinion that Mr. Howard knew nothing. They shut him out, as they did me. But no one has tried to grab and interrogate *me*. Perhaps Howard was working for the Fenians himself, and they turned on him."

"One of the fellows who caught me said *Orders, weren't it?*" I warmed my hands on my teacup, trying to still the shaking that threatened to overtake me again. "There is someone pulling the strings for reasons they didn't know or care about. These men weren't Irish though, I don't think."

"Not all the anarchists are," Daniel said. "Ruffians can be hired by anyone, and many don't care who they work for as long as they are paid."

I swallowed a sip of tea. "I hadn't realized such hard men existed."

Daniel shrugged. "I've known they have for years, which is why I wanted to join the police. To stop them."

Daniel's attempt to enter the police hadn't gone well and had led to him being obligated to and working for Mr. Monaghan.

I set down my teacup and reached for Daniel's hand, which rested as a fist on the table. "You were trying to do good."

Daniel met my gaze with a bleak one. "I was also trying to escape my past and at the same time learn more about it. I thought that eventually becoming a detective constable would give me access to knowledge about villains that I could use. I still want the man who ordered the murder of Carter, even after all these years."

Daniel, and Mr. Fielding too, had been taken in by Mr. Carter, a South London villain who'd been kind to them. Both had been very young, and they'd been devastated by Mr. Carter's death.

"You *have* done a lot of good, Daniel," I told him. "In spite of Monaghan's ruthlessness."

"Or because of it." Daniel let out a breath. "Life never follows the paths one expects. But as I said, I'm finished with all that, at least, once we've thwarted the bombers and learn why Lord Peyton died."

"He saw something out the window," I said. "I'm certain of it."

"So you said. I did ask Fagan about it, and he had no idea. He was emphatic that he was nowhere near the man, and neither was anyone else in that household."

I gave Daniel's hand a pat. "You will find out. And when you do, I will arrange a picnic for us, and Grace and James. To celebrate. As a family."

Daniel's eyes flickered when I said the word *family*, but he studied me with amused skepticism. "You sound as though you are going to leave the rest to me."

"I am." I carried the empty plates to the scullery and returned to pour more tea. "I learned my lesson today. I will remain here, cooking and baking, and visit Grace on my days out under the watchful eye of Mr. Grimes and his toughs. I want no more excitement."

Daniel's brows rose. "You mean it."

"I do." I sat down again, lifting my cup. "I came very close to death today. I nearly left Grace alone and unprotected—Sam and Joanna can only do so much. I will not do that to my child. So here I stay."

"Good." The word was soft. Daniel reached across the table and smoothed my hair from my forehead. "When I heard what happened to you, it nearly killed me. I'd been closeted with Peyton's friends and Fagan all day, and only learned of your ordeal when Monaghan finally released me this evening. Grimes found me and told me. That's when I decided I was done."

I turned my head and kissed his wrist. "I am sorry I caused

you such worry." I sent him a smile. "I imagine it is rather like the worry you cause me."

Daniel laughed. "Oh, Mrs. Holloway, you always know how to strike a blow. Let us both give up excitement and live as plain working people, laboring during the day, nodding at each other over apricot tarts at night."

I rested my forehead against his. "I'd like nothing more, Mr. McAdam."

I meant to keep to my word and not stray a step from the house until Monday, when I'd return to Grace. I sent footmen the next day to shop for produce, and though they bought exactly what I told them, they did not know a good specimen of asparagus from a poor one. But I did not scold them, only accepted the vegetables without fuss.

Tess made another apricot tart, showing me how she'd brushed the crust with preserves before layering in the fruit, with another coating of preserves over that. I began another star bread with garlic and fresh herbs, ready for the evening meal.

Friday morning passed quietly. I'd bade Cynthia to stay home and to tell her friends to do likewise, as there would be danger about. I heard no word from Daniel, so I did not know whether the bombs had been found or prevented. I had to tell Cynthia all, which took some time, the two of us shut in the housekeeper's parlor for a long while after breakfast.

She was alarmed enough to send notes to Miss Townsend and other friends, and to stress that I should remain indoors as well.

Which I planned to do. Mrs. Bywater would host a large gathering of her charity group on Sunday, and I decided to do a fine tray for it, giving the guests a choice of plain, lemon-scented, and currant scones. Tess and I would make mini apricot tarts and add those to the selection of petits fours.

I had every intention of adhering to my vow to remain home and out of harm's way, until Adam turned up Friday afternoon, fear in his eyes.

"Something's amiss with me mum," he said when I answered the door. "Will you come, missus? I'm that worried."

27

Adam's plea alarmed me greatly, but I did not let myself simply race away after him. I went up to the street and signaled for my lads, then I made many preparations.

Only after that did I leave off my cap and apron, fetch my coat, and follow Adam, who was unashamedly terrified. I tried to make him explain clearly what had happened, but he only danced with impatience and raced off along Mount Street toward Park Lane.

When we reached Piccadilly, we turned west to Knightsbridge and south into Belgravia. We arrived in Belgrave Square to find that every front window in Viscount Peyton's house was muffled, the knocker removed from the front door. All signs told us the house was deserted.

We made our way around to the back, entering an unnaturally quiet mews. No grooms moved about tending horses or repairing coaches or harnesses. Mr. Fielding's man was nowhere in sight, and I wondered if Mr. Fielding had pulled him from his watch, assuming the danger was done.

The entire lane was eerily silent, the windows of Lord Peyton's house once again blocked by heavy draperies. At the far end of the mews, where it dead-ended against homes in Upper Belgrave Street beyond, a man and dog sauntered into one of the carriage houses and vanished. No one else was there.

Adam and I ventured to the narrow, protected passageway that took us to the back door of number 38. The solid door rang with my knock, but as the seconds ticked by, no one answered.

"She might not be here," Adam said worriedly.

I arrested my balled hand in the act of knocking again. "Then where? Did she accompany Lady Fontaine to wherever she is staying next?"

Adam shook his head. "When I came this morning, Mum was in front, arguing with the lady about something, and Mum shooed me away. When I came back later, this house was shut up, and no one would answer, no matter how much I banged."

I listened in disquiet, then left the passageway for the mews again. There I studied the back walls of both Lord Peyton's house and the one next door, where Lord Downes lived.

His house also contained a shielded passageway, which I plunged down without hesitation, pounding on the door at the end of it.

We waited a long time. I was beginning to believe this house deserted too, when the door was pulled open and a sullen kitchen maid looked out. Her sand-colored hair under its cap was wildly curly and also a bit greasy.

"What?" she asked without much interest.

"Is Lady Fontaine here?" I asked. "Come to visit, perhaps with her maid?"

The maid shrugged. "Dunno, do I?"

"Ask your housekeeper," I commanded. "Or a footman. It's important."

"They ain't here," the kitchen maid announced.

She started to shut the door, but I put my foot into it. "What do you mean, they aren't here? Where are they?"

"Well, I don't know." The maid regarded me with scorn from tired brown eyes. "The master sent them off. Cook said I had to stay and finish scrubbing the pots, which I am. Then I'm going."

I went cold. "Why did your master send everyone away?"

The maid scowled at my persistence. "He wouldn't be telling the likes of me, would he? Now clear off. I'm busy."

She tried to close the door again, but I shoved it open. "Not until we find Lady Fontaine and her maid."

I strode past her, Adam following without delay. The maid watched us, open-mouthed, but there wasn't much she could do against our determination.

"You can't just push in," she shouted after us. "Anyone asks, it weren't me that opened the door. I ain't getting the sack."

Her voice faded as I clattered down the short flight to the kitchen and servants' area, all deserted, as the maid had claimed. Pots that definitely could use a bit of scrubbing lay near the sink in the scullery.

I easily navigated my way to the back stairs, as most London houses had similar layouts. I hastened up them and pushed open the green baize door at the top.

This house was identical to Lord Peyton's, with a long staircase and a landing with a large window directly above me.

Three doors lined the lower hall, which led to a fan-lighted front door.

All was silence.

I felt Adam's warm body behind mine as he peered around me. Dust motes swam in the afternoon light from the landing's window, but nothing else stirred.

I motioned to Adam to remain quiet, and we climbed the main stairs, taking care to not let our footsteps ring. Adam proved expert at moving noiselessly. He stayed close behind me, as though a plump London cook could protect him from all danger.

We reached the next floor, finding all quiet there as well. I was about to continue upward when I heard a muffled noise.

Adam darted around me and raced to the first door off the staircase. He opened it but obviously found nothing inside, because he backed out and ran to the second. He ducked inside this room and did not return.

I hurried to its door and peered in.

Hannah sat on a straight-backed chair in the very middle of an otherwise pretty sitting room. Her hands were bound behind her, her feet lashed to the bare legs of the chair, a cloth tied over her mouth. Her eyes, above the gag, held both relief and fury.

Adam already had a pocketknife out and was sawing through the thick ropes. They were tough and wiry, the kind a country steward might use to bind up a pole on a sagging fence.

As Adam kept cutting, I closed the door, moved quickly to Hannah, and eased the gag from her mouth. "My dear, what happened?"

Hannah wet her lips and swallowed, grimacing. "'E's lost 'is mind, that's what 'appened." Her voice was hoarse and dry.

"Bleedin' arse." She still wore her black maid's gown and pale muslin apron, but she'd dropped all pretense of prudishness.

"Lord Downes?" I asked.

"None other. He's got Lady Fontaine upstairs. Heard 'em tramping over me. His tough put me in here when I tried to pull her out of this house." Hannah's expression held rage, disgust, and some fear. "What's our Sean doing 'ere? This bloke's dangerous."

Adam didn't answer. He kept his head down and continued working.

"He came to fetch me," I told her. "Good job he did, eh? Adam—I mean, Sean—take your mum out when she's free. I'll find Lady Fontaine."

"Not a bit of it." Hannah kicked at the bonds Adam had loosened, managing to extract one foot. "You're not going up there by yourself. I told you 'e's a madman."

"Did *he* murder Lord Peyton?" I asked.

"If he did, he did it without coming into the house," Hannah said, sounding disappointed to admit this. "Everything was bolted up that night—I swear to it. I checked the doors every night before I let meself go to sleep."

Adam cut through a cord that bound her hands, and Hannah flailed until she disentangled one wrist. She and I helped Adam loosen the other ropes, and between the three of us, she was soon free.

I caught Hannah when she stood up and half collapsed. "I'm all pins and needles," she complained. "Damn the wretch."

"It will wear off soon." I held her until she nodded at me that she could stand.

There were welts around Hannah's wrists, and her mouth was red where the gag had pressed. Adam regarded the signs of bondage with murder in his eyes.

"He'll pay," I assured the boy. "Why did he dismiss everyone?" I asked Hannah.

"So he could continue his heinous plan," she answered grimly. "Why else?"

Once Hannah could walk without stumbling, I opened the door again and peeked out into the hall.

All was as quiet as before. I heard no one upstairs and wondered if Lord Downes had departed with Lady Fontaine. If so, where would he have taken her? And did she go with him willingly?

I led the way to the next flight of stairs, Adam aiding Hannah as the circulation returned to her legs and feet. I knew neither she nor Adam would sensibly flee back to their own home, wherever it might be, so I didn't bother arguing with them.

We crept up the stairs, all three of us tense and listening, but we heard nothing. The normal sounds of a house this size were absent, and I knew the maid spoke the truth when she said the entire staff had been sent away. I wondered if Lord Downes realized the cook had instructed the kitchen maid to remain behind to finish the cleaning.

Hannah pointed to a door that led to the room directly above the chamber where she'd been imprisoned. I tiptoed to the entrance, put my ear to the door, and listened.

"When are we off to Paris?" Lady Fontaine's voice came readily to me, but she sounded eager, not frightened. "I will have to shop quite a bit once we reach there. I'll need new frocks, because the ones I have now aren't good enough for Paris."

"Soon," a gravelly voice answered. I heard a click, as though someone consulted a pocket watch. "Once I know all has gone well."

"You aren't taking all that with us are you?" This question held a touch of nervousness. "I'm not certain they'd allow us on the train."

"No," the man barked. "It's staying. To erase all my sins."

I did not like the sound of that.

Nor was I certain a man who'd had Hannah tied and gagged, ordered the murder of a private secretary, and caused the death of Lord Peyton would tolerate Lady Fontaine's prattling for long. He'd leave her somewhere, or perhaps kill her along the way. The train to Dover went through long stretches of countryside, with perfect places to roll a body out of a carriage in a lonely area.

"No, you don't, you old bastard," Hannah snarled under her breath.

I realized we'd not best Lord Downes by subterfuge. Direct action was needed. He was an elderly man, and I heard no one else in the room but Lady Fontaine. Any guard with them would make some sort of noise—loud breathing, clearing his throat, or asking for orders.

Despite his fondness for shotguns, I knew the elderly Lord Downes could not prevail against the three of us.

I thrust open the door, and we burst inside, only to halt in dismay.

Lady Fontaine glanced up from where she sat on a horsehair sofa, which was pulled against the back of a desk. We were in an office, with filled bookshelves, comfortable chairs, and a smattering of papers on the large desk.

Lord Downes, the bearded man I'd watched descend from his carriage yesterday, was indeed the only other person in the room. He was dressed in a dark suit and coat, of the sort one might wear for traveling. He held no shotgun, for which I was grateful.

What stopped us as we crossed the threshold was not a shotgun or a tough waiting to bully us away.

It was the piles of dark tubes of dynamite that were piled against the bookshelves on every wall, with another stacked under the window in the back of the room.

Lord Downes faced us. He held another stick of the deadly substance in one hand, a meerschaum pipe, lit and trickling smoke, in the other.

28

Lady Fontaine rose in surprise as we hovered on the threshold. "Mrs. Crowe?" she said to me in amazement. "Marjory? Where did *you* get to? And who is this urchin?"

"Come away with me, your ladyship," Hannah said, holding out a hand and ignoring Lady Fontaine's disparagement of her son. "It ain't healthy in here. We'll get you far away."

Lady Fontaine's eyes sparkled. "Nonsense. Lord Downes and I are eloping. It is quite exciting, though scandalous, I know. We will live in Paris a while until the fervor dies down."

"He has no intention of marrying you, Lady Fontaine," I broke in. "I would guess he is taking you with him, because what could be more innocuous than a proper lady and gentleman journeying to the docks in Dover?" I turned to Lord Downes. "Are you waiting for the bombs your lackeys have planted to go off? Hoping that in the confusion, the police will not notice you slipping away?"

"Bombs?" Lady Fontaine asked in bewilderment. "What are

you talking about? Lord Downes uses this dynamite on his estate, to clear out the burrowing animals from his fields. He told me."

"The police know about them," I said, keeping Lord Downes and his lit pipe in my view. "They have the locations of all the devices supposed to go off today and will render them harmless. You've lost this round."

I spoke with confidence I did not feel. I had no doubt that Inspector McGregor, Daniel, and Monaghan and his men would make certain the explosives were found, but I could not say whether Lord Downes would set off the dynamite in this room in a moment of madness.

My hope was that he wanted only to get away and had no intention of topping himself, but he might light the stick he held if he became desperate. Not only would the dynamite end him, the blast would kill the rest of us, and if the lot went off, this side of Belgrave Square would become a smoking hole in the street.

I was fairly certain Lord Downes did mean to detonate the piles around him, perhaps using a slow match to give himself time to get away. The collapse of the house would bury evidence of his crimes, but inhabitants of the houses along this row, along with anyone walking or driving by outside, would be hurt or killed.

Meanwhile, Lord Downes would escape to France, either ridding himself of Lady Fontaine along the way or finding a way to do it once he was on the Continent.

He'd have left Hannah tied up in the room below, ensuring she was the first person to die.

The last thought made me furious. "If you name the conspirators to the police, they will possibly be more lenient to you," I said in a hard voice. "You are a peer of the realm and won't have to scrabble for your bread in Newgate. The police only want to stop the bombings."

"What I'm doing will be considered treason," Lord Downes said with eerie calmness. "I don't think they'll go easy on me, young woman, whoever you are."

"Why are you helping the Fenians?" I countered. "Are you Irish? I quite understand their cause, but—"

Lord Downes snorted a laugh. "I'm no Fenian. I'm from Bedfordshire, born and bred. My family were here before the Normans." He regarded me with arrogance in his small, dark eyes. "But this country has gone to hell. So-called British gentlemen swarming over the world, riding roughshod over anyone in their way. It's embarrassing. Not because they want to bestow Christianity on these nations and give them railways and so forth. It's so they can grab tea, cotton cloth, and opium without having to pay fortunes for them. The so-called empire is a disgrace. Home Rule." He snorted again. "More pompous gents pretending to give Irishmen what they want while still holding the reins. Ireland's a powder keg ready to go off. Might as well give them a leg up." He brandished the dynamite with a chilling smile.

"Blowing up everyone at home isn't likely to change that," I said rapidly. "You're in the House of Lords. You can introduce bills or whatever it is you do to stop those who are running roughshod."

"You are a stupid woman," Lord Downes informed me. "You can have no idea what difficulty it is to bring legislation to a body of gentlemen who care for nothing but reposing in soft chairs in their clubs with the best brandy. A few explosions will gain their attention. That and having their womenfolk who are no better than they ought to be leverage the slovenly lords to do whatever I wish."

"Told ya he were mad," Hannah muttered.

"Well," I said in what I hoped was a reasonable tone. "I quite understand. If you want to flee to France and obliterate part of Belgrave Square, I can hardly stop you. I ask only that you allow us to take Lady Fontaine away and warn the inhabitants of the surrounding houses to clear out first."

"You three can run if you like," Lord Downes said. "Lady Fontaine stays with me. She's up to her neck in my schemes, and if she remains in London, I will make certain everyone knows what she's done and why."

Lady Fontaine stared at him in confusion. "In your schemes? Cyril? What are you talking about?"

"You used her information to write the blackmail letters," I stated. "Probably collected it over the years, every time she came to visit her brother. Your groom told me you let her speak to you almost nonstop."

Lord Downes sent me a faint smile. "She knows so many whose husbands, brothers, and fathers are in the cabinet and high government positions—the gentlemen who guide Britain's policies. Dear Mary told me all the scandalous secrets of their wives, sisters, and daughters. I kept it all cataloged, knowing it would come in handy one day."

Color drained from Lady Fontaine's face. She was not the cleverest of women, but it was at last dawning on her that Lord Downes's attentions to her were less than honest.

Astonishment was quickly followed by anger and humiliation. "You horrible little man," she exclaimed.

Lord Downes ignored her. "It is sad how many great men have women who betray and belittle them, who have secrets that would topple them if known."

"Did you truly believe blackmailing their wives would help you?" I asked, my skepticism evident. "That they would harangue their husbands to put policies in place that would make you happy? That Miss Townsend would actually beg her father to tell the police to cease investigating?"

Lord Downes shrugged, looking like nothing more than an impatient gentleman explaining his reasoning to the slow-witted. "It couldn't hurt. The police are disgusting too. Spying on their fellow countrymen, writing up reports on them whether they've done anything to warrant investigation or not. Britain is supposed to be a shining example of freedom to the cowed peoples of the Continent and beyond. How pathetic. Even Peyton didn't trust the police. He gathered all his proof about me right under my nose, or so he thought. Believed his boyhood friend capable of treachery but not smart enough to know what he was doing."

"You *are* treacherous," Lady Fontaine said in outrage. "You made me believe you cared for me."

Lord Downes took no notice of her. "Peyton's machinations were all for naught," he said to me. "I am only sorry he isn't here to be buried in his own house together with any evidence in mine."

"You made certain of that," I said. "He saw you out the window, didn't he? You frightened him, and he fell."

Lord Downes chuckled, nodding. "That he did. I only meant to taunt him, but I couldn't have planned a better end if I'd tried. I never laughed so hard."

His lack of compassion was chilling. "Did you aim your shotgun at him?"

"No, no, nothing so obvious. I rolled a stick of dynamite toward his back door, pretending to light it first."

Lord Peyton had seen that, had believed that his house was about to be destroyed, all inside it in danger. He'd risen in shock, tried to warn the others, and fell to his death for his pains.

"You murdered him," I said sharply.

Lord Downes laughed again. "No court in the land can prove that."

"You murdered Mr. Howard as well. That might be easier to prove, if your hired ruffians confess."

"*If* they do," Lord Downes agreed. "There is no reason I should kill Peyton's secretary, is there?"

I hated that he was right. There was no obvious connection between Lord Downes and Mr. Howard, the secretary, but I'd been thinking things through.

I'd first believed Mr. Howard had been killed because he knew too much about Lord Peyton's schemes. However, after my conversation with the groom and Daniel's information that Lord Peyton was actually trying to prevent the bombings, I'd shifted my attention from Lord Peyton to Lord Downes. I'd realized, during my restlessness last night, that Mr. Howard had been killed because of the letters. Lord Downes had used Mr. Howard to prepare them as much as he'd used Lady Fontaine.

"Mr. Howard wrote out the first batch of envelopes for you," I said. "I suppose you came up with some excuse, or simply said you had no secretary of your own, and he helped you out of kindness. Lady Fontaine, I imagine, was happy to carry the envelopes back and forth for you. Did you have Mr. Howard post the letters as well? Did he discover what was inside them?"

"Howard was a compliant young man," Lord Downes said. "He did know what I was doing, so do not call him *kind*. He helped me because I promised him a cut of the money I'd get from these pitiful ladies. He bundled up the letters and posted them, so I wouldn't have to touch them. He was impressed with how clever I was. Then he made a mistake."

"He posted the letter to Lady Rankin," I said. "We wondered why *she'd* received a letter when she's been gone these last three years. You wrote the letters with Lady Fontaine's information over a long stretch of time, hoarding them, as you said, until you decided the time was ripe. Mr. Howard must have included it when he sent a batch for you, not knowing who Lady Rankin was, or that she was deceased. The direction only said, *To the Lady of the Household*, after all. But the information in it was very specific."

"Which meant it would be opened by someone else in the house," Lord Downes snapped. "Who'd wonder why it was threatening a woman long dead, and maybe they'd go to the police. Jeopardizing everything. Howard was an idiot, and now he knew too much. He had to go."

I felt sick. "The secretary who replaced Mr. Howard didn't find you out. You'd grown wiser and made certain he saw only the envelopes, with no letters inside them."

Lord Downes's eyes narrowed. "How the devil do you know all this? Have they recruited women for the secret police now? How appalling."

"She's not with the police," Lady Fontaine said faintly. "She's a medium."

Lord Downes shot her an incredulous look. "Whoever she is, she's a ridiculous, interfering busybody, and I am tired of talking to her. Leave now," he commanded me. "Lady Fontaine will remain behind. It is the best thing she can do, unless she wants the world to know she was a blackmailer as well as a petty thief." He turned a sneer on her. "You should be grateful I intend to destroy your house—no one will find all the bits and pieces you stole."

"You deceitful, odious *liar*," Lady Fontaine cried in outrage. "I trusted you. I *loved* you."

She lunged at him. Hannah shrieked and dove for her, and Lord Downes backed swiftly from both of them, holding his pipe closer to the dynamite.

Adam, brave lad, went after *him*, and I leapt for Adam, terrified the boy would provoke Lord Downes into lighting the stick.

"I'd stay away," Lord Downes said. "Unless you want us all to go up."

Lady Fontaine, her anger becoming a frenzy, twisted from Hannah, lifted a heavy paperweight from the desk and threw it at Lord Downes.

He ducked the missile, which thudded into the bookcase behind him, but as he swerved, his boot heel caught on the carpet, and he tripped. He flailed as he started to fall, a terrified light in his eyes.

I knew in an instant Lord Downes had no wish to light that dynamite while he held it. He'd planned only to flee, cover his crimes, and start again as an innocuous English lordship relaxing in the cafés of Paris.

He'd sip coffee and reminisce about the English countryside, while his friends informed him what a lucky escape he'd had from his home in Belgrave Square. The Fenians would be blamed for the bombs, and Lord Downes would never be connected to their crimes.

As he desperately tried to right himself, Lord Downes clutched the pipe in his hand so hard that its bowl broke. Burning embers singed his fingers, and he cried out.

Lord Downes hit the floor, the single stick of dynamite falling to the carpet. A glob of burning tobacco burst from the broken pipe and plunged toward the pile of explosives behind him.

I flung myself at the small glow of fire, batting Adam and Lord Downes aside. I grabbed the bright clump, which burned my hand something fierce, and took it down to the floor with me. I beat out every spark into the carpet, and kept beating, the pile of dynamite inches from my face.

I heard pounding footsteps as I lay face down, my hands smarting, my body aching. Lady Fontaine was sobbing, Hannah trying to persuade her out. Lord Downes floundered like a bug on his back. He struggled to rise, and Adam stepped on his stomach.

Men poured into the room, responding to the summons I'd put forth before I'd followed Adam to Belgrave Square.

"No!" I shouted. "There's dynamite everywhere." One spark from a policeman's boot would send the lot of us up.

A hand in a thick leather glove reached to me. I looked up to behold Daniel, his forbidding expression mixed with one of relief that he'd found me alive.

I folded my burned right hand to my chest and clutched at him with my left. I let out a gasp when that one stung as well.

"Kat, what the devil?" Daniel pulled me to my feet, then gently unfolded my hands to reveal the hot red marks from where I'd pounded at the wad of fiery tobacco.

"Better stinging skin than going up with this house," I said shakily. I cast my gaze to the policemen who surrounded the dynamite in a respectful manner. "Tell them to be careful."

"They know what to do," Daniel assured me. "They were already dismantling explosives at the base of Nelson's Column when your lads found us. Now come away and let them work."

"Lord Downes organized everything," I babbled as Daniel helped me stumble from the room. "He confessed as much. He would have been happy to kill us all while he ran free. I hope

you dig a deep hole and drop him into it," I finished adamantly.

Daniel steered me into the hall, where I wilted against him,
my legs weak. Two brushes with death within a week were not
good for me.

"I heard him," Daniel said. "More importantly, Monaghan
did." He nodded at the gray-haired gent with round spectacles
giving orders in his unfeeling tones. "I've had my eye on
Downes for a while. There had to be some way information
was getting to and from the Fenians, and if it wasn't Lord Peyton or his friends, then who? Lord Downes was a bit too much
the anti-Irish, anti-Catholic, anti-anyone-but-men-exactly-
like-himself cliché to be believed."

"Yet, he is that," I said, my voice scratchy. "But not for the
reasons one would think."

"Hush, now." Daniel towed me away, past the constables,
Inspector McGregor with his usual glower, Sergeant Scott's
cool efficiency, and the chill stare of Mr. Monaghan.

Hannah and Adam were leading Lady Fontaine, who wept
and asked anyone within hearing why she'd deserved Lord
Downes to be so horrible to her. We made it downstairs and
finally emerged from the house, a curious crowd filling the
street. London loved a spectacle.

Adam, or rather, Sean—I had to remember to call him by
his correct name—ran to me and flung his arms around my
waist.

"Thank you, Mrs. Holloway." His words were tremulous.
"Thank you."

He broke from me then and raced after Hannah, who was
assisting Lady Fontaine along the street and across into the
park. It wouldn't be safe for Lady Fontaine to go back into

Lord Peyton's house, as much as she protested she wanted to, until Lord Downes's home was cleared of all explosives.

Daniel would not let me linger and propelled me gently onward. I saw Mr. Fielding's groom among the crowd, along with youths big and small who'd been protecting me all these weeks. Lord Downes's kitchen maid, I was happy to see, was among them. He'd not have spared her if she'd lingered too long over her pots.

I spied Mr. Grimes as well, who pushed through the onlookers and lumbered to us.

"All right then, Mrs. H.?" he said in his big voice. "I'm that glad you sent for us. We was ready to rush inside, but the coppers came, and we decided to step back and let them pass. Daniel was with them, so I knew you'd be all right."

Mr. Grimes made to clasp my hands, but I pulled them back fearfully. Mr. Grimes sent Daniel a questioning look, and Daniel opened my palms to show him the blistering skin.

"She burned them," Daniel said grimly. "Preventing dynamite from going off."

Mr. Grimes gazed at me in awe. "She's right brave, ain't she? Better marry her, Danny, me boy, so she can look after you proper."

"Oh, I intend to," Daniel said, to my amazement, then he waved for a hansom, bundled me into it, and took me away.

W e did not go directly to Mount Street, but to a small house in Kensington that lay not far from its gardens. There, Daniel doctored my burns as competently as any surgeon, rubbing my skin with a greasy balm that quickly soothed me.

He bound my hands in bandages, while the quietness of

the little house, which was one of Daniel's hideouts, did me more good than medicine.

"Did you mean that?" I asked softly as Daniel tucked in the ends of the bandages. I'd have to find some means to explain my injury to Mrs. Bywater, and poor Tess would have to assist me until I healed.

"Did I mean what?" The flush on Daniel's cheekbones told me he knew exactly to what I referred.

"That you intended to marry me."

Daniel finished the last bandage and put his fingers under my chin so I'd look directly at him. "Yes. I did mean it."

"I see."

I could think of nothing else to say. Too many distressing things had happened to me in the past few days for me to grasp the entirety of his declaration.

I glanced about the sitting room, with its paneled walls, comfortable chairs, small collection of books, and fireplace that would snap with a cozy blaze in the winter.

"Can we live here?" I asked.

"We can live anywhere you like." Daniel caressed my cheek with his calloused thumb. "That is, if you cease throwing yourself at villains. Kat, my love, when I saw you leap *toward* the dynamite, my world stopped."

"It's a mercy I did," I pointed out. "That dreadful man would have killed every one of us."

"Why the devil did you go to Belgrave Square at all?" Daniel demanded. "When your message reached me, I feared the worst. I couldn't race straight to you—I had to put together a team of constables and fetch McGregor and Monaghan. And instead of waiting for us, you charged directly inside."

I eyed him in indignation. "He had Hannah bound up in a room, where he meant to leave her to die. Her poor son was scared to death, and rightly so. Lady Fontaine was in danger as well. Waiting would have possibly been the worst thing I could do. Lord Downes might have fled with Lady Fontaine and lit his slow match, blowing up the house with Hannah in it, and taking down much of the street. I kept him talking to give you plenty of time to reach us."

"Logically, I agree with you." Daniel pressed a fist to his chest. "Inside, I'm surprised *this* is still beating."

"When you marry me, if you mean to keep me sequestered at home instead of out helping others, I will say no."

Daniel stilled. "When?"

"Indeed, I had a husband who thought to enforce obedience, and I will not go through that again."

He gazed at me with unreadable eyes. "Kat, you said *when* I marry you. Not *if*."

I started, realizing I'd spoken without thought.

I hadn't needed to think.

"Of course I did," I said softly.

Daniel let out a sound like a groan. He carefully lifted my bandaged hands and kissed my fingertips. "You love to torture me. Do you really mean to let me marry you?"

I sent him an impish smile. "You have to do it proper, you know. On one knee and everything."

Daniel slid so swiftly from the chair where he'd perched, it was comical. He knelt on the carpet and pressed one hand to his heart, his blue eyes sparkling.

"Kat Holloway," he said with warm earnestness. "Will you do me the honor of becoming my wife?"

My heart thumped, the audacity of what I was doing flooding me with fear as well as excitement and anticipation. I suppose giddiness from my brushes with death also compelled me.

"I will, Mr. McAdam." My words were shaky but sincere.

Daniel leapt to his feet and pulled me up with him, his arms going around me.

"Then I declare myself the luckiest man on earth," he said fervently. "I am madly in love with you, Kat. Do you mind?"

"Not at all." I wanted to dance and shout in my relief and sudden flood of happiness, but that would hardly be dignified. "I believe I love you too, my dearest Daniel."

29

I had to explain my burned hands at home, and I simply said I'd accidentally laid them on an iron kettle that was too hot. Mrs. Bywater tutted at my clumsiness, but she sent a salve down via Mrs. Redfern that soothed my skin once Daniel's had worn off.

It could have been much worse, I knew.

I told Tess and Lady Cynthia the entire story after supper Friday night, and they listened, agog. Both praised me for my courage and scolded me for taking any risks at all.

Tess, who'd nipped out to speak to Caleb that afternoon, was full of the news that a few bombs had indeed gone off in various places around London—one near the Carlton Club in Pall Mall, another in front of an MP's home, and one at a pub that shared a wall with Scotland Yard. Caleb had been summoned to help, and Tess had run home.

There had been some injuries, Mr. Davis announced while

reading his newspapers on Saturday morning, but warnings had come soon enough that there had been no deaths and those hurt were expected to recover. Other bombs had been dismantled before they could go off, and the stack of dynamite at Nelson's Column had been defused entirely, as Daniel had told me.

Tess beamed at me as she rolled out tart dough, believing I had been the heroine who'd saved the day.

Daniel hadn't visited Friday after he'd seen me back to Mount Street, and I did not expect him on Saturday either, though I planned to wait up, in case. On Saturday afternoon, I baked an entire batch of crullers and a whole lemon cake—with Tess's ample help—using my own money for the ingredients, and gave it all to Mr. Grimes, who waited in the street that evening.

Mr. Grimes was amazed and thankful, and generously said he'd share with his men who'd helped keep me safe. I warmed as he walked away, happy that I had such a friend.

I'd sent a batch of currant buns across the city to Mr. Fielding, with instructions to give them out to his groom and the lads Mr. Fielding had recruited to look after me.

Mr. Fielding sent a note with his thanks and explained that the groom, when he'd seen Hannah go after Lady Fontaine into Lord Downes's deserted house, had immediately run to fetch help. Lord Downes had tried to dismiss him that day, along with the rest of his staff, but the groom had lingered, suspecting something was very wrong.

I also rewarded Albie and my other lads well. Baking the things was costly, but I dipped into the ten guineas Lady Fontaine had given me and sent Charlie, the boot boy, out to the shops to fetch me the ingredients.

I hadn't seen nor heard from Hannah since Daniel had taken me from Belgrave Square, but I assumed she and Sean had returned home to recover from the ordeal.

I did not do much on Saturday night after the rest of the staff went to bed. My hands hurt too much to hold my knives properly to sharpen them, and I had no desire to jot thoughts in my book. Tess had been more than generous with her assistance, doing the extra chopping, slicing, peeling, stirring, and kneading without complaint, and I'd sent her early to bed with my gratitude.

Tea steeped in the pot, and two cups and a plate of crullers with slices of lemon cake rested on the table. I'd made several extra cakes, one of which would go with Lady Cynthia to Mr. Thanos, the other to Miss Townsend. I'd told Cynthia to have Miss Townsend spread the word that the blackmail victims need worry no more.

Near midnight, when I was about to give into my exhaustion and go to bed, Daniel tapped on the door, and I hurried to answer it.

Daniel greeted me with a kiss, insisted on examining my hands, which he proclaimed were better, then let me lead him to the table.

We'd been shy with each other yesterday after our declarations, the pair of us who could chatter without ceasing suddenly with nothing to say. We were as quiet tonight, the tea trickling into cups the only sound as we settled at the table.

"Ah, your famous lemon cake," Daniel said as he drew a slice toward him. "I knew something lured me here this night."

"It's naught but pound cake," I said modestly, though I was proud of the recipe I'd perfected. "Scented with lemon and vanilla, and made with a bit of buttermilk."

"When you bake it, it is heavenly."

I sent him a wavering smile. "You needn't pile on the flattery. I have already accepted you."

Daniel's brows rose. "So now that I have your pledge, I should be callous and disagreeable? That will never happen, I assure you." He savored another bite. "My praise is not to gain things from you, my Kat. It is truth and well deserved."

I hid my flush of pleasure by quickly lifting my teacup. "You'll turn my head."

Daniel winked. "I hope so."

"I do have something serious to tell you," I said.

Daniel laid down his fork, his teasing tone abruptly vanishing. "Are you throwing me over already? If so, state it quickly, and be done."

"Not at all," I said in surprise. "Except . . ." I let out a breath. "I do think we should wait a bit. Not rush into things."

Daniel studied me with quiet watchfulness. "Are we rushing? I've been trying to woo you for nearly five years now."

"I've thought it over all last night and through today, and I think we should wait at least a year before we wed."

"Why a year?" He spoke in curiosity, but I heard the wariness behind the question.

"That will give me opportunity to settle some things." I took a sip of tea as though I weren't speaking about the most important matters in my life. "I can't leave Tess too soon. She's coming along well, but I don't want her to break into hysterics at the thought of being left on her own too quickly. She needs to grow used to the idea. Mrs. Bywater will likely promote Tess to head cook, but she'll try to save money by not employing another assistant. I will have to work to convince Mrs. Bywater that her kitchen needs two to function well."

"I see that," Daniel said. "You are right that Tess will need time to train further and grow more confident in her role."

"Also, I want to give plenty of notice so I can receive all the pay I'm owed. Mrs. Bywater would find some way to convince Lord Rankin to cut me off if I suddenly announced I was marrying. We do need money to live on, Daniel. If I cease working to look after you, and you have only what you make as a deliveryman, we will be pinched to make ends meet."

Daniel's focus on me sharpened as I laid out my argument. "My love, I have no intention of locking you into my house to take care of me. I know it's what wives are trained to do, but you are like no woman I know. You have always wanted to have a tea shop—do not give up that dream for me."

"What I want is a place to be with Grace," I said, though I warmed with gratitude at his understanding. "And you."

"Even so. You have a talent, and I'll not selfishly deny it to the world, or deny you the recognition for it." Daniel's good humor returned. "As long as you save a good portion of what you cook for me."

"Of course I will, you daft man." I lifted my teacup again. "But thank you."

"As it happens, I came here with the purpose of suggesting we wait a bit as well."

The sting of his words surprised me. I'd taken much trouble to convince myself that this course was best, but for some reason, I was a bit hurt that he'd drawn the same conclusion.

"Oh? Why?"

"Not only for the reasons you stated so well, but because there are things I also need to take care of. Monaghan, with pressure from McGregor and a detective chief super, actually did release me from my obligation to him."

The relief his statement brought made me want to sag in my chair, but I forced myself to remain upright.

"Well, of course he should have. You brought in a cruel and

unfeeling man and saved many people from being hurt by his explosives."

"With a hefty amount of assistance from you," Daniel said. "You found that map, which was crucial, and alerted half of London that a madman was about to flee."

"I hadn't anticipated he'd turn his own home into an incendiary device," I said.

"Neither had I. I did insist you take credit for your help, which McGregor grudgingly acknowledged. Monaghan growled that you had inserted yourself too much in this case, and he'll be happy to see the back of me for that reason."

"How rude." I should not care what a heartless man like Monaghan thought of me, but his dismissal rankled. "You do not know how glad I am that you are finished with him."

"But . . ."

My relief fled. "But what?"

Daniel ran his thumb along the handle of his fork. "But—I thought I'd stay on. With Special Branch, I mean. Working my way into CID when they have a place for me."

"I see," I said.

"I'm good at it, Kat. I can insert myself into a gang of villains without them being the wiser and stop them doing terrible things. Monaghan chose the worst assignments he could find for me, yet I accomplished them. I wouldn't be working under Monaghan anymore—he made it clear he is finished with me—but there are others willing to take me on."

"Ah." I sat back in uncertainty.

While I agreed that Daniel was quite talented at his job, better than Scotland Yard gave him credit for, it was dangerous, and I'd hoped I was finished with worrying. Daniel would become a delivery driver for always, I'd decided, and I'd bake treats for him and enjoy surprising him with what I made.

"You don't want this." Daniel's statement was simple, with no disappointment and no surprise.

"I don't want you to be hurt, is all. Perhaps they'll let you sit behind a desk and growl at constables, like Inspector McGregor does."

Daniel chuckled. "I'd be terrible at sitting behind a desk."

"I know. You like to move about London as you please, being in the thick of things."

"If I hadn't done that, I would never have met you."

We studied each other. I blessed the day Daniel had happened into my kitchen, with his wide grin and blue eyes I'd not been able to forget. I continued to bless my luck every day that Daniel was there to walk alongside me and to catch me when I fell. He'd seen a part of me that I dared show no one else, and he knew me better than anyone but Grace.

"You are unwilling to keep me from my dreams," I said slowly. "I should be unwilling to keep you from yours."

"I admit that baking for a tea shop will be less dangerous than infiltrating anarchist gangs."

I huffed a laugh. "You've not encountered ladies in tea shops who are displeased with what they have been served. It will not be as easy as you imagine."

Daniel acknowledged this with a nod and smile as he tucked into his lemon cake once more.

I glanced into my cup, saw that it was empty, and refilled both it and his. "I suppose I can learn to be the wife of a policeman."

"And I suppose I can be husband to a grand baker in a tea shop."

I lifted my cup in toast to him.

We were both still uncertain, but something had been settled between us. We'd carry on, each of us not giving up our entire lives for the other, but being there for each other whenever needed.

"There is another reason I want to wait," Daniel announced.

I stiffened, but answered casually. "And what is that?"

"I want to investigate my own life. Find out where I came from, how I ended up on the streets, and what exactly happened to Carter. What my real name is."

Because Daniel didn't know. In his life, he'd never found the answer to any of these things.

It struck me, as I listened to him, that I'd always been secure in the knowledge of myself, no matter what had happened—losing my mother, entering a false marriage with a brutal man, fearing I'd have to give my child to strangers, working my fingers raw to keep her.

Through it all, I'd always been me, Kat Holloway of Bow Lane, daughter of a good-hearted woman and a man my mother had loved to her dying day, though she'd lost him soon after my birth.

Daniel had never possessed the sense that, no matter what, he was rooted in himself.

I reached for him, squeezing the broad hands that had held me up so many times. "So you should," I said softly. "I will help you any way I can."

"It might be dangerous," Daniel warned.

I raised one of his hands to my lips and kissed the backs of his fingers. "If it involves you, of course it will be. But I am going to help. You can depend upon it."

When Monday afternoon came, I left Tess baking scones for yet another of Mrs. Bywater's infernal teas and sailed forth to enjoy my half day out.

Daniel met me at the end of Mount Street, and we traveled by hansom to Cheapside. We'd agreed to keep silent to our friends about our betrothal—how strange to be betrothed!—for a time, until we worked out our precise plans.

However, I would tell Grace. I'd not hide from my daughter an event that would change her life. She could be trusted to keep the secret. Besides, I wanted to celebrate with her.

We said little when we entered Joanna's house and again as we took another hansom back across the city with Grace to Portobello Road.

I carried some of my folded banknotes in my pocket, ready to spend them on cloth for my new frock. I'd argued with myself that I ought to return Lady Fontaine's fee, as I'd only pretended to be a medium. But then, I truly had figured out how her brother had died, so perhaps I was right to keep it. I wasn't certain what had become of Lady Fontaine, in any case.

We wandered through the market, Grace enchanted with the many stalls with all their wares. Daniel and I walked with her between us, halting often to let her browse the tables.

I took my time looking over bright bolts of cloth a few vendors displayed. I wanted fabric that would be durable but would also drape well and make a pretty frock. Daniel waited with the patience of a man letting his female friends pore over and reject choices that likely seemed perfectly fine to him.

Grace and I at last chose a dark blue broadcloth and added black piping and blue-violet lace to trim it. It was satisfying to pay over the cash for the fine cloth, without having to quibble about the price.

Daniel tucked my packages under his arms without complaint, and we continued up the hill to the stall near the top.

I hadn't been certain she'd be there, but two stout ladies in

front of her table listened as Hannah charmed them with im-
probable tales about the trinkets she was goading them to buy.
The women took their purchases and strolled on, while Hannah, dressed again in her bright blue skirt and black jacket,
feathered hat on her dark hair, straightened up the wares.

When she lifted her head and saw us, she gasped in delight,
then moved swiftly around her table and flung her arms
around me.

"Here you are, Katie, me darling. She saved me life," she informed startled passersby and neighboring stallholders. "I'd
be in a pile of bits if not for this lady rushing to my rescue."

"And if not for your son," I said when Hannah released me
from her crushing hug. "I'd never have come at all if he hadn't
realized something was wrong."

"Don't I know it, and hasn't he been scolding me something
fierce?" Hannah turned and called into the draperies behind
her stall. "'Ere. Our Sean. Come out and say good afternoon."

Adam—Sean—emerged from where I assumed Hannah
kept her excess stock, his young face bearing a scowl. "Yeah?
What'ye want?"

"Is that any way to greet our friends?" Hannah admonished
good-naturedly. "He won't bugger off and let me get on with
things," she informed us. "He's sure I'll fall into the hands of
some ruffian once I'm out of his sight."

"Well, you did already, didn't you?" Sean demanded.
"Haven't got the sense not to run into a villain's house and get
yourself tied up. You should be smarter, like Mrs. Holloway.
She sent for help."

"Don't be so cheeky to your old mum," Hannah chided, but
I saw her pride in him. "Now, Katie, this must be your little
girl. She's the spitting image of you, ain't she?"

"This is Grace, yes," I said, my heart swelling.

Hannah bent to Grace. "How are you, young lady? I'm Hannah, your mum's old mate. I used to be a tea leaf, but otherwise, I ain't a bad sort."

"How do you do?" Grace said formally, and the two shook hands. "My mum's told me all about you."

"That is probably not good." Hannah laughed. "Now, Grace, you look over me wares and take anything you want home. My gift to you."

Grace glanced to me for confirmation, and I gave her a nod. Grace eagerly began scanning the trinkets, and Sean joined her, pointing out a few of the nicer bits. His claim that they came from a princess's dressing table didn't take in Grace.

Hannah turned from them and gave Daniel a bold once-over. "And here *you* are, looking like an ordinary bloke. Is that the true you? Or another disguise?"

Daniel spread one hand. "I am as you see me." He wore his workingman's clothes with a light woolen jacket against the spring breeze. It was the first of June, and the days would soon warm, but the wind still kept us cool.

"I have to say, I like you better than that ever-so-haughty and rather dim-witted gentleman's son, don't you know." Hannah let her accent become toffy before she relaxed into another grin. "Nice to make your acquaintance, Danny McAdam."

"And you," Daniel said. "I will say I prefer *you* to Marjory, the stuffy maid."

"She were a one, weren't she?" Hannah returned her attention to me. "By the way, I introduced Lady Fontaine to a mate of mine, a woman who is used to looking after genteel old ladies. Me pal used to run confidence games herself, and she's well acquainted with those who can't help themselves stealing. She'll look after her ladyship and help her get a pension of some kind out of Lord Peyton's heir. Her ladyship is in good hands, you can be sure."

"I am glad," I said in true relief. "Lady Fontaine is silly but doesn't deserve to be shifted about like she was."

"Or used by a mean old man," Hannah said decidedly. "I gave Lord Downes a nice kick as he was dragged away. Of course, the police took me in with them to ask all sorts of questions, but since I was still prissy Marjory I went along with it. Was terribly shocked by it all and worried for her ladyship. They released me and let me take her home."

"You are kinder than you know," I told her.

Hannah shrugged. "Maybe. But I think I'll stick to me table of trinkets for a time now. Sean is a great one for helping."

"I've been giving some thought to your idea of having a stall here for my baked goods," I said. Daniel, who'd been watching Grace look over Hannah's things, turned to me in curiosity. I hadn't mentioned this to him yet.

"Have ye, now?" Hannah eyed me speculatively. "You'd do well with it, I'd wager."

"Not every day," I said quickly. "Or even every week. I'd start with perhaps one day a month, and see how things go."

"Good on you." Hannah pressed her hands together. "I'll help you any way I can, Katie. You can depend on it. And I know just the spot."

Before we took our leave, Hannah showed me the place she had in mind, a space halfway down Portobello Road she said she could help me get the lease for. There was plenty of foot traffic in that area and no other food stalls too close.

I collected Grace, who'd chosen a porcelain brush and comb set from Hannah's stock. Grace thanked Hannah sincerely, and I handed Hannah a half dozen scones I'd brought for her in my basket. Hannah accepted them with eager thanks, already sharing them out with Sean as the three of us started back down the road.

Once in the hansom, packages piled around us, I turned to Grace.

"What would you say if I told you your old mum has decided to marry Daniel?" I asked her.

Grace studied me, her blue eyes serene. "I would say it was about time."

I stared at her in surprise. I'd worried mightily over this moment, but I should have known Grace would take the news without turning a hair.

"Is that all?" I demanded, while Daniel chuckled in high amusement.

"No, I think it is splendid." Grace pulled me into a firm hug. "I've wanted this for so long. You and Daniel belong together."

I held my daughter tightly, fears easing. "I'm glad," I whispered. "Thank you, my love."

Grace released me and turned to embrace Daniel, who returned the hug with wonder.

"Does this mean James will be my brother?" Grace asked when we all were finished gushing.

"I suppose it does," I answered, watching her carefully.

"Good. I've always wanted a brother." Grace leaned to me, confiding. "Though I believe he's sweet on Jane. He's always finding an excuse to come around for a visit."

"Is he?" Daniel asked in consternation. "Well."

I tried not to laugh at Daniel's expression, but it was no use. Grace and I both fell about while Daniel shook his head, a father befuddled by his swiftly growing son.

When we reached Joanna's, she raved about my choice of

fabric and trimmings, and immediately fetched her scissors and sewing box.

I gazed about her sitting room as we unfolded the fabric and began to fit the pattern pieces I'd copied from the book I'd bought, and realized how rich I was.

The houses of luxury on Belgrave Square couldn't compare to Joanna and Sam's happy and crowded abode, with Grace next to me and Joanna's daughters eagerly reaching for pins to help start my new gown.

Daniel sat apart with a cup of tea, chatting to Joanna's boys with unfeigned ease. Daniel, who'd known no parents, had learned to find family and enjoy them wherever he could.

As the afternoon waned, Sam returned from his new post at the solicitor's office and joined in the male conversation, smiling at his wife with true joy. Daniel's gaze at me held the same amount of tenderness.

My life was full and stood to become even fuller. As I basked in the warmth of my friends, my daughter, and my love, I knew that there was no woman in London better off than I was at this moment.

Photo by Silvio Portrait Design

Jennifer Ashley is the *New York Times* bestselling author of more than one hundred and twenty novels and novellas in mystery, romance, and historical fiction. Jennifer's books have been translated into more than a dozen languages and have earned starred reviews in *Publishers Weekly* and *Booklist*. When she is not writing, Jennifer enjoys playing music (guitar, piano, flute), reading, hiking, gardening, knitting, and building dollhouse miniatures.

Ready to find
your next great read?

Let us help.

Visit prh.com/nextread